THE
WORLD'S
ONE HUNDRED
BEST SHORT STORIES

VOLUME TWO
ROMANCE

THE
WORLD'S
ONE HUNDRED
BEST SHORT STORIES

[IN TEN VOLUMES]

GRANT OVERTON
EDITOR · IN · CHIEF

VOLUME TWO
ROMANCE

FUNK & WAGNALLS COMPANY
NEW YORK AND LONDON

CONTENTS

THE WORLD'S 100 BEST SHORT STORIES

THE STAR SPANGLED MANNER

By Peter B. Kyne

HEIGHO! NOT ALL THE LOCHINVARS COME OUT OF THE WEST. SOME DO THEIR WOOING RIGHT ON THE HOME GROUNDS

The annual task of breaking new saddle stock follows the beef round-up at Dad Tully's ranch. Dad usually invites me up to the rodeo. Upon my arrival last fall I discovered, greatly to my satisfaction, that no longer would I be required to view the excitement from the top rail of Dad Tully's circular breaking corral. Dad had very thoughtfully constructed on top of the eight-foot fence a solid platform three feet wide by about six feet long, and to this rude throne he had fastened the discarded rear seat of an old spring wagon, with the cushions still in a fair state of preservation.

When I expressed my appreciation of his nice attention to the comfort of a guest, Dad apologized because he had not thought of it sooner.

"As a man grows older he gets horse sense," the old cattleman explained. "I reckon I was most forty years old before the thought come to me that I'd busted a number of bones twice too often in a brave but misguided effort to ride disrespectful horses. All them sad years it never occurred to me once that I had more than enough substitutes on the ranch pay roll at forty dollars a month, notwithstandin' the fact that employers' liability insurance wasn't even thought of in them days.

"For that matter," he concluded sadly, "if a rider got broke up in a fellow's service, he'd have shot the lawyer that suggested maybe it would be a good idea to sue the old man. However, times change, an' we got to keep up with them. I got the idea of this here platform from Bill Emlow eight years ago, but it's took all that time to get the idea to congeal in my fool head. Bill had a stairway with a hand-railin' leadin' up to his private box, but I reckon, until my rheumatism gets worse, I'll continue to climb the fence to my reserved roost. I never was much of a hand at luxuries. We didn't have 'em on cow ranches when I learned my trade. But this here Bill Emlow I'm tellin' you about wouldn't have nothin' else but.

"I never did see such a hand for indulgin' himself as Bill was, an' when, takin' advantage o' my years, I reprove him for his extravagance, he just looks at me sort o' solemn an' says: 'Dad, it is the manifest duty of every gentleman to do himself well. Personally,' he adds with a ghost of a smile, 'I find it's a good investment. Now, here you are,' says Bill, 'a-visitin' me for the avowed purpose of buyin' three hundred head o' pure-bred Hereford two-year-old bulls. You can buy those bulls almost as cheap a thousand mile closer to your ranch, but do you do it? You do not. The answer is you get a lot of enjoyment buyin' 'em from me, because that gives you an excuse to come up an' look 'em over—an' a visit's all you're really concerned about. You could trust me to send you down just as good bulls as you can select your own self, an' thereby save travelin' expenses. But do you do it? You do not.

"'The fact is you like to see a ranch with a real home on it, not an unpainted shanty designed to keep the elements off'n you. You like the way my ranch home is furnished. After years of red tablecloths (or maybe yellow oilcloth) you like white linen. You like to look at the family crest on my silver, an' you sure do revel in the culinary art of my Chink cook. What if I do pay that exile from Far Cathay a hundred and a quarter a month? Ain't that cheaper than maintainin' a wanderin' white drunkart at sixty-five a month to ruin my digestion with starches an' fries? It pleases you no end to note that my cook doesn't heave his dishwater out into the front yard an' that flies in his kitchen ain't.

"'The Belfast linen sheets on my guestroom bed are mighty soothin' to an old-timer who's slept between woolen blankets all his life, an' my three-hundred-dollar graphophone an' three-thousand-dollar player piano interest you somethin' scandalous. You got a habit o' pickin' a rose from my garden to pin in your lapel right after breakfast, an' while it pleases you to make fun o' my fancy ridin' britches you know in your ancient heart they're a heap more comfortable than overalls. You come rovin' up here ostensibly to buy bulls, an' you never look at 'em. You take whatever the boys drive in for you.'

"'Ain't much choosin' between them, I'll admit, Bill,' I says.

" 'Well, why don't some other Hereford breeder closer to home get your trade?' he demands.

" ' 'Cause they haven't any ancestors, Bill,' I says, an' that was the truth. 'I can trust a man with a proud ancestry to be proud of his morals an' proud o' the quality an' breedin' of his livestock. An' I don't know another cowman in North America who has so many expensive paintings of defunct ancestors lookin' down at him as you have. Hell's fire, man, it's as good as goin' to the circus just to prowl around your house an' look at 'em.'

" 'We go back to William the Conqueror,' says Bill Emlow. 'Come now, Dad. Admit you like the way I do myself.'

" 'I admit it and I enjoy it, Bill,' says I, lyin' not bein' one of my noticeable faults. 'I certainly do like to come an' spend a few weeks with you in the slack season. I admit you have the best barns in the United States an' you paint 'em instead of whitewashin' 'em, or let 'em go entirely. I admit you never leave your hayin' equipment out in the weather when you finish with it in the autumn, an' I'll tell the world you paint that equipment every year when you've done with it an' then keep it in a shed till you use it again. I admit you've got the finest ranch in the Northwest, that you run it right an' make it pay, but there's one crime for which I've got you unanimously convicted an' no hope o' clemency from the court. Why'n hell don't you get married?"

" 'A cow ranch is a sort o' lonesome place for a woman,' he protests.

" ' 'Tain't neither,' I says. 'Anyways, not such a place as you've got here—all tucked away serene an' beautiful in a subirrigated evergreen valley with the

hills just far enough away so they don't give you the
notion you're hemmed in. An' it's only twenty miles
to a sizable town an' a day's run to Spokane. An'
you with an imported English automobile!'

"'I reckon it's because I ain't met up with the
right girl, Dad,' says Bill.

"'Oh,' I says, 'so that's the way of it,' an' then I
shut up, because I see right away it wasn't no use
wastin' any more breath on that subject."

And then Dad proceeded to tell the story of Bill
Emlow:

You understand, son [said Dad], this Bill, tho
a fine, upstandin' American citizen, was a whole lot
different from the average American, corral count.
The average American's a mixture of breeds—what we
call a grade in the pure-bred cattle business—but Bill
Emlow was pure-bred. Folks who don't know have
a habit of referrin' to his kind as Anglo-Saxons, but
as a matter of fact Bill was a Norman. He had
a pedigree runnin' back to William the Conqueror,
who was a Norman, an' he had the pedigree of every
family the male Emlows had ever married into, an'
they all showed the Norman strain strong enough to
have been registered. The Anglo-Saxon is a blond,
but Bill Emlow was dark-completed, which you'll find
plenty of brunets in Norway.

Bill's old man was the youngest son of the tribe
of Emlow, back in the old country, an' when they give
him his choice as to whether he'd enter the church,
the army or the navy, he had a reversion to type an'
declared he wouldn't do neither, nohow. He wasn't
for havin' his destiny cut an' dried for him, just
because it had got to be the fashion to dispose of

younger sons that way. So he hung around home, after graduating from Oxford, an' took a postgraduate course in plain an' fancy hell-raisin' until the old earl, his father, was inexpressibly shocked.

At a family council it was decided that Bill's future parent was in a fair way to disgracin' the family. As near as I ever got the straight of it, the young man's crime consisted of a hell-bent yearnin' to marry a girl the earl disapproved of. Her family tree was O. K., but her father was in trade, consistin' of whole-sale tobacco. Bill the Thirteenth, which was then as not yet father of my young friend Bill the Fourteenth, hasn't anything to marry on unless the earl gives it to him, which the earl won't do, an' in order to bust up this love affair he quietly but with considerable passion informs Bill the Thirteenth that to-night he must leave England forever.

There's a ticket to Australia, New Zealand, Canada or any other section of Britain's far-flung battle line waitin' for him at the office of the family solicitor, together with a modest bit of get-away money, an' if Bill the Thirteenth will have the goodness to call for same and use both to put distance between himself and impendin' disgrace, the earl will agree to send him fifty pounds monthly so long as he stays away. Accordin' to Bill the Fourteenth, the young man bows low, shakes hands with the earl very cordially, tells him an' the family solicitor to take a jump in the Thames, there bein' no lake handy, an' emigrates to the U. S. A. via the stokehold of a cattle boat he finds at a Liverpool dock.

This bein' the only means he has of makin' an' savin' enough money to send for the tobacconist's girl an' marry her, Bill the Thirteenth sticks to it an' in

the course of time he crosses the Atlantic a number
of times with cattle, which in them days was mostly
long-horned, long-legged, narrow-hipped scrub steers
that didn't think no more of jumpin' a six-foot fence
than I do o' spittin' off into space. Comparin'
these lean critters with the Herefords of his native
Albion an' points farther north, say Scotland, Bill
the Thirteenth sees a chance to uplift the cattle business in the rebellious colonies an' at the same time
make some money for himself.

So he continues to shovel coal, meanwhile havin'
made application for American citizenship, an' then
some kind of a war comes along and three of his
brothers, includin' the oldest, who are all in the army,
go down to Africa and get killed off.

The shock of this polishes off the earl, an' the family
solicitor starts huntin' for the heir to the earldom, Bill
the Thirteenth. Through the tobacconist's daughter he
gets in touch with the wanderin' boy, who comes home,
shuts up all the earl's houses he can't sell, cleans out
the kitty, marries his heart's desire an' pulls out for
the land of his adoption. He buys an empire east of
the Cascades, in Washington State, an' the northern
boundary of the Emlow ranch is part of the international boundary between the United States and Canada,
or, to be exact, between Washington and British
Columbia. And here he breeds pure-bred Hereford
cattle an' Bill the Fourteenth; from here he sends his
heir to Oxford, after he's finished in the University
of Washington, and allows that if young Bill should
come home with any of the characteristics most promi-
nent on an earl he'll take a quirt to him.

As far as the earl business is concerned, the Emlow

family have declared for a new deal in a new land.
Bill the Thirteenth has fallen so low he's even lost
his Oxford accent.   However, while now thoroughly
American an' desirous of havin' his son even more
so, Bill the Thirteenth can never get his ancestors out
of his head, he's that proud of them. In the matter
of ancestor worship he's worse than a Chinaman,
an' his wife, rememberin' she'd be an earless if she'd
had her rights, never at no time trumps Bill the
Thirteenth's ace when he's dealin' a hand to his prog-
eny on the blood that's back of him.

Well, when Bill the Fourteenth is about fifteen
his mother dies, an' about a year after he returns from
Oxford and is rapidly bein' kidded out of his shawn'ts
and cawn'ts and I-say-old-fellows by a rude lot o'
grade Americans known as cowboys, Bill the Thirteenth
joins his ancestors an' Bill the Fourteenth is lord
of three hundred thousand acres, mostly rolling grass
lands, an' some fifty thousand head of Herefords, as
broad as box cars—which, as Bill Emlow told me
himself, had the earl business beaten to death.

"Which, if I wasn't a good American," says Bill,
"I'd be settin' in the House o' Lords this minute surrounded by a lot of peers with titles so new a feller
could smell the paint on 'em, whereas here I set, on
my own throne, on top of this here breakin' corral,
an' me a cattle king. Got any chewin' tobacco, Dad?"

That was Bill Emlow the Fourteenth. As plain an'
democratic a cowman as you'll ever meet, an' yet
an aristocrat net. I knew mighty well why he hadn't
married. He hadn't met any girl with enough worth-
while ancestors to be the father of Bill the Fifteenth.

Bill finally found a gal with the right kind of
ancestors, tho, so he took her to bosom, as the poet

says, but not until he'd had more fuss an' trouble
than ever his old man had. I seen Bill the Fifteenth
when I was up there last. The heir to the earldom
is risin' five year old now an' looks like a kid with
a lot o' breedin' back of him. Tall for his age, not
too thick an' plenty wide between the ears where his
brains are. An' whereas Bill the Fourteenth waited
until the blush of youth was a trifle faded before he
picked him a wife, when he does elect to pick her it
develops he's no mean picker, so I reckon it's just
as well he waited a spell.

Angela's sure loverlier'n eight aces in a pinochle
hand, and as for ancestors—well, they got the portraits of her ancestors hung up alongside Bill's an'
jedgin' by the faces of some of them Angela runs
clear back to Bloody Mary, for they sure are a pi-
ratical-lookin' crew—all with long faces an' hawk
noses.

Bill says they all look like natural-born undertakers,
an' he's mighty glad Bill the Fifteenth takes after his
father's people, otherwise he'll sure have to bed him
in a coffin instead of a crib.

Fate so ordains that I'm present when Bill Emlow
meets the Lady Angela Hadley. It's late October
of 1913, when I find myself sighin' for the comforts
of the Fourteen Ranch. Yes, fourteen's his brand,
on account of him being the fourteenth Bill Emlow.
Bill's wired me that he has a lot of registered two-
year-old bulls he's willin' to sell at a reasonable price,
so I descend upon him from the train at Spokane,
where he meets me with his French car. The following
morning he mounts me on Tango, which Tango is a

heavy, active, but gentle and sensible old hoss Bill keeps special for aged visitors.

Bill mounts up on a black thoroughbred, and we amble up toward the northern boundary of his ranch to look at the bulls he's got in a field up that way. We've reached a rise of ground, and right before us is one of the monuments that mark the international boundary, so I pull up to read what's on it, when from quite a ways up in British Columbia I hear the belling of all the foxhounds in the world, and pretty soon they heave into sight.

Scattered out behind the hounds, visible here an' there through the patches of willow an' an occasional sycamore or alder, me and Bill makes out the red coats of the huntsmen.

"Here comes the Hadleycroft Hunt," says Bill Emlow, cockin' one leg up over his pommel an' scratchin' a match on his leathern chaps. "The fires o' hell can't change an Englishman, even when he emigrates to Canada. Here they come, all in uniform and ridin' postage stamp saddles. Most of them are remittance men, chasin' coyotes (no, there ain't no red foxes in this country) on the family bank roll. They won't work. They won't even look at work. They lie down alongside of it. Honest, Dad, I wouldn't have one of them on the Fourteen Ranch for a free gift."

"What's these here Hadleycroft Hunt?" says I.

"There's an old duffer name o' Hadley—The Hon. Sir Humphrey A. J. C. Hadley, Bart., to give him all his customary names, a retired colonel of the Fifth Punjab Lancers. He's stuck pigs and Pathans in India, shot tigers afoot in Burma and Ceylon, and now he's chasing coyotes in Canada. He's by way of being a rawncher, don't you know. Has a little stock farm of about ten thousand acres up yonder: a sort of glorified nester. Raises polled Angus cattle and running horses, crosses his running horses on Canadian range mares and gets polo ponies; ships the polo ponies to England and gets half what they're worth. Proud old cove. Must have a lot of money, the way he wastes it on that rawnch of his. Keeps open house. I heard last year he imported a flock of Irish hunters."

"An interestin' neighbor," says I, feelin' Bill out on account o' the contempt I sense in his remarks.

"An interestin' jackass," says Bill, savage like. "His black Angus bulls have a habit of breakin' out of their pasture an' crossin' the line without a passport. Most generally they cross it where my fence marks the boundary, and they breach right through that. Me, I don't like black Herefords with white faces, an' the last calf round-up showed me quite a number with blots on their escutcheons. I like my Herefords a deep cherry red with white faces, the way God intended them to be; and since this retired English army colonel settled in British Columbia the Almighty seems sort of powerless to preserve His handiwork.

"After standin' for this outrage two years in succession, I wrote the colonel all about my grievance, and the first thing I knew he sent half a dozen of his remittance men over to me with orders to buy all my half-bred Hereford-Angus cow critters at my price an' drive 'em away. Also one of these pink-faced remittance men (the foreman, by the way) is the bearer of a most courteous letter from the colonel, apologizin' for his Angus bulls and statin' that while it don't seem possible for him to build fences strong enough to keep his bulls to home, the next best thing

he can do to make the nuisance bearable is to keep
my fences in repair where his bulls breach them an'
furnish me with a steady, dependable and profitable
market for any Herefords with a tinge of black in
them.

"To this communication," Bill adds, "I reply with
equal courtesy, suggestin' a new plan: I offer to stock
him up with registered Herefords at a reasonable price,
provided he gets rid of his black Anguses; then if his
cattle mix with mine the result will be agreeable to me
and I'll relieve him of the responsibliity of buying the
calves. To this the colonel replies that for the past
two years divers of his black Angus cows have been
presenting him with white-faced calves, from which he
judges that some of my Hereford bulls are afflicted
with the wanderlust, and perhaps we'd better call the
battle a draw and let it go at that.

"Not knowing what else to do, I accept his proposition, but not before I've written him again reminding
him that black Angus bulls without horns are frequently found dead in my pastures, on account of my
Hereford bulls having horns. Then I go on to tell
him how much money he'll lose breeding Angus cows.
They're wild and won't be driven, and the best a
feller can expect from Angus cattle is a 40 per cent
calf crop. The colonel came back with the retort
that the Hadleys had always raised Angus cattle, so I
knew that settled it. These dog-goned Britishers don't
do a thing because it's the correct thing to do, although
they spread a lot of propaganda to that effect. They
do a thing because their ancestors did it. That's why
the colonel and his neighbors are at this moment
ridin' to hounds!"

I was sympathizin' with Bill on account of his havin'

unreasonable neighbors residin' in a foreign country where he couldn't sue them for maintainin' a nuisance, when he interrupts. "I wonder whose coyote they're runnin'," he says to himself. "If that's a Canadian coyote, well an' good, but if it's an American coyote I don't aim to have that gang of red-coated wasters ride across my range an' frighten my pure-bred cows most to death with that pack of yelpin' foxhounds."

So we jog down the slope, parallel with the fence, an' presently I catch a glimpse of the quarry—at least I can see flashes of the white on the under side of his tail, as he lopes ahead of the hounds, occasionally leaping a bush. We're ridin' straight across the coyote's path, an' pretty son Bill puts his fingers in his mouth an' whistles. Right off the coyote answers with a friendly yip and heads toward us. Under the fence he crawls and lopes up to Bill, who stoops down, picks him up by the nape of the neck and drapes him across his saddle.

"The trail's lost, Dad," says Bill. "Let's mosey along about our business. This here's an American coyote, and I aim to give him the protection of Old Glory. Yes, sir. This coyote certainly has consular representation."

"Which he's most certainly goin' to need it, Bill," I says, because lookin' back just then I saw a girl, ridin' a side-saddle, come flyin' across a wide irrigation ditch. She's a quarter of a mile ahead of the field an' right up with the hounds. In about a minute the hounds came through the fence like the German army came through Belgium—an' behind them comes that girl on a horse as tall as an elephant. I hear her give a little cry of encouragement to her mount, and then she's over that barbed-wire fence and pounding straight toward us. The next thing I know old Tangos goin' high, wide an' handsome in the middle of forty foxhounds; by the time he'd bucked himself out of the mess and I can look around them forty hounds is tryin' to get in the saddle with Bill Emlow and he is holdin' the coyote over his head with both hands an' tryin' to control his horse with the other.

"So sorry," says the girl, and slips off her monument of an Irish hunter. She lays into the pack with her ridin' crop; they know her voice and after each of the forty has been struck as much as half a dozen times each, the pack backs off whimperin' and sit around in circles to see what'll happen next. What happens is that this Diana grabs Bill's thoroughbred by the bridle and steadies him—and when that's done she and Bill Emlow look straight into each other's eyes —and both pair of eyes are flashin'.

"Well," says the girl, "what have you got to say for yourself, spoilin' the sport as you have?"

"All I've got to say, young lady," says Bart. Emlow, "is that every post on this line fence carries a sign pointin' toward British Columbia and conveyin' the information to all and sundry that trespassin' is not only not desired but is also forbidden by the owner of this ranch."

"I didn't see your foolish sign," says the girl. "I was comin' too fast. And I'd have been in at the death in another minute if you hadn't picked up this exhausted coyote—"

"You're cruel an' bloodthirsty," says Bill. "Have a heart."

"It's not cruel and bloodthirsty to kill a coyote.'

"I'll admit most coyotes are a walking misdemeanor," says Bill, "but not this one. This is an American coyote. His name is Jeff, an' he happens to belong to me. Look! Here's his name and my name and address on his collar."

"Oh-h-h!" says the girl. "Sorry! By the way, aren't you English?"

"Listen to the woman," says Bill Emlow, horrified. "If I was English, I'd have sacrificed little Jeff rather than kill the hunt."

"Pardon! I rather thought—from your accent, you know, and if you were English I was at a loss to understand—"

"Quite so, quite so," says Bill, "unfortunately educated at Oxford, but an American just the same—only more so. My name is Bill Emlow."

"I haven't asked you for your silly name," says the girl with spirit.

"I'm a free giver," says Bill. "I don't have to be asked for anything. What kind of a hatrack is that you're ridin'? An Irish hunter?"

"Yes," says my lady. "Isn't he simply toppin'?

"He's all of that," says Bill. "In fact, I never saw a horse with more top to him. He must be eighteen hands high. Where did you pick up my little Jeff coyote?"

"About eight miles from here."

Bill cuffs Jeff. "You little sneakin' devil," he says, "What do you mean by moseyin' up to Hadleycroft to steal the colonel's prize chickens, eh? Don't you get enough to eat at home? First thing you know I'll restrict your freedom." He looks down at the girl. "Much obliged for savin' my life," he says. "If you hadn't caught up my horse, I might have had to let Jeff go to save myself."

They looked at each other again—and then the girl commenced to laugh—the healthiest, merriest, friendliest laugh I ever did hear. "So you're the quaint American who writes Father the funny letters?" she says.

"Lady Angela Hadley," says Bill risin' in his stirrups and bowin' very low over Jeff.

"Who told you I'm a Lady?"

"Well, I can see that with my eyes shut, and if that ain't reason enough I must inform you that I read in the last issue of the Times to reach me that your father's grandfather had popped off, which shoves the colonel up a notch in the peerage and consequently makes his daughter a Lady whether she is or not."

"You're so droll," says Lady Angela.

"I am remiss in my manners, Lady Angela," says Bill. "Permit me to present one of my good friends and a fellow cowman, Mr. Tully."

Lady Angela gives me a cool look that sets me in my place, but she's politer'n hell, I'll say that for her. Without tellin' me so she lets me know I aint in her class. Bill passes me the ghost of a wink.

"How is the coyote runnin' in British Columbia these bright days, Lady Angela?" he asks.

"Awful, Mr. Emlow. We cannot seem to raise a coyote, and as a result the last three meets of the Hadleycroft Hunt have been dismal failures."

"I'll have to stop all that, Lady Angela. Just let me know what days you hunt, and I'll send one of the boys up with Jeff. All I ask is a fair chance an' no favor for the little feller, because I'm right fond o' Jeff, havin' raised him from a pup. He's got to be turned loose half a mile from the start and after that if any member of the hunt gets Jeff's brush I'm agreeable. Jeff's got to be taught that Hadleycroft ain't a healthy place for him. Ain't nature wonderful, Lady Angela? I feed Jeff all a coyote can eat, yet he prefers to wander ten miles on the off chance of stealin' some grub." An' he cuffs Jeff some more.

"I think you're an awfully good sport," says Lady Angela. "One doesn't expect that sort of thing in your country, you know."

"Quite so, quite so," says Bill, goin' all out, as they say in London, with his disused Oxford accent. "But we always expect that sort of thing in our country, eh, what? This hands-across-the-sea business is going to be all off until you jolly Britishers get cured of the notion that you can patronize us. And while we're getting acquainted, let's settle our social standing once and for keeps. While I haven't any more use for a title than Jeff has for your hounds, I'll have you know that my tribe was makin' an' unmakin' the kings of Britain centuries before the sport had become popular with the masses of runnin' your tribe down to take 'em out of bearskins and put 'em into petticoats."

"We're rather old, you know," says Lady Angela with a noticeable chill in her eyes.

"I've looked you up in Burke's Peerage," says Bill, "and you're mere Johnnies-come-lately. All of the best families didn't settle north of that monument. Not by a considerable! My friend Mr. Tully, for instance, may, for purely social purposes, refer to himself as the Earl of Pawtucket."

Lady Angela burst out laughing. "I've seen the play, old thing," she said. "Do let's be friends. Here comes my father and the other gentlemen of the hunt. I should so much like to have them meet you."

"With all the pleasure in life. Bring 'em over," says Bill. But Lady Angela looked at that barbed-wire fence. "One doesn't jump such obstacles unless one happens to be up to them before one notices them— as I did."

"Ain't you goin' to jump back home?" says Bill, surprised.

"Is it worth the risk, Mr. Emlow?"

Bill passes me Jeff to hold, removes his chaps and drapes 'em along the top wire of that fence, so her horse can see what he's bein' asked to hurdle. "Thanks awfully," says Lady Angela, an' sails over like a bird. Bill mounts up an' sails over after her, seein' which I follow with old Tango, and we're all presented to the Hadleycroft Hunt. Everybody's most polite, but I noticed that when Bill turned Jeff over to the master of the hounds, with permission to sick the hounds on him the first time they felt like it, he receives a lot of thanks an' praise for his sportin' attitude, but neither Lady Angela nor the old man invites him to join in the next hunt or attend the hunt breakfast.

Bill explains the etiquet of this hunting business as we ride back to his place. Durin' lunch I suggests to Bill that his action in bawlin' Lady Angela out like he done wasn't calculated to make her cheer for him none whatever.

"Don't you make no bets on that proposition, Jed," he says. "A Britisher knows exactly where he or she belongs in the body politic, and any time he or she gets out of that class and finds somebody smart enough to remind 'em of it, it's never an occasion for hard feelings. The only crime I could commit with Lady Angela would be in lettin' her get away with murder. Whether a feller is right or wrong doesn't matter. It's lowerin' the tail an' bendin' the neck that gravels that class of Britisher. They hate an Anglo-maniac worse than I do. If that girl has a motto on her family crest, I'll bet it reads: 'Be yourself.'" He was silent, sippin' his tea, an' finally he says:

"She'll do."

"Do for what?" I asks.

"For my wife, you old idiot! I'm goin' to marry her as sure as death and taxes. She doesn't know she's going to marry a mere cow waddy, and the bare thought of it now would make her sick, but—she'll do it.

"Why not save trouble and expense by sendin' her over your pedigree to peruse?" I suggest. "Once she finds you're really the Earl of Sub Rosa, Baron Bill of Nux Vomica and High Lord Chancellor of your own Exchequer, the chances are she surrenders without firin' a shot."

"I'd die a bachelor first. Me, I'm tradin' on what I am, not what my ancestors was. But still I got some pride o' race an' lineage. If you had a horse that was a world beater over a mile an' a half course and you wanted to reproduce him, you wouldn't breed him to a range mare, would you? If you did, most likely you'd get a quarter horse that'd have hairy fetlocks. The Lady Angela's a thoroughbred, which is advantage No. 1, and I'm madly in love with her, which is advantage No. 2. My family tree, which is advantage No. 3, I decline to use. This game has got to be played accordin' to the rules of a country with

horizons in it, and that goes for the entire continent
of North America. Did you see any Canadians in
that hunt this morning?"

I had to admit I hadn't, because one of them beastly
colonials is almost if not impossible to tell from one
of us and the only two men resembling us there present
was me an' Bill Emlow.

The next morning Bill turned me over to Jim Yeager,
his foreman, in lieu of better human society, and
motored over to Spokane. He's back, that night, and
a week later, while we're settin' on the front porch
chewing the rag, Jeff comes lopin' in and without even
a nod to Bill passes on through the house to the
kitchen. Pretty soon we hear the bellin' of hounds,
and before I could say knife (which I wouldn't, although Bill always did) that hell-anointed pack o'
hounds boils into the yard, up over the veranda an'
plumb back into the kitchen. The Chinese cook hears
'em comin' just in time to open a little door and let
Jeff pop in under the sink; then, as the first three tiers
of hounds crashes the door leadin' to the dinin'-room
that Chink lights out the back door an' makes for a
tree. Bill never says nothin' or makes a move. Just
keeps on smokin', an' the next thing we know Lady
Angela comes poundin' up to the foot of the stairs
on her Irish hunter.

Bill rises an' bows. "Ride right in through the hall-
way," he says. "Jeff has gone to earth in the kitchen.
My Chinese cook will lend you a cleaver to remove
his brush."

Before she can quit laughin' the rest of the hunt
arrives, and the M. F. H., which he's the dog man in
charge, goes back into Bill's kitchen and shoos the
pack out. Bill makes all hands welcome to the Four-

teen Ranch, the Chink is induced to come down out of the tree and serve a flock of drinks, and when that's done Bill says:

"I had an idea Jeff would head for home and that you folks would arrive hotfoot in his wake, all steamed up and hungry as panthers. So I decided to have the hunt breakfast all ready an' waitin' for you."

"Oh, but, my dear, dear chap," says old Hadley, which he's as fine an' upstandin' an old boy as I ever see, "we're having the hunt breakfast at Hadleycroft. We must be riding back."

"You're doin' nothin' of the sort. I'm the boss of this ranch, and what I say goes here. What do you suppose I had rails nailed on the top of that boundary fence for? Why, so your horses could see what they had to jump—and jump it. Otherwise I wouldn't have had anybody except Lady Angela for my hunt breakfast."

"But really," says the colonel, but Lady Angela put her hand over his mouth.

"Hasn't Jeff got some rights in this party, pater?" she asks. "I'm certain if Jeff furnishes the sport, Jeff's master has every right to claim us as his guests—particularly," she adds bravely, "since he has so delicately taught us a lesson in neighborliness and courtesy. Mr. Emlow, I do hope you understand why you were not invited to help pursue your own coyote. We British aren't really rude, but a bit shy—a bit standoffish. We like to know strangers rather well before we—"

"And of course," says the colonel, "it never occurred to us that you might care to ride to hounds."

"I don't care to ride to them. I have to ride to cows so much horseback ridin' is a business with me,

not a pastime. What I do like, however, is the society
of my own kind."

"Then you mustn't blame us for having negelected
to invite you, Mr. Emlow. With the utmost appreciation and admiration of your kind, we're not it—eh,
what, what?"

"When do we eat?" says Lady Angela. She realizes
Bill has slapped the Hadleycroft Hunt on the wrist in
the nicest and most delicate way; she can't slap back
and like a good sport she's willing Bill shall know
how well she can take a lickin'.

"We eat as soon as my guests can titivate themselves," says Bill, and rings for his Chinese house boy
to direct the ladies to a guest chamber where they
can powder their noses, as the saying goes. He has
a couple of hands come over and take the horses to
the barn, and he looks after the gentlemen himself.
Bill don't bother to remove his chaps and spurs, but
out of deference to the company he does put on his
coat. Come to think of it, Bill always did eat with
his coat on. Then he sits at the head of the table,
with Lady Angela at his right and the colonel at his
left and proceeds to pull off a party that would have
done credit to the Prince of Wales.

He even gives the customary toast to the jolly old
king, God bless him, whereupon Colonel Hadley toasts
the President of the United States; then Jeff is brought
in and drinks a toast to the guests, lapping a little
hooch out of a saucer, and all is merry as hell.

Bill's hard to beat as a host. His manners is perfect,
his grace something to conjure with. He's a good
storyteller and a good talker, and our British cousins
find him devilish quaint, don't you know. Charming

chap, eh, what! And when the meal is finished and all hands retire to the veranda for liqueurs an' coffee, Lady Angela starts wanderin' around the shack and runs into Bill's ancestors in the drawing-room.

I knew she had because she came out and drug her old man in for a look, and I reckon them ancestors must have been ugly enough an' ancient enough to please the most exactin', because just before the Hadleycroft Hunt mounts up for the ride home, the old colonel makes a motion, which is instantly seconded by Lady Angela and unanimously carried by all an' sundry, that Mr. Emlow hunt with them the following Thursday and stay over for the hunt breakfast at Hadleycroft Lodge. As the start will be early, Mr. Emlow must come over on Wednesday and remain all night.

"Sure, I'll come," says Bill. "I been bankin' on bein' asked. So much so, in fact," he adds with that amazin' innocence that's so devastatin' to Lady Angela, "that last week I drove over to Spokane and give a tailor an order for my coyote huntin' clothes. When in Rome do as the jolly old Romans do, is my motto."

Well, the Hadleycroft Hunt was certainly laughin' as they said good-by.

On Tuesday Bill motored to Spokane again, and on Wednesday after lunch he treated the Fourteen Ranch to a surprise, by unpackin' a pigskin ridin' saddle as flat as stale beer, an' orderin' Jim Yeager, the foreman, to see that it was plastered on that thoroughbred of his. Also he has a bridle with two bits and two sets of reins, which certainly beat Jim's time, an' he said so.

Jim was so curious as to future events that he brought the saddled horse over to the house himself,

and incidentally all the hired help quit whatever jobs
they was on to follow Jim and the horse. And well
are they rewarded, for what their eager eyes rest
on is Bill Emlow all dressed up to shame the lilies
of the field. He has black ridin' boots armed with
little nickeled steel spurs without rowels; his pants
is whiter'n the driven snow, his coat has a long tail
an' is red as fire an' he's wearin' a red jocky cap an'
carryin' a ridin' crop. His face is calm an' dignified
as he comes walkin' majestically down the steps.

"Your Majesty," says Jim Yeager, "there is a horse
without."

"Shut up," says Bill Emlow, very snappish.

"Yes, good m'lord," says Jim—and then Jim an'
his followers lets out mournful cries an' falls flat on
their faces in the dust. "Which any waddy that dares
to cast human eyes upon this godly sight gits fired muy
pronto," said Jim Yeager. Bill Emlow gives Jim an
undignified root in the tail. "Arise, Sir Knight," says
he, "an' hustle back here with my Jeff coyote."

Presently, with Jeff spraddled out in front of him,
Bill rides away to Hadleycroft, leavin' mental chaos
an' desolation behind him. Jim Yeager allows it ain't
dignified for him to work for Bill Emlow no longer,
and thinks he'll quit. As for me, all of my affairs
are in the capable hands of my foreman, so as there
ain't no reason why I should hurry home I elect to
linger an' ride herd on this love affair of Bill Emlow's.

Bill gets home for supper Thursday night, all wet
an' sloppy as a coon that's been huntin' goldfish. His
white pants is now black, his white stock is wilted
an' unclean, an' there's mud spots all over his red coat,
which is badly torn. An' I notice he's a mite stiff
as he climbs off his horse, but what I notice in particu-

lar is that Bill's sperrits has sagged to zero. All
through dinner he refrains from mentionin' the hunt.
So, naturally, I didn't mention it. However, just
before bedtime he sighs an' says:

"Dad, I had a hell of a time. Them dod-gasted
dogs all but cornered Jeff, an' the little feller got
so hard pressed he just naturally give up an' doubled
right back to me. I couldn't lean out o' that hell-
anointed English saddle to pick him up, so I got off
to pick him up, an' not a minute too soon. I had to
hold him over my head, at arm's length, while them
hounds kept jumpin' for him an' ever an' anon takin'
a nip out o' me or my coat. Jeff had took us through
some rough country an' at the finish there was only
me an' Angela present—me to save Jeff an' Angela
to save me. Finally I got Jeff tucked up in the forks
of an alder tree, where the dogs could jump at him to
their hearts' content while Angela and yours truly discussed sport. Angela allows that my thoroughbred is
the fastest long-distance runner an' the best jumper
she's ever seen; also she allows that for a novice at
hounds I'm just a plain devil. I can see she likes
me an' admires me some, so as there wasn't the least
bit of use waitin' an' wastin' time, right then and there
I propositioned her for her hand in the bonds of holy
matrimony."

"And she refused you, Bill?" says, I, most sympathetic.

"All she says, Dad, is: 'My word! You *are* fast.'"
So I told her that was the American way o' doin'
things an' renewed the offer of my hand, includin'
with it all my goods an' chattels an' takin' care to
inform her they ain't encumbered for more than a
fifth of their value. I said that I'd be a High Church
Episcopalian if I worked at it an' if my early youth

hadn't been blighted by cows an' cowboys. I tell her
I come of good, solid British stock originally an' none
of us has ever been in jail or executed except for
political offenses, the only reason they were offenses
bein' that the revolutions failed, so that what was magnificent patriotism to-day was treason to the king
to-morrow.

"All the time I'm talkin' to her she's laughin' at
me, an' when I'm through she tells me I'm so droll
I'm better than a doctor's prescription in a dry county.
Finally she gets the notion I'm dead serious, so she
lays her little hand on my arm an' says: 'Look here,
old thing, I'm sorry. Really. I'm engaged to Lord
Bardleigh.'

"Well, Dad, I'd met this Lord Bardleigh at dinner
the night before an' took an active dislike to him.
I can see he's got a Hanoverian strain in him—a
heavy, stocky man, with a lot o' beam across his
southern elevation an' a neck that runs up too straight
an' quick in back. So naturally I'm interested in his
pedigree an' question him more or less on the subject.
He seems disinclined to discuss it, but, like all Americans, I'm dead interested an' I *will* ask questions, so
by the time the black coffee comes on I have his
family tree all square in my mind. Evidently he gets
weary answerin' questions because presently he starts
talkin' French to Lady Angela, askin' her all about
me an' expressin' himself quite freely about my native
Americanisms. I'd studied French four years at Oxford an' a year in Paris, an' while I reckon I speak
with a foreign accent I never had no difficulty gettin'
along in French society. An' I notice that Lord
Bardleigh's learned his French in Heidelberg, although
it being no affair of mine I don't mention it, nor do I

tip it off that I'm drinkin' in every word o' French
he's spoutin'. It never occurs to me, until Lady
Angela slips me the fatal tidings, that Lord Bardleigh's
in my way. When she does I says: 'Lord Bardleigh,
eh? Who did his folks tend bar for?"

"'That,' says Lady Angela, 'is not at all nice of
you, Mr. Emlow.'

"'I don't like him,' I says. 'And I don't intend
that you shall marry him. You're too good for him.'

"She has another laughin' spell at this, and informs
me I'm too simply delicious for anything and consequently she can't quarrel with me. Then she gets
serious and tells me all about Lord Bardleigh, his fine
old family, his wealth an' his estates in Sussex, an'
how he's been a sort of wanderer. Been an officer
in the French Foreign Legion in Morocco an' commanded a cavalry regiment in the Bulgarian-Turkish
war an' fought with the Italians at Tripoli. He's a
big game hunter an' has just come down from a trip
up into the Arctic Circle.

"When I ask her who told her all this she says he
did an' when I tell her I'll have to have corroborative
evidence before I'll believe it, she says he has all kinds
of credentials and I can look him up in Burke's Peerage,
if I doubt him. She ends up by hopin' us two will get
to be good friends, but I tell her straight there ain't
a Chinaman's chance o' that. Then we ride back to
pick up the stragglers and when we hit a road an'
the grooms are there to take charge of the horses,
the hunt goes back to Hadleycroft in automobiles.

"Nice place, Hadleycroft, and the colonel certainly
has about five hundred of the finest horses in Canada.
His half thoroughbreds, which he sells for polo ponies

are a bit big for polo—about fifteen two. More suited
for cavalry than polo.

"At the hunt breakfast Lady Angela had Lord
Bardleigh on her right an' I'm told off to amuse an old
maid that can't talk a thing but sports an' is deaf
into the bargain."

"I reckon then, Bill," I says, "you didn't have a very
good time."

"Not exactly," he says, "but I think I have a good
time comin'. I ain't afraid none of this Lord Bardleigh.
A feller can fool some of the people all of the time and
all of the people some of the time, but it just don't
lay in nature that he can fool all of the people all of
the time—an' Lord Bardleigh didn't fool me. He's
goin' to receive a telegram callin' him away on important business, an' in order to make sure that he does
I'm goin' to write that horse thief a letter."

So sayin' Bill goes to his typewriter an' writes as
follows:

Lord Bardleigh,
Hadleycroft Lodge,
Dear August:
Beat it for Berlin. All is discovered. Leave your
title behind, because it belongs to somebody else. I
am coming to Hadleycroft the day after to-morrow
and if I find you there I'll certainly make you hard
to catch.

Cordially yours,
EMLOW.

P. S.—Even if I am an American cowman, I speak
better French than you do and not with a Heidelberg
accent.

Bill sits ponderin' a minute, then he drags out another sheet of his ranch stationery and writes in longhand to Lady Angela:

Dear Lady Angela:
Twenty-four hours after you receive this letter that big piece of weinerwurst you are engaged to marry is going to receive a telegram calling him away. He isn't coming back either, so you might as well forget him and give serious consideration to the proposition I made you this morning. Jeff has more nobility than that bird. Bet you anything his lordship's father runs a brewery in Berlin. Sorry to jolt you like this, but I can't see you and the colonel hornswoggled while I stand idly by. That wouldn't be playing the game.
Lovingly yours,
BILL EMLOW.

The next morning Bill sends one of his hands over to Hadleycroft Lodge with these letters, and the following day he mounts up, without bothering to use his new saddle and fancy clothes, and rides over to Hadleycroft himself. There's an automobile drawn up in front of the house when Bill rides in, and Lord Bardleigh is on the steps takin' a fond farewell of the Colonel and Lady Angela. Bill tells me his lordship gets very red an' then very pale at sight of him. Doffin' his sombrero to all hands, Bill says gayly:

"Why, is his lordship not gone yet? Must have been a break in the telegraph line somewhere?"

Lady Angela is in what Bill later refers to as a regal rage. "Mr. Emlow," she says, "this situation requires an explanation. You have made certain charges derogatory to Lord Bardleigh—"

"Herr Augoost von Twinkletoes, Lady Angela," says Bill, interruptin'. "Watch his dust."

"Mr. Emlow," says the colonel, "your levity is always delightful, but what we require here is facts. Lord Bardleigh denies the charge made in the extraordinary letter you saw fit to send my daughter yesterday, and inasmuch as he is her fiance—"

"Pardon the interruption, Colonel," says Bill, "but Augoost is not her fiance. I am. Lady Angela doesn't know this yet, but I put my application on file yesterday, and as soon as Augoost is out of the way I've naturally got to come up for consideration."

"If I remain to listen to the silly chaff of this vulgar fellow," says Lord Bardleigh, "I shall miss my train. Have him explain himself by all means, my dear Colonel. I'll be back to-morrow, never fear." And with a smile and a lift of his hat, he enters the car and says to the chauffeur, "Let's go, my man."

So they went, and Bill clumb down off his horse an' set down on the steps an' rolled a cigaret, contemplative like. "So you still believe in Lord Bardleigh eh?" he says. "Lady Angela, I warned you that he would receive a telegram calling him away very suddenly. Did he receive it?"

"He did, Mr. Emlow. Naturally he would—when you sent it!"

"I dislike to appear inhospitable, Mr. Emlow," says the colonel, "but unless you can substantiate your allegations I must ask you not to call again at Hadleycroft Lodge."

"All right. I'll substantiate them," says Bill, an' with a jump he's in his saddle. He don't stop to open any gates. He goes over 'em, an' across the colonel's fields to cut Lord Bardleigh off on the highway leadin' to the railroad. His lordship sees him comin' an' tells the chauffeur to step on the gas, but on account of him not payin' the chauffeur's wages (it's the colonel's car) the boy can't see any reason why he should run away from a friend of the colonel's! He protests an' wants a reason, most likely, he says, Mr. Emlow is the bearer of some final message from the colonel, so he'd better stop and wait. This not suitin' Lord Bardleigh a little bit, he picks the boy up from back o' the wheel an' roughly drops him overside into the roadside ditch, after which he slides in behind that wheel himself an' moves on at sixty miles an hour.

Seein' he's goin' to lose him, Bill pulls up, an' Lord Bardleigh, looking back, sees that Bill has abandoned the chase, so he slows down and takes it easy.

Bill waits until he'd turned a bend, an' then straight across the road he goes, taking the fences on each side an' up the hillside, for he knows the highway runs ahead about a mile along the west slope of the hill, turns the toe of it an' doubles back on the east side.

Bill gets over the hill and comes chargin' down the other slope as Lord Bardleigh appears in the distance, an' although Bardleigh speeds up an' passes the spot where Bill's course intercepts the road, Bill doesn't slack up this time. So his lordship takes to emptyin' a gun at him. But this doesn't stop Bill a-tall, an' when Bardleigh's gun's empty he can't take his hands off'n the steerin' wheel to reload it.

Pretty soon he comes to a place in the road where a gang of men are at work. They've plowed up the highway an' are about to grade it, an' Lord Bardleigh has half a mile of this goin' ahead of him. He can't help easin' up; if he don't come down to ten miles an hour, he'll bust the car and jar himself out on his ear. He toots long an' loud to clear the road, and while his tootin' gets him immediate action from the men at work, it don't cause Bill Emlow to side-step none. On he comes.

Bill, he has his rope out now—an' just as Bardleigh reaches the smooth goin' again Bill's twine settles over him—a jerk an' his arms are tight aganist his side, and he has to put on the brakes or get jerked out of the car. Bill's horse holds him taut while Bill dismounts, climbs into the car an' hogties his lordship. Then he casts off his rope, climbs in behind the wheel an' with his horse jogging along behind he returns peaceably to Hadleycroft.

On the way back he talks to Lord Bardleigh an' tells him just what he wants, so when presently Lady Angela faces him it ain't any use for him to deny he's a faker. The chauffeur's already made his way back to the house with his report and the colonel has his opinion, anyhow, of any sprig of the nobility that'll treat his host's servant like that an' help himself to his host's automobile.

Lord Bardleigh knows he's nabbed—not an out in the world—so he confesses he ain't Lord Bardleigh, but on account of findin' that title is real but hasn't been in active use for more'n twenty years an' nobody knows who or where the real Lord Bardleigh is, if any, he familiarizes himself with the family history an', backed up by Burke's Peerage, he gets away with the deal and manages to induce a lot of responsible people to give him letters of introduction an' vouch for him.

The English are hell on letters of introduction, anyhow, an' I don't know why, because the only one I

ever give a fellow cost me four hundred and ten dollars to square the debts he contracted with my friends
before leavin' for parts unknown.

Well, of course Lady Angela and the colonel are
justly indignant and can't get shut of this maverick
quick enough, so Bill pilots the late lamented over to
the railroad and at partin' gives him a smack on
the ear and a boot on the widest part of him, and thus
the rivals part.

Bill, returnin' to Hadleycroft with the car to get
his horse, is greeted like the Prodigal Son. Of course
Lady Angela's a lot fussed and embarrassed and cries
some for her lost love, because it seems, even accordin' to Bill, that, to give the devil his due, this bogus
lord has a mighty takin' way about him an' is as
handsome as a human bein', almost. But as for the
colonel, he is no end set up about Bill now, as they say
in England.

"Egad," says the colonel, "one cawn't pull the leg of
a Yank and come it over him, eh, what?" He asks
Bill how come he sniffs the fraud out so quick, and
Bill says that's just his art, that all his life he's been
trained to notice little, unimportant things that most
folks overlooks, and besides he happens to have been
at Oxford with the real Lord Bardleigh, which the
genuine article is a lot taller'n the substitute an' much
thinner, looks an' acts more like an American than a
German soldier of fortune and is commonplace an'
ornery in his habits, bein' just as much at home with
plain folks as he is with the nobility.

Bill stays for dinner an' rides home in the moonlight, but when he leaves Hadleycroft that night he's
top-hole with the colonel and his daughter, as they
say in perfidious Albion. At partin' he allows he won't

be over for a week or two on account of havin' his annual horse-breakin' stunts to perform. So he performs
them, an' I stay on a week longer to observe the fun
and watch Bill build a throne upon top of his breakin'
corral, where the colonel and his daughter can sit an'
watch the performance.

Bill rides everything in the corral to a squealin'
finish, and Angela's right proud of him, but she's been
hard hit by that wanderin' scion of an ignoble house
and she ain't the sort of girl that can off with the old
love an' on with the new just because some hard-drivin'
American insists on it. I tell Bill so, and he agrees
with me that his chances of makin' the grade are
better if he don't crowd his hand at this embarrassin'
time.

Well, all of Bill's broomtails have been topped except one miserable little blue-roan cayuse with a china
eye, but as it's gettin' late the colonel and Lady Angela mount up and start home. A little matter of
fifteen mile across country was duck soup to them.
Bill saw them off an' then came back and run a specu-
lative eye over that blue-roan cayuse.

"Better let that rat go, Bill," I suggested. "You've
been shook up more'n usual to-day, what with the job
n' showin' off before your lady love. You're tired, an'
this excuse for a horse may swap ends with you successfully."

But Bill's British blood makes him bull-headed. My
advice sounded too much like quittin' talk, an' Bill has
all the reverence of his ancestors for playin' the game
to the finish. So he tops this blue-roan critter an' gets
the ride of his life. What he'd had durin' the day was
mere sheep jumpin' to what that cayuse gave him, an'
I was sure sorry Lady Angela had gone home an'

missed the sight of as fine a bit o'ridin' as I ever did
see. About ten seconds later, however, I'm glad she
ain't there, because that critter turned a complete
somersault and when he rose up Bill Emlow had been
rolled on good an' plenty an' was lyin' mighty white
an' still in the dirt of the breakin' corral.

Well, we toted Bill over to the house an' telephoned
to town for a doctor, who found a broken collarbone,
right arm fractured in two places, both legs busted an'
a couple o' ribs sprung out from the backbone. The
medico allows Bill's inner works must be squashed
up a lot and that the boy'll die. However, Bill don't
die that night, an' as there ain't no sense in movin' him
I have a couple of trained nurses sent out, and at the
end of a week it appears Bill is goin' to live. His
fractures are all clean breaks, so, as I ain't much in
a sickroom and have my own ranch to look after
besides, I bid Bill Emlow good-by and go home.

The nurses write me favorable reports right regu-
larly, and bimeby I get a letter from Bill sayin' he's
likely to last till spring, but no matter how long he
lives he ain't never goin' to have no more familiar
doings with unbroke horses. He says Lady Angela and
the colonel used to ride over right frequent to cheer
his lonely state, but that business connected with his
new title an' the entailed estate has now took them to
England. They won't be back till summer, an' Hadleycroft's been left at the mercy o' them remittance men
employees.

Bill allows that the thought of Lady Angela
being in London, completely surrounded by genuine
lords, dukes an' earls, is most maddenin' to him while
he's confined to the house, but come the day he can
chuck his crutches he's goin' to leave Jim Yeager in

charge of the Fourteen Ranch an' beat it to London to
look after his interests. Jim's been on the ranch so
long he's become part of the assets an' is perfectly
capable of runnin' it right.

Time passes. Then I get another letter from Bill,
an' it seems the colonel has written him that things
ain't goin' so well at Hadleycroft, and can he lend him
Jim Yeager to look after things until him and Angela
returns in July? Of course Bill can't refuse this request, altho it makes him b'ilin' mad to let Jeff go,
on account of not havin' anybody to take Jim's place,
thereby necessitatin' Bill's remainin' home instead of
chasin' to London after Lady Angela. However, he
composes his soul as best he can an' on the first of
August Colonel Hadley (now what you call a vee-
count) and Angela return to Hadleycroft.

Bill is practically his old self by this time, but when
he calls at Hadleycroft things ain't the same. The war
has busted out in Europe, an' all them remittance men,
an' other Britishers that was under contract at nothing
a month to learn rawnchin' in Canada, has all beaten
it away to get into the army. Vee-count Hadley ain't
no sooner home than he has to leave again. He's on
the retired list, but a grateful government says yes
when he cables his request for active service, and as
things don't look right in India, he's shot back there
to his old job as colonel of the Punjab Lancers, and
Lady Angela is left in charge of Hadleycroft.

She's all for bein' a nurse or drivin' an ambulance
or makin' recruitin' speeches, but the old man declares
her job is at home lookin' after them horses and Angus
cattle. It developed that the Germans have been
buying up all the horses available for months, an, if

the British cavalry are to have replacements the vee-
count figures on furnishin' his quota. So Lady Angela
settles down at Hadleycroft an' Bill Emlow tells Jim
Yeager he just naturally has to work for her until the
war is over. Of course this makes his own ranch
duties fall heavy on Bill, so the best he can do is one
visit a week to Hadleycroft, where Lady Angela has
her aunt chaperonin' her by now.

I run up to visit Bill that fall because I'm curious
to see whether his politics is British or American. On
account of dwellin' alone in his house with all them
beak-nosed ancestors, I figured Bill would be cussin'
the U. S. A. to beat four of a kind.

To my surprise, I find him the most rabid American
in America, an' I ain't long findin' out who's responsible. It's the Lady Angela. Bill is in low sperrits
when I arrive, but a feller can't carry a grouch around
when there's an old man handy to unload it on, so presently Bill unloads his grief. It seems Lady Angela
gets to prowlin' around British Columbia makin' recruitin' speeches an' sendin' them Canucks to their
deaths, an' pretty soon she's cleaned up all the available man power an' crosses the international border
looking for sympathy. First she tells Jim Yeager how
glorious it would be if Jim would die for king and
country, an' Jim tells her straight out it ain't his country and to hell with the king. So Lady Angela fires
him and when he comes back to the Fourteen Ranch
Bill rides over to Hadleycroft to argue with the girl.

First off he tells her p'intedly she ain't the one to
fire Jim, because Jim ain't been hired at all. He's
been lent as a favor and at her paw's request, an even
if he is a grade American he's one of the best and an
A No. 1 cowman, which he's not used to havin' his

feeling's hurt, added to which Hadleycroft can't be
run without him, so if she'll apologize to Jim Yeager
he'll overlook her impertinence an' come back.

Every word of this bein' the whole truth an' nothing
but, naturally Lady Angela flies into what Bill calls a
royal rage an' changes the subject of conversation.
I've noticed that all women, whether ladies or scrub-
women, pull this line on a man when he has them run
into a corner. Lady Angela says:

"Mr. Emlow, some months back, when I expressed
mild surprise that you had not, out of respect an'
veneration for your ancient line of British ancestry,
enlisted in our forces at the outbreak of the war, you
informed me you couldn't do that because you had
nobody to leave in charge of your ranch. Well, you've
got your Mr. Jim Yeager back now, so what are you
goin' to do about this war?"

"That," says Bill Emlow, "is none of your business.
I'm an American citizen an' I love my country, an' I
don't love yours. I don't see why we should bust a
leg runnin' wild to horn in on your fight, just because
it seems you're goin' to get licked. In our Civil War
almost 35,000 Germans fought for the Union, but
there were less than 3,000 Englishmen. The rest of
your countrymen were busy lendin' aid an' comfort to
the Confederacy, tryin' to bust up our country. A lot
of us Americans remember that, an' we think back even
farther."

"But this war threatens civilization," says Lady
Angela. "If the Germans win it, they'll be tackling
your country next."

"Well, I'm willin' to wait until they give us reason
to dislike 'em more than we do," says Bill. "I'm not

goin' to let my ranch an' cattle go to glory for the privilege of hornin' in on a fight that's none of my business—yet."

"You Americans are impossible," says Lady Angela.

"When are you goin' to marry me?" says Bill.

"After you return from this war," says Lady Angela.

"I don't want you bad enough to win you that way," says Bill, provin' his blood by sayin' just exactly what he thought regardless of her feelin's.

"I think your country is acting contemptibly, Mr. Emlow."

"If yours would do more fightin' an' less complainin', it might get somewhere," Bill fires back at her. "The trouble with you British is that you're so doggoned dull you couldn't see this thing comin' and now you're rattled an' runnin' in circles like a pup chasin' its tail. Anyhow, you haven't done any real fightin' yet. The French are fightin' your war for you now. Maybe the French *are* crazy, but they had sense enough to know this thing might happen an' they got an army in the field quicker'n you could say knife." Not receivin' any reply Bill barged on.

"The idea of you people railin' at us because we won't join in your war!" he says. "Why, a feller can't throw a rock up in the air without havin' it fall on a German citizen of the U. S. A., whereas you couldn't find an Englishman with naturalization papers if you get out a search warrant for him. You dislike us so much you won't emigrate to our country, an' the few that do won't accept the burden of citizenship, an' we Americans have to sit around an' be polite an' listen to you folks scold us an' patronize us an' tell us openly how inferior we are an' what bad manners we got an' what all."

So then Lady Angela paints him a picture of some Middle West tourists in London, an' how the watchmen at Westminister Abbey an' St. Paul's Cathedral are worked to death keepin' Americans from carvin' their undistinguished monikers on ancient an' holy tombs, etc. All this verbal barrage she lets out through her nose an' accuses Bill's countrymen of bein' stand-ardized an' sayin' they "guess" when they "think" an' of murderin' the beautiful English language. She says they're a mucky lot of souvenir hunters an' dollar idolators.

Bill then allows that her people are a flock of tip hounds an' says they say horse pistol when they mean hospital and al-u-min-i-um when they mean aluminum an' they never sent over a candidate for pugilistic honors that didn't come a long ways for a lickin'. And, of course, when sensible folks get talkin' that way to each other the dove of peace starts moltin'; so the result of it all was that Lady Angela begs Bill please to do her the favor to stay to home hereafter, an' Bill goes home an' stays there.

"I reckon you've changed your mind about marryin' that damsel, Bill," I suggest to the boy.

Bill sighed. "No," he says, "us Emlows don't give up that easy." Then he spills me a line of Latin, which he allows is the motto on the Emlow shield an' means "To grab and to get." "Of course," he adds, "this doggoned war has come between me an' my love, but time'll heal that. However, if I have to join the British army to win her fair hand I'll be a bachelor all my days."

Well, things drifted along until the Kaiser pulled his bonehead play of sinkin' neutral commerce. When

we stood for that Bill began to get restless, an' when
Kaiser Bill, mistakin' our love of peace for cowardice,
bars us from the freedom of the seas, Bill commenced
slippin', an' when the Lusitania was sunk an' the President sent the Kaiser a polite note about it instead of
the United States fleet, Bill couldn't wait no longer.
He was one American who wasn't too proud to fight
an' he figured he'd start then an' there. So he put his
affairs in order an' told Jim Yeager to take good care
of the ranch until he come back—if an' when—never
expectin' any opposition from Jim. However, he got
it. Jim's fed up on peace at any price too, so he quits
his job an' is over the border an' into the Canadian
army while Bill Emlow is sayin' knife. An' three of
Bill's top riders go with the foreman.

The Chink cook tells me Bill sat down an' cried like
a child. There he was, thirstin' for German gore, an'
tied to his ranch an' a vast smear of Hereford cows.
When he could think he sent for me. Wired me he
was in a heap o' big trouble an' would I come up an'
help him out? Of course I would an' I did, an' when
I got to the Fourteen Ranch Bill says to me mighty
plaintive:

"Dad, you got a hell-fired good foreman to run your
ranch?"

I allow I have the best obtainable an' that I have
every confidence in him.

"How old is he?" says Bill.

"Risin' fifty."

"Then he won't be runnin' off to war," says Bill
gratefully. "Dad, I want you to let your foreman run
your ranch an' you take charge of mine. Name your
own salary an when you want to collect it sell some
Herefords. The Chink likes you an' he'll stay, an'

with a dozen of the old hands an' a smear of Indian
riders you can get along fine. I'll get you a lot of new
phonograph records an' teach you how to play the automatic piano an' the French car is yours. This here war
is no longer a private fight. Anybody can bulge into
it, an' I'm goin'. I can't live here with my ancestors
no longer. Why, Dad, the night I made up my mind
to do this the old pirate in the gold frame yonder
actually smiled at me. He was with Nelson at the
battle of the Nile."

I saw it was up to me whether I broke the boy's
heart or not, so I says: "Bill, I'll oblige you, but only
on condition that you answer me one question an'
answer it to my satisfaction. Do you aim to go over
to Hadleycroft an' clean yourself with Lady Angela
before you go?"

"I should say not!" Bill Emlow yells. "Catch me
swankin' around her, showin' off what a brave Yank
I am an' all for her smile an' favor. No, sir'ee. This
here is my own bright little idea, an' she had nothin'
to do with it."

"Then, Bill," I says, "go where glory waits thee an'
when fame elates thee think of me."

He went away a week later, an' he took two of his
best horses with him. "Which I've heard a lot about
the rain an' mud of France," he explains, "an' I like
a dry climate to do my fightin' in. All the Emlow
fightin' men were in the cavalry, an' there's nothin'
doin' with cavalry in France. But there's a whole lot
of cavalry opportunity in Mesopotamia an' Egypt an'
Palestine. There's always been an Emlow commandin'
a troop of Berks Yeomanry, an' the Berks are down
that way somewhere. I'm bringin' my own mounts because that country is hard on a horse an' the thorough-

bred is the only type that will stand up under hard service."

So he runs his horses down to the railroad in a truck, expresses them to Seattle, ships 'em on a steamer to Manila, reships 'em on various steamers an' eventually lands in Suez. He calls upon the commandin' officers of the Egyptian Expeditionary Force an' presents his family archives to prove that he's an Emlow of the Emlows an' entitled to be called my lord. Yes, sir, Bill's no longer a plain American hombre now. He's a British gentleman the minute he enlists as a private in the British army. However, it seems it's a British gentleman's job to lead Tommy Atkins, so Bill is commissioned a second lieutenant right off, and as vacancies are frequent it ain't long before he's Captain William Emlow, V. C.

Me, I run his ranch for him, an' if I do say so I run it right. The price of beef went sky-high, an' I was surely storin' up the dollars against Bill's homecomin', when one bright day who should ride in on me but Lady Angela.

"Where's Bill Emlow?" she says.

"He ain't here."

"When will he be back, Mr. Tully?"

"Can't tell. He's off on some Kathleen Mavourneen business, which it may be for years an' it may be forever. What can I do for you, Lady Angela?"

"I've got to borrow Jim Yeager," she says. "I thought I could get along without him, but I can't."

"Jim Yeager's been fertilizin' the soil of France for mebbe a year," I says. "Won't somebody else do?"

She looks down at me mighty solemn, an' I seen a

mist in her fine eyes. So to change the conversation I says: "An' how's your father?"

"Killed in action at Gaza," she says, as careless as if the old man had only been laid up with an attack of rheumatism. "Led his regiment in the charge, got the charge home and died among the enemy's **cannon.** I'm the last of the Hadley's, Mr. Tully."

"An' you need help?"

She nods an' tries to smile, but there's tears behind that smile. "The ranch is too much for me, Mr. Tully. I should have retained Jim Yeager. By the way. Mr. Tully, where *is* Mr. Emlow? I should like to have his address if it appears he will not be home for some time. On the last occasion he and I met we quarreled dreadfully—and I—I—well, I rather thought I'd apologize. It was this beastly war, you know."

"Well, Lady Angela," I says, "you address Captain William Emlow, V. C., Berks Yeomanry, Egyptian Expeditionary Force, Egypt or Palestine or Mesopotamia. The last letter I had from Bill he was livin' in back of a pawnshop in Jerusalem; he says that in view of all the advertising the River Jordan has had since B. C., that stream certainly was a disappointment to him. To anybody that's ever seen the Columbia River the River Jordon's just a creek."

Lady Angela sits her horse starin' at me. "So he didn't wait," she says presently, in a little funny voice.

"As far as I can make out, the Emlows never wait to be asked into a fight, provided the fightin's good an' it ain't a private row."

"What a perfectly ripping old sport he is, to be sure!" says Lady Angela. "If he had come to say good-by to me, I'd have hated him. And, by the way, do you know you Americans got into the war yes-

terday? All England is thrilled to death, and I came
over to see if I could borrow an American flag from
Mr. Emlow. I wanted to fly it with the Union Jack
at Hadleycroft."

Well, Bill got through the war all right, an' in due
course he come back—with one of his horses.
Both Bill and his mount was pretty well used up.
They'd both been shot an' carved more or less, but not
fatally, an' Bill had a lot of ribbons on his manly breast
an' looked mighty doggoned particular in his uniform.
The day he come home he folded up his uniform an'
put it away in moth balls along with his memories,
an' along after dinner that night, when we're settin'
out on the porch havin' a quiet smoke, Bill says all of
a sudden:

"By the way, I haven't seen Jeff. What became of
him?"

"Jeff's moved over to Hadleycroft. Seems as though
Lady Angela wanted him to keep her company, so I
give Jeff to her," I says.

"Hum-m-m!" says Bill. Then, a little later: "Thanks,
Dad." He smoked a long time and then he said: "By
the way, I met the late 'Lord Bardleigh' in Palestine.
He was with Allenby's forces as a military observer of
the United States Army—forged passport and credentials, and all that sort of thing. German spy, you
know. Clever chap, Bardleigh. He was getting away
with it beautifully until he ran into me . . . we shot
him. His name was Augoost, after all—August Hein-
rich von Detmer. Just before we shot him he told
me that but for me he'd have married Lady Angela and
bought all the Hadley horses for the German army.
He was curious to know how I managed to smell him

out so quickly and attributed it to the typical alertness of the American. I let it go at that. What good would it have done him to tell him the truth?"

"Speakin' of Lady Angela," I says, "I've been sort of helpin' her out, marketin' her cattle an' horses for her an' lendin' her some labor when she had to have it. After I heard you were comin' back I got workin' on her to sell those danged Angus cattle, and she allowed she'd do it, in the interests of peace. I suppose you're goin' over to Hadleycroft to call on the girl."

"I suppose I ain't that big a boob," Bill Emlow snaps. "If I was to call on her, I'd be makin' a gesture of surrender, an' after that I could never call my soul my own. Unless she takes a notion to call at the Fourteen Ranch an' apologize for what she said about me and my country, it sort of looks as if the name Emlow will die with this generation."

I knew it would! And I knew Lady Angela would never stoop to conquer, as the feller says. So I bring to work my native American wit to save the situation. I write Lady Angela to meet me at the international boundary about at the monument where she first met Bill Emlow, and to bring Jeff. All on a certain day. And on that day I induce Bill to ride up there with me to look at some yearlin' bulls—some tops I'd held out on the last calf round-up. As we come up toward the monument little Jeff gets up out of the grass and lopes over to Bill. The fact that the little varmint recognizes his old master touches Bill an' puts him in a tender humor, and when a minute later Lady Angela is discovered gettin' her horse on the Canadian side of that monument I seen I'd done all that was humanly possible and from now on nature must take her course.

So I tell Bill Emlow I have some business over the hill an' ride away.

Bill gets back to the ranch late for lunch, an' his Chink scolds hell out of him for it, which is a habit with Chinks when they like a feller well enough to die for him. But Bill only grins and all through luncheon he continues to grin, and finally he says:

"Well, Dad, I suppose you're glad the war is over and you can go back to your own ranch an' run it, eh, what?"

"Oh, I'm in no hurry, William," I says. "I don't want to leave you here to get lonesome."

"No feah," says Bill, just like one of his ancestors might. Soldierin' with Allenby has revived his accent. "I say, old fruit! I've some deucedly jolly news for you. I' going to marry Angela right away—and you'd be a bit in the way, following the wedding. So I dare say you'd better go home, eh, what?"

"You're an ingrate. However, I don't mind. Was this peace powwow pulled off in the state of Washington or in British Columbia?"

"We had quite a discussion as to that," says Bill. 'When I told her she'd have to abandon the jolly old king and become an American, and to signify her surrender by stepping across the line, she revolted. Said if I wanted her bad enough I'd come after her, and she headed back for Hadleycroft at top speed. So I galloped after her, picked her off her horse and carried her across the line to American territory, and kissed her. She was so angry she cried. Gave me Hail Columbia for going off to war without stopping to say good-by, and then gave me more Hail Columbia for not callin' on her when I got back, and—"

"Bill," I says sternly, "this woman is a fraud."

"Is she?" says Bill innocently. "Well, she has a temper, at any rate. But I'll cure her of that. I won't have a titled British wife puttin' it over me because I'm a plain dub of an American. I ain't sayin' nothin' yet, Dad, but directly after the preacher's muttered over me an' Angela I'm going to get out the family record an' prove to her that I could have been Lord Bardleigh once if I'd cared to claim it, and that I'm at this moment the Earl of Emlow, so I outrank her. And when she knows that the Emlows were searchin' for the Holy Grail an' getting drunk with King Arthur at a time when the Hadleys were still chasin' each other around stumps with knobby clubs she won't feel so bad about becomin' an American by marriage. And I'll make that woman vote for a Democratic Presidential candidate if I have to larrup her with a quirt."

"Bill," I says, lookin' at him long an' earnestly, "who won the war?"

"Why, we did, fool," says Bill. "Nobody can deny that!"

"What do you mean by this we stuff?"

"Why, we British!"

I didn't argue with him. What would have been the use? You can't argue with our late allies nohow. That's their story and they're going to stick to it, and as far as Bill Emlow and Lady Angela were concerned I was mighty glad Bill took this one-sided view of the matter, because it convinced me they were going to be mighty happy together. However, after the wedding and just before I left the Fourteen Ranch, I took Bill to one side and said:

"Bill, be honest with me, old-timer. You know dog-gone well who won the war. Own up."

"Listen, Dad," says Bill, "the war's over, and I don't give a hoot in a hollow who won it, but just between ourselves, and not to be repeated to my wife"—Here he interrupts himself long enough to turn the face of his principal an' most hook-nosed ancestor to the wall—"we won the war!"

YOUTH

By Joseph Conrad

This could have occurred nowhere but in England, where men and sea interpenetrate, so to speak—the sea entering into the life of most men, and the men knowing something or everything about the sea, in the way of amusement, of travel, or of bread-winning.

We were sitting round a mahogany table that reflected the bottle, the claret-glasses, and our faces as we leaned on our elbows. There was a director of companies, an accountant, a lawyer, Marlow, and myself. The director had been a *Convoy* boy, the accountant had served four years at sea, the lawyer—a fine crusted Tory, High Churchman, the best of old fellows, the soul of honor—had been chief officer in the P. & O. service in the good old days when mail-boats were square-rigged at least on two masts, and used to come down the China Sea before a fair monsoon with stun'-sails set alow and aloft. We all began life in the merchant service. Between the five of us there was the strong bond of the sea, and also the fellowship of the craft, which no amount of enthusiasm for yachting, cruising, and so on can give, since one is only the amusement of life and the other is life itself.

Marlow (at least I think that is how he spelt his name) told the story, or rather the chronicle, of a voyage:—

"Yes, I have seen a little of the Eastern seas; but what I remember best is my first voyage there. You fellows know there are those voyages that seem ordered for the illustration of life, that might stand for a symbol of existence. You fight, work, sweat, nearly kill yourself, sometimes do kill yourself, trying to accomplish something—and you can't. Not from any fault of yours. You simply can do nothing, neither great nor little—not a thing in the world—not even marry an old maid, or get a wretched 600-ton cargo of coal to its port of destination.

"It was altogether a memorable affair. It was my first voyage to the East, and my first voyage as second mate; it was also my skipper's first command. You'll admit it was time. He was sixty if a day; a little man, with a broad, not very straight back, with bowed shoulders and one leg more bandy than the other, he had that queer twisted-about appearance you see so often in men who work in the fields. He had a nut-cracker face—chin and nose trying to come together over a sunken mouth—and it was framed in iron-gray fluffy hair, that looked like a chin-strap of cotton-wool sprinkled with coal-dust. And he had blue eyes in that old face of his, which were amazingly like a boy's, with that candid expression some quite common men preserve to the end of their days by a rare internal gift of simplicity of heart and rectitude of soul. What induced him to accept me was a wonder. I had come out of a crack Australian clipper, where I had been third officer, and he seemed to have a prejudice against crack clippers as aristocratic and high-toned. He said to me, 'You know, in this ship you will have to work.' I said I had to work in every ship I had ever been in. 'Ah, but this is different, and you gentlemen out of

them big ships; . . . but there! I dare say you will
do. Join to-morrow.'

"I joined to-morrow. It was twenty-two years ago;
and I was just twenty. How time passes! It was one
of the happiest days of my life. Fancy! Second mate
for the first time—a really responsible officer! I
wouldn't have thrown up my new billet for a fortune.
The mate looked me over carefully. He was also an
old chap, but of another stamp. He had a Roman
nose, a snow-white, long beard, and his name was
Mahon, but he insisted that it should be pronounced
Mann. He was well connected; yet there was something wrong with his luck, and he had never got on.

"As to the captain, he had been for years in coasters,
then in the Mediterranean, and last in the West Indian
trade. He had never been round the Capes. He could
just write a kind of sketchy hand, and didn't care for
writing at all. Both were thorough good seamen of
course, and between those two old chaps I felt like a
small boy between two grandfathers.

"The ship also was old. Her name was the *Judea*.
Queer name, isn't it? She belonged to a man Wilmer,
Wilcox—some name like that; but he has been bank-
rupt and dead these twenty years or more, and his
name don't matter. She had been laid up in Shadwell
basin for ever so long. You may imagine her state.
She was all rust, dust, grime—soot aloft, dirt on deck.
To me it was like coming out of a palace into a ruined
cottage. She was about 400 tons, had a primitive
windlass, wooden latches to the doors, not a bit of
brass about her, and a big square stern. There was
on it, below her name in big letters, a lot of scroll-
work, with the gilt off, and some sort of a coat of arms,
with the motto 'Do or Die' underneath. I remember

it took my fancy immensely. There was a touch of romance in it, something that made me love the old thing—something that appealed to my youth!

"We left London in ballast—sand ballast—to load a cargo of coal in a northern port for Bankok. Bankok! I thrilled. I had been six years at sea, but had only seen Melbourne and Sydney, very good places, charming places in their way—but Bankok!

"We worked out of the Thames under canvas, with a North Sea pilot on board. His name was Jermyn, and he dodged all day long about the galley drying his handkerchief before the stove. Apparently he never slept. He was a dismal man, with a perpetual tear sparkling at the end of his nose, who either had been in trouble, or was in trouble, or expected to be in trouble—couldn't be happy unless something went wrong. He mistrusted my youth, my common-sense, and my seamanship, and made a point of showing it in a hundred little ways. I dare say he was right. It seems to me I knew very little then, and I know not much more now; but I cherish a hate for that Jermyn to this day.

"We were a week working up as far as Yarmouth Roads, and then we got into a gale—the famous October gale of twenty-two years ago. It was wind, lightning, sleet, snow, and a terrific sea. We were flying light, and you may imagine how bad it was when I tell you we had smashed bulwarks and a flooded deck. On the second night she shifted her ballast into the lee bow, and by that time we had been blown off somewhere on the Dogger Bank. There was nothing for it but go below with shovels and try to right her, and there we were in that vast hold, gloomy like a cavern, the tallow dips stuck and flickering on the beams,

the gale howling above, the ship tossing about like
mad on her side; there we all were, Jermyn, the captain, every one, hardly able to keep our feet, engaged
on that gravedigger's work, and trying to toss shovel-
fuls of wet sand up to windward. At every tumble of
the ship you could see vaguely in the dim light men
falling down with a great flourish of shovels. One of
the ship's boys (we had two), impressed by the weird-
ness of the scene, wept as if his heart would break. We
could hear him blubbering somewhere in the shadows.

"On the third day the gale died out, and by and by
a north-country tug picked us up. We took sixteen
days in all to get from London to the Tyne! When
we got into dock we had lost our turn for loading,
and they hauled us off to a tier where we remained for
a month. Mrs. Beard (the captain's name was Beard)
came from Colchester to see the old man. She lived
on board. The crew of runners had left, and there
remained only the officers, one boy and the steward, a
mulatto who answered to the name of Abraham. Mrs.
Beard was an old woman, with a face all wrinkled and
ruddy like a winter apple, and the figure of a young
girl. She caught sight of me once, sewing on a button,
and insisted on having my shirts to repair. This was
something different from the captains' wives I had
known on board crack clippers. When I brought her
the shirts, she said: 'And the socks? They want
mending, I am sure, and John's—Captain Beard's—
things are all in order now. I would be glad of something to do.' Bless the old woman. She overhauled
my outfit for me, and meantime I read for the first
time *Sartor Resartus* and Burnaby's *Ride to Khiva*.
I didn't understand much of the first then; but I
remember I preferred the soldier to the philosopher at

the time; a preference which life has only confirmed.
One was a man, and the other was either more—or
less. However, they are both dead and Mrs. Beard is
dead, and youth, strength, genius, thoughts, achieve-
ments, simple hearts—all die. . . . No matter.

"They loaded us at last. We shipped a crew. Eight
able seamen and two boys. We hauled off one evening
to the buoys at the dock-gates, ready to go out, and
with a fair prospect of beginning the voyage next day.
Mrs. Beard was to start for home by a late train.
When the ship was fast we went to tea. We sat rather
silent through the meal—Mahon, the old couple, and
I. I finished first, and slipped away for a smoke, my
cabin being in a deck-house just against the poop. It
was high water, blowing fresh with a drizzle; the double
dock-gates were opened, and the steam-colliers were
going in and out in the darkness with their lights
burning bright, a great plashing of propellers, rattling
of winches, and a lot of hailing on the pier-heads. I
watched the procession of head-lights gliding high and
of green lights gliding low in the night, when suddenly
a red gleam flashed at me, vanished, came into view
again, and remained. The fore-end of a steamer loomed
up close. I shouted down the cabin, 'Come up, quick!'
and then heard a startled voice saying afar in the dark,
'Stop her, sir.' A bell jingled. Another voice cried
warningly, 'We are going right into that bark, sir.'
The answer to this was a gruff 'All right,' and the next
thing was a heavy crash as the steamer struck a glancing blow with the bluff of her bow about our fore-
rigging. There was a moment of confusion, yelling,
and running about. Steam roared. Then somebody
was heard saying, 'All clear, sir.' . . . 'Are you all
right?' asked the gruff voice. I had jumped forward

to see the damage, and hailed back, 'I think so.' 'Easy astern,' said the gruff voice. A bell jingled. 'What steamer is that?' screamed Mahon. By that time she was no more to us than a bulky shadow maneuvering a little way off. They shouted at us some name—a woman's name, Miranda or Melissa—or some such thing. 'This means another month in this beastly hole,' said Mahon to me, as we peered with lamps about the splintered bulwarks and broken braces. 'But where's the captain?'

"We had not heard or seen anything of him all that time. We went aft to look. A doleful voice arose hailing somewhere in the middle of the dock. *'Judea* ahoy!' . . . How the devil did he get there? . . . 'Hallo!' we shouted. 'I am adrift in our boat without oars,' he cried. A belated water-man offered his serv- ices, and Mahon struck a bargain with him for half-a- crown to tow our skipper alongside; but it was Mrs. Beard that came up the ladder first. They had been floating about the dock in that mizzly cold rain for nearly an hour. I was never so surprized in my life.

"It appears that when he heard my shout 'Come up' he understood at once what was the matter, caught up his wife, ran on deck, and across, and down into our boat, which was fast to the ladder. Not bad for a sixty-year-old. Just imagine that old fellow saving heroically in his arms that old woman—the woman of his life. He set her down on a thwart, and was ready to climb back on board when the painter came adrift somehow, and away they went together. Of course in the confusion we did not hear him shouting. He looked abashed. She said cheerfully, 'I suppose it does not matter my losing the train now?' 'No, Jenny— you go below and get warm,' he growled. Then to us:

'A sailor has no business with a wife—I say. There I was, out of the ship. Well, no harm done this time. Let's go and look at what that fool of a steamer smashed.'

"It wasn't much, but it delayed us three weeks. At the end of that time, the captain being engaged with his agents, I carried Mrs. Beard's bag to the railway-station and put her all comfy into a third-class carriage. She lowered the window to say, 'You are a good young man. If you see John—Captain Beard—without his muffler at night, just remind him from me to keep his throat well wrapped up.' 'Certainly, Mrs. Beard,' I said. 'You are a good young man; I noticed how attentive you are to John—to Captain——' The train pulled out suddenly; I took my cap off to the old woman: I never saw her again. . . . Pass the bottle.

"We went to sea next day. When we made that start for Bankok we had been already three months out of London. We had expected to be a fortnight or so—at the outside.

"It was January, and the weather was beautiful—the beautiful sunny winter weather that has more charm than in the summer-time, because it is unexpected, and crisp, and you know it won't, it can't, last long. It's like a windfall, like a godsend, like an unexpected piece of luck.

"It lasted all down the North Sea, all down Channel; and it lasted till we were three hundred miles or so to the westward of the Lizards: then the wind went round to the sou'west and began to pipe up. In two days it blew a gale. The *Judea* hove to, wallowed on the Atlantic like an old candle-box. It blew day after day: it blew with spite, without interval, without

mercy, without rest. The world was nothing but an
immensity of great foaming waves rushing at us, under
a sky low enough to touch with the hand and dirty
like a smoked ceiling. In the stormy space surrounding us there was as much flying spray as air. Day
after day and night after night there was nothing
round the ship but the howl of the wind, the tumult
of the sea, the noise of water pouring over her deck.
There was no rest for her and no rest for us. She
tossed, she pitched, she stood on her head, she sat on
her tail, she rolled, she groaned, and we had to hold
on while on deck and cling to our bunks when below,
in a constant effort of body and worry of mind.

"One night Mahon spoke through the small window
of my berth. It opened right into my very bed, and
I was lying there sleepless, in my boots, feeling as
tho I had not slept for years, and could not if I
tried. He said excitedly—

"'You got the sounding-rod in here, Marlow? I
can't get the pumps to suck. By God! it's no child's
play.'

"I gave him the sounding-rod and lay down again,
trying to think of various things—but I thought only
of the pumps. When I came on deck they were still
at it, and my watch relieved at the pumps. By the
light of the lantern brought on deck to examine the
sounding-rod I caught a glimpse of their weary, serious
faces. We pumped all the four hours. We pumped
all night, all day, all the week—watch and watch. She
was working herself loose, and leaked badly—not
enough to drown us at once, but enough to kill us
with the work at the pumps. And while we pumped
the ship was going from us piecemeal: the bulwarks
went, the stanchions were torn out, the ventilators

smashed, the cabin-door burst in. There was not a dry spot in the ship. She was being gutted bit by bit. The long-boat changed, as if by magic, into match-wood where she stood in her gripes. I had lashed her myself, and was rather proud of my handiwork, which had withstood so long the malice of the sea. And we pumped. And there was no break in the weather. The sea was white like a sheet of foam, like a caldron of boiling milk; there was not a break in the clouds, no—not the size of a man's hand—no, not for so much as ten seconds. There was for us no sky, there were for us no stars, no sun, no universe—nothing but angry clouds and an infuriated sea. We pumped watch and watch, for dear life; and it seemed to last for months, for years, for all eternity, as tho we had been dead and gone to a hell for sailors. We forgot the day of the week, the name of the month, what year it was, and whether we had ever been ashore. The sails blew away, she lay broadside on under a weather-cloth, the ocean poured over her, and we did not care. We turned those handles, and had the eyes of idiots. As soon as we had crawled on deck I used to take a round turn with a rope about the men, the pumps, and the mainmast, and we turned, we turned inces-santly, with the water to our waists, to our necks, over our heads. It was all one. We had forgotten how it felt to be dry.

"And there was somewhere in me the thought: By Jove! this is the deuce of an adventure—something you read about; and it is my first voyage as second mate—and I am only twenty—and here I am lasting it out as well as any of these men, and keeping my chaps up to the mark. I was pleased. I would not have given up the experience for worlds. I had

moments of exultation. Whenever the old dismantled
craft pitched heavily with her counter high in the air,
she seemed to me to throw up, like an appeal, like a
defiance, like a cry to the clouds without mercy, the
words written on her stern: '*Judea*, London. Do or
Die.'

"O youth! The strength of it, the faith of it, the
imagination of it! To me she was not an old rattle-
trap carting about the world a lot of coal for a freight
—to me she was the endeavor, the test, the trial of
life. I think of her with pleasure, with affection, with
regret—as you would think of someone dead you have
loved. I shall never forget her. . . . Pass the bottle.

"One night when tied to the mast, as I explained,
we were pumping on, deafened with the wind, and
without spirit enough in us to wish ourselves dead, a
heavy sea crashed aboard and swept clean over us.
As soon as I got my breath I shouted, as in duty
bound, 'Keep on, boys!' when suddenly I felt something hard floating on deck strike the calf of my leg.
I made a grab at it and missed. It was so dark we
could not see each other's faces within a foot—you
understand.

"After that thump the ship kept quiet for a while,
and the thing, whatever it was, struck my leg again.
This time I caught it—and it was a saucepan. At
first, being stupid with fatigue and thinking of nothing
but the pumps, I did not understand what I had in
my hand. Suddenly it dawned upon me, and I shouted,
'Boys, the house on deck is gone. Leave this, and
let's look for the cook.'

"There was a deck-house forward, which contained
the galley, the cook's berth, and the quarters of the
crew. As we had expected for days to see it swept

away, the hands had been ordered to sleep in the cabin
—the only safe place in the ship. The steward, Abraham, however, persisted in clinging to his berth, stu-
pidly, like a mule—from sheer fright I believe, like an
animal that won't leave a stable falling in an earth-
quake. So we went to look for him. It was chancing
death, since once out of our lashings we were as
exposed as if on a raft. But we went. The house
was shattered as if a shell had exploded inside. Most
of it had gone overboard—stove, men's quarters, and
their property, all was gone; but two posts, holding a
portion of the bulkhead to which Abraham's bunk was
attached, remained as if by a miracle. We groped in
the ruins and came upon this, and there he was, sitting
in his bunk, surrounded by foam and wreckage, jabber-
ing cheerfully to himself. He was out of his mind;
completely and for ever mad, with this sudden shock
coming upon the fag-end of his endurance. We
snatched him up, lugged him aft, and pitched him
head-first down the cabin companion. You understand
there was no time to carry him down with infinite
precautions and wait to see how he got on. Those
below would pick him up at the bottom of the stairs
all right. We were in a hurry to go back to the pumps.
That business could not wait. A bad leak is an
inhuman thing.

"One would think that the sole purpose of that
fiendish gale had been to make a lunatic of that poor
devil of a mulatto. It eased before morning, and next
day the sky cleared, and as the sea went down the
leak took up. When it came to bending a fresh set
of sails the crew demanded to put back—and really
there was nothing else to do. Boats gone, decks swept
clean, cabin gutted, men without a stitch but what they

stood in, stores spoiled, ship strained. We put her head for home, and—would you believe it? The wind came east right in our teeth. It blew fresh, it blew continuously. We had to beat up every inch of the way, but she did not leak so badly, the water keeping comparatively smooth. Two hours' pumping in every four is no joke—but it kept her afloat as far as Falmouth.

"The good people there live on casualties of the sea, and no doubt were glad to see us. A hungry crowd of shipwrights sharpened their chisels at the sight of that carcass of a ship. And, by Jove! they had pretty pickings off us before they were done. I fancy the owner was already in a tight place. There were delays. Then it was decided to take part of the cargo out and caulk her topsides. This was done, the repairs finished, cargo reshipped; a new crew came on board, and we went out—for Bankok. At the end of a week we were back again. The crew said they weren't going to Bankok—a hundred and fifty days' passage—in a something hooker that wanted pumping eight hours out of the twenty-four; and the nautical papers inserted again the little paragraph: 'Judea. Bark. Tyne to Bankok; coals; put back to Falmouth leaky and with crew refusing duty.'

"There were more delays—more tinkering. The owner came down for a day, and said she was as right as a little fiddle. Poor old Captain Beard looked like the ghost of a Geordie skipper—through the worry and humiliation of it. Remember he was sixty, and it was his first command. Mahon said it was a foolish business, and would end badly. I loved the ship more than ever, and wanted awfully to get to Bankok. To Bankok! Magic name, blessed name. Mesopotamia wasn't a patch on it. Remember I was twenty, and it was my first second-mate's billet, and the East was waiting for me.

"We went out and anchored in the outer roads with a fresh crew—the third. She leaked worse than ever. It was as if those confounded shipwrights had actually made a hole in her. This time we did not even go outside. The crew simply refused to man the windlass.

"They towed us back to the inner harbor, and we became a fixture, a feature, an institution of the place. People pointed us out to visitors as 'That 'ere bark that's going to Bankok—has been here six months— put back three times.' On holidays the small boys pulling about in boats would hail, '*Judea*, ahoy!' and if a head showed above the rail shouted, 'Where you bound to?—Bankok?' and jeered. We were only three on board. The poor old skipper mooned in the cabin. Mahon undertook the cooking, and unexpectedly developed all a Frenchman's genius for preparing nice little messes. I looked languidly after the rigging. We became citizens of Falmouth. Every shopkeeper knew us. At the barber's or tobacconist's they asked familiarly, 'Do you think you will ever get to Bankok?' Meantime the owner, the underwriters, and the charterers squabbled amongst themselves in London, and our pay went on. . . . Pass the bottle.

"It was horrid. Morally it was worse than pumping for life. It seemed as tho we had been forgotten by the world, belonged to nobody, would get nowhere; it seemed that, as if bewitched, we would have to live for ever and ever in that inner harbor, a derision and a byword to generations of long-shore loafers and dishonest boatmen. I obtained three months' pay and a five days' leave, and made a rush for London. It took me a day to get there and pretty well another to come back—but three months' pay went all the same. I don't know what I did with it. I went to a music-hall, I believe, lunched, dined, and supped in a swell place in Regent Street, and was back to time, with nothing but a complete set of Byron's works and a new railway rug to show for three months' work. The boat-man who pulled me off to the ship said: 'Hallo! I thought you had left the old thing. *She* will never get to Bankok.' 'That's all *you* know about it,' I said scornfully—but I didn't like that prophecy at all.

"Suddenly a man, some kind of agent to somebody, appeared with full powers. He had grog-blossoms all over his face, an indomitable energy, and was a jolly soul. We leaped into life again. A hulk came along-side, took our cargo, and then we went into dry dock to get our copper stripped. No wonder she leaked. The poor thing, strained beyond endurance by the gale, had, as if in disgust, spat out all the oakum of her lower seams. She was recaulked, new coppered, and made as tight as a bottle. We went back to the hulk and reshipped our cargo.

"Then, on a fine moonlight night, all the rats left the ship.

"We had been infested with them. They had destroyed our sails, consumed more stores than the crew, affably shared our beds and our dangers, and now, when the ship was made seaworthy, concluded to clear out. I called Mahon to enjoy the spectacle. Rat after rat appeared on our rail, took a last look over his shoulder, and leaped with a hollow thud into the empty hulk. We tried to count them, but soon lost the tale. Mahon said: 'Well, well! don't talk to me about the intelligence of rats. They ought to have

left before, when we had that narrow squeak from
foundering. There you have the proof how silly is the
superstition about them. They leave a good ship for
an old rotten hulk, where there is nothing to eat, too,
the fools! . . . I don't believe they know what is
safe or what is good for them, any more than you or I.'

"And after some more talk we agreed that the wisdom of rats had been grossly overrated, being in fact
no greater than that of men.

"The story of the ship was known, by this, all up
the Channel from Land's End to the Forelands, and
we could get no crew on the south coast. They sent
us one all complete from Liverpool, and we left once
more—for Bankok.

"We had fair breezes, smooth water right into the
tropics, and the old *Judea* lumbered along in the sunshine. When she went eight knots everything cracked
aloft, and we tied our caps to our heads; but mostly
she strolled on at the rate of three miles an hour.
What could you expect? She was tired—that old ship.
Her youth was where mine is—where yours is—you
fellows who listen to this yarn; and what friend would
throw your years and your weariness in your face?
We didn't grumble at her. To us aft, at least, it
seemed as tho we had been born in her, reared in
her, had lived in her for ages, had never known any
other ship. I would just as soon have abused the old
village church at home for not being a cathedral.

"And for me there was also my youth to make me
patient. There was all the East before me, and all life,
and the thought that I had been tried in that ship
and had come out pretty well. And I thought of men
of old who, centuries ago, went that road in ships that
sailed no better, to the land of palms, and spices, and

yellow sands, and of brown nations ruled by kings more
cruel than Nero the Roman, and more splendid than
Solomon the Jew. The old bark lumbered on, heavy
with her age and the burden of her cargo, while I lived
the life of youth in ignorance and hope. She lumbered on through an interminable procession of days;
and the fresh gilding flashed back at the setting sun,
seemed to cry out over the darkening sea the words
painted on her stern, '*Judea*, London. Do or Die.'

"Then we entered the Indian Ocean and steered
northerly for Java Head. The winds were light.
Weeks slipped by. She crawled on, do or die, and
people at home began to think of posting us as overdue.

"One Saturday evening, I being off duty, the men
asked me to give them an extra bucket of water or
so—for washing clothes. As I did not wish to screw
on the fresh-water pump so late, I went forward
whistling, and with a key in my hand to unlock the
forepeak scuttle, intending to serve the water out of
a spare tank we kept there.

"The smell down below was as unexpected as it was
frightful. One would have thought hundreds of
paraffin-lamps had been flaring and smoking in that
hole for days. I was glad to get out. The man with
me coughed and said, 'Funny smell, sir.' I answered
negligently, 'It's good for the health they say,' and
walked aft.

"The first thing I did was to put my head down the
square of the midship ventilator. As I lifted the lid
a visible breath, something like a thin fog, a puff of
faint haze, rose from the opening. The ascending air
was hot, and had a heavy, sooty, paraffiny smell. I
gave one sniff, and put down the lid gently. It was
no use choking myself. The cargo was on fire.

"Next day she began to smoke in earnest. You see it was to be expected, for tho the coal was of a safe kind, that cargo had been so handled, so broken up with handling, that it looked more like smithy coal than anything else. Then it had been wetted—more than once. It rained all the time we were taking it back from the hulk, and now with this long passage it got heated, and there was another case of spontaneous combustion.

"The captain called us into the cabin. He had a chart spread on the table, and looked unhappy. He said, 'The coast of West Australia is near, but I mean to proceed to our destination. It is the hurricane month, too; but we will just keep her head for Bankok, and fight the fire. No more putting back anywhere, if we all get roasted. We will try first to stifle this 'ere damned combustion by want of air.'

"We tried. We battened down everything, and still she smoked. The smoke kept coming out through imperceptible crevices; it forced itself through bulkheads and covers; it oozed here and there and everywhere in slender threads, in an invisible film, in an incomprehensible manner. It made its way into the cabin, into the forecastle; it poisoned the sheltered places on the deck, it could be sniffed as high as the mainyard. It was clear that if the smoke came out the air came in. This was disheartening. This combustion refused to be stifled.

"We resolved to try water, and took the hatches off. Enormous volumes of smoke, whitish, yellowish, thick, greasy, misty, choking, ascending as high as the trucks. All hands cleared out aft. Then the poisonous cloud blew away, and we went back to work in a smoke that was no thicker now than that of an ordinary factory chimney.

"We rigged the force-pump, got the hose along, and by and by it burst. Well, it was as old as the ship—a prehistoric hose, and past repair. Then we pumped with the feeble head-pump, drew water with buckets, and in this way managed in time to pour lots of Indian Ocean into the main hatch. The bright stream flashed in sunshine, fell into a layer of white crawling smoke, and vanished on the black surface of coal. Steam ascended mingling with the smoke. We poured salt water as into a barrel without a bottom. It was our fate to pump in that ship, to pump out of her, to pump into her; and after keeping water out of her to save ourselves from being drowned, we frantically poured water into her to save ourselves from being burnt.

"And she crawled on, do or die, in the serene weather. The sky was a miracle of purity, a miracle of azure. The sea was polished, was blue, was pellucid, was sparkling like a precious stone, extending on all sides, all round to the horizon—as if the whole terrestrial globe had been one jewel, one colossal sapphire, a single gem fashioned into a planet. And on the luster of the great calm waters the *Judea* glided imperceptibly, enveloped in languid and unclean vapors, in a lazy cloud that drifted to leeward, light and slow; a pestiferous cloud defiling the splendor of sea and sky.

"All this time of course we saw no fire. The cargo smouldered at the bottom somewhere. Once Mahon, as we were working side by side, said to me with a queer smile: 'Now, if she only would spring a tidy leak—like that time when we first left the Channel—

it would put a stopper on this fire. Wouldn't it?' I remarked irrelevantly, 'Do you remember the rats?'

"We fought the fire and sailed the ship too as carefully as tho nothing had been the matter. The steward cooked and attended on us. Of the other twelve men, eight worked while four rested. Everyone took his turn, captain included. There was equality, and if not exactly fraternity, then a deal of good feeling. Sometimes a man, as he dashed a bucketful of water down the hatchway, would yell out, 'Hurrah for Bankok!' and the rest laughed. But generally we were taciturn and serious—and thirsty. Oh! how thirsty! And we had to be careful with the water. Strict allowance. The ship smoked, the sun blazed. . . . Pass the bottle.

"We tried everything. We even made an attempt to dig down to the fire. No good, of course. No man could remain more than a minute below. Mahon, who went first, fainted there, and the man who went to fetch him out did likewise. We lugged them out on deck. Then I leaped down to show how easily it could be done. They had learned wisdom by that time, and contented themselves by fishing for me with a chain-hook tied to a broom-handle, I believe. I did not offer to go and fetch up my shovel, which was left down below.

"Things began to look bad. We put the long-boat into the water. The second boat was ready to swing out. We had also another, a 14-foot thing, on davits aft, where it was quite safe.

"Then, behold, the smoke suddenly decreased. We redoubled our efforts to flood the bottom of the ship. In two days there was no smoke at all. Everybody was on the broad grin. This was on a Friday. On

Saturday no work, but sailing the ship of course, was done. The men washed their clothes and their faces for the first time in a fortnight, and had a special dinner given them. They spoke of spontaneous combustion with contempt, and implied *they* were the boys to put out combustions. Somehow we all felt as tho we each had inherited a large fortune. But a beastly smell of burning hung about the ship. Captain Beard had hollow eyes and sunken cheeks. I had never noticed so much before how twisted and bowed he was. He and Mahon prowled soberly about hatches and ventilators, sniffing. It struck me suddenly poor Mahon was a very, very old chap. As to me, I was as pleased and proud as though I had helped to win a great naval battle. O! Youth!

"The night was fine. In the morning a homeward-bound ship passed us hull down—the first we had seen for months; but we were nearing the land at last, Java Head being about 190 miles off, and nearly due north.

"Next day it was my watch on deck from eight to twelve. At breakfast the captain observed, 'It's wonderful how that smell hangs about the cabin.' About ten, the mate being on the poop, I stepped down on the main-deck for a moment. The carpenter's bench stood abaft the mainmast: I leaned against it sucking at my pipe, and the carpenter, a young chap, came to talk to me. He remarked, 'I think we have done very well, haven't we?' and then I perceived with annoyance the fool was trying to tilt the bench. I said curtly, 'Don't, Chips,' and immediately became aware of a queer sensation, of an absurd delusion,—I seemed somehow to be in the air. I heard all round me like a pent-up breath released—as if a thousand giants simultaneously had said Phoo!—and felt a dull concussion which made my ribs ache suddenly. No doubt about it—I was in the air, and my body was describing a short parabola. But short as it was, I had the time to think several thoughts in, as far as I can remember, the following order: This can't be the carpenter—What is it?—Some accident—Submarine volcano?—Coals, gas!—By Jove! we are being blown up—Every body's dead—I am falling into the after-hatch—I see fire in it.'

"The coal-dust suspended in the air of the hold had glowed dull-red at the moment of the explosion. In the twinkling of an eye, in an infinitesimal fraction of a second since the first tilt of the bench, I was sprawling full length on the cargo. I picked myself up and scrambled out. It was quick like a rebound. The deck was a wilderness of smashed timber, lying crosswise like trees in a wood after a hurricane; an immense curtain of soiled rags waved gently before me—it was the main-sail blown to strips. I thought, The masts will be toppling over directly; and to get out of the way bolted on all-fours towards the poop-ladder. The first person I saw was Mahon, with eyes like saucers, his mouth open, and the long white hair standing straight on end round his head like a silver halo. He was just about to go down when the sight of the main-deck stirring, heaving up, and changing into splinters before his eyes, petrified him on the top step. I stared at him in unbelief, and he stared at me with a queer kind of shocked curiosity. I did not know that I had no hair, no eyebrows, no eyelashes, that my young moustache was burnt off, that my face was black, one cheek laid open, my nose cut, and my chin bleeding. I had lost my cap, one of my slippers, and my shirt was torn to rags. Of all this I was not aware. I was amazed to see the ship still afloat, the poop-deck whole —and, most of all, to see anybody alive. Also the peace of the sky and the serenity of the sea were distinctly surprising. I suppose I expected to see them convulsed with horror. . . . Pass the bottle.

"There was a voice hailing the ship from somewhere —in the air, in the sky—I couldn't tell. Presently I saw the captain—and he was mad. He asked me eagerly, 'Where's the cabin-table?' and to hear such a question was a frightful shock. I had just been blown up, you understand, and vibrated with that experience, —I wasn't quite sure whether I was alive. Mahon began to stamp with both feet and yelled at him, 'Good God! don't you see the deck's blown out of her?' I found my voice, and stammered out as if conscious of some gross neglect of duty, 'I don't know where the cabin-table is.' It was like an absurd dream.

"Do you know what he wanted next? Well, he wanted to trim the yards. Very placidly, and as if lost in thought, he insisted on having the foreyard squared. 'I don't know if there's anybody alive,' said Mahon, almost tearfully. 'Surely,' he said, gently, 'there will be enough left to square the foreyard.'

"The old chap, it seems, was in his own berth winding up the chronometers, when the shock sent him spinning. Immediately it occurred to him—as he said afterwards—that the ship had struck something, and he ran out into the cabin. There, he saw, the cabin-table had vanished somewhere. The deck being blown up, it had fallen down into the lazaret of course. Where we had our breakfast that morning he saw only a great hole in the floor. This appeared to him so awfully mysterious, and impressed him so immensely, that what he saw and heard after he got on deck were mere trifles in comparison. And, mark, he noticed directly the wheel deserted and his bark off her course—and his only thought was to get that miserable, stripped, undecked, smoldering shell of a ship back again with her head pointing at her port of destination. Bankok! That's what he was after. I tell you this quiet, bowed, bandy-legged, almost deformed little man was immense in the singleness of his idea and in his placid ignorance of our agitation. He motioned us forward with a commanding gesture, and went to take the wheel himself.

"Yes; that was the first thing we did—trim the yards of that wreck! No one was killed, or even disabled, but everyone was more or less hurt. You should have seen them! Some were in rags, with black faces, like coal-heavers, like sweeps, and had bullet heads that seemed closely cropped, but were in fact singed to the skin. Others, of the watch below, awakened by being shot out from their collapsing bunks, shivered incessantly, and kept on groaning even as we went about our work. But they all worked. That crew of Liverpool hard cases had in them the right stuff. It's my experience they always have. It is the sea that gives it—the vastness, the loneliness surrounding their dark stolid souls. Ah! Well! we stumbled, we crept, we fell, we barked our shins on the wreckage, we hauled. The masts stood, but we did not know how much they might be charred down below. It was nearly calm, but a long swell ran from the west and made her roll. They might go at any moment. We looked at them with apprehension. One could not foresee which way they would fall.

"Then we retreated aft and looked about us. The

deck was a tangle of planks on edge, of planks on end,
of splinters, of ruined woodwork. The masts rose from
that chaos like big trees above a matter undergrowth.
The interstices of that mass of wreckage were full of
something whitish, sluggish, stirring—of something that
was like a greasy fog. The smoke of the invisible fire
was coming up again, was trailing, like a poisonous
thick mist in some valley choked with dead wood.
Already lazy wisps were beginning to curl upwards
amongst the mass of splinters. Here and there a piece
of timber, stuck upright, resembled a post. Half of a
fife-rail had been shot through the foresail, and the
sky made a patch of glorious blue in the ignobly soiled
canvas. A portion of several boards holding together
had fallen across the rail, and one end protruded overboard, like a gangway leading upon nothing, like a
gangway leading over the deep sea, leading to death—
as if inviting us to walk the plank at once and be
done with our ridiculous troubles. And still the air,
the sky—a ghost, something invisible was hailing the
ship.

"Someone had the sense to look over, and there was
the helmsman, who had impulsively jumped overboard,
anxious to come back. He yelled and swam lustily
like a merman, keeping up with the ship. We threw
him a rope, and presently he stood amongst us streaming with water and very crestfallen. The captain had
surrendered the wheel, and apart, elbow on rail and
chin in hand, gazed at the sea wistfully. We asked
ourselves, What next? I thought, Now, this is something like. This is great. I wonder what will happen.
O youth!

"Suddenly Mahon sighted a steamer far astern.
Captain Beard said, 'We may do something with her

yet.' We hoisted two flags, which said in the inter-national language of the sea, 'On fire. Want imme-diate assistance.' The steamer grew bigger rapidly, and by and by spoke with two flags on her foremast, 'I am coming to your assistance.'

"In half an hour she was abreast, to windward, within hail, and rolling slightly, with her engines stopped. We lost our composure, and yelled all together with excitement, 'We've been blown up.' A man in a white helmet, on the bridge, cried, 'Yes! All right! all right!' and he nodded his head, and smiled, and made soothing motions with his hand as tho at a lot of frightened children. One of the boats dropped in the water, and walked towards us upon the sea with her long oars. Four Calashes pulled a swinging stroke. This was my first sight of Malay seamen. I've known them since, but what struck me then was their unconcern: they came alongside, and even the bowman standing up and holding to our main-chains with the boat-hook did not deign to lift his head for a glance. I thought people who had been blown up deserved more attention.

"A little man, dry like a chip and agile like a mon-key, clambered up. It was the mate of the steamer. He gave one look, and cried, 'O boys—you had better quit.'

"We were silent. He talked apart with the captain for a time,—seemed to argue with him. Then they went away together to the steamer.

"When our skipper came back we learned that the steamer was the *Somerville*, Captain Nash, from West Australia to Singapore *via* Batavia with mails, and that the agreement was she should tow us to Anjer or Batavia, if possible, where we could extinguish the fire

by scuttling, and then proceed on our voyage—to Bankok! The old man seemed excited. 'We will do it
yet,' he said to Mahon, fiercely. He shook his fist at
the sky. Nobody else said a word.

"At noon the steamer began to tow. She went
ahead slim and high, and what was left of the *Judea*
followed at the end of seventy fathom of tow-rope,—
followed her swiftly like a cloud of smoke with mast-
heads protruding above. We went aloft to furl the
sails. We coughed on the yards, and were careful
about the bunts. Do you see the lot of us there, putting a neat furl on the sails of that ship doomed to
arrive nowhere? There was not a man who didn't
think that at any moment the masts would topple over.
From aloft we could not see the ship for smoke, and
they worked carefully, passing the gaskets with even
turns. Harbor furl—aloft there!' cried Mahon from
below.

"You understand this? I don't think one of those
chaps expected to get down in the usual way. When
we did I heard them saying to each other, 'Well, I
thought we would come down overboard, in a lump—
sticks and all—blame me if I didn't.' 'That's what I
was thinking to myself,' would answer wearily another
battered and bandaged scarecrow. And, mind, these
were men without the drilled-in habit of obedience.
To an onlooker they would be a lot of profane scally-
wags without a redeeming point. What made them do
it—what made them obey me when I, thinking con-
sciously how fine it was, made them drop the bunt of
the foresail twice to try and do it better? What?
They had no professional reputation—no examples, no
praise. It wasn't a sense of duty; they all knew well
enough how to shirk, and laze, and dodge—when they

had a mind to it—and mostly they had. Was it the two pounds ten a-month that sent them there? They didn't think their pay half enough. No; it was something in them, something inborn and subtle and everlasting. I don't say positively that the crew of a French or German merchantman wouldn't have done it, but I doubt whether it would have been done in the same way. There was a completeness in it, something solid like a principle, and masterful like an instinct—a disclosure of something secret—of that hidden something, that gift of good or evil that makes racial difference, that shapes the fate of nations.

"It was that night at ten that, for the first time since we had been fighting it, we saw the fire. The speed of the towing had fanned the smoldering destruction. A blue gleam appeared forward, shining below the wreck of the deck. It wavered in patches, it seemed to stir and creep like the light of a glowworm. I saw it first, and told Mahon. 'Then the game's up,' he said. 'We had better stop this towing, or she will burst out suddenly fore and aft before we can clear out.' We set up a yell; rang bells to attract their attention; they towed on. At last Mahon and I had to crawl forward and cut the rope with an axe. There was no time to cast off the lashings. Red tongues could be seen licking the wilderness of splinters under our feet as we made our way back to the poop.

"Of course they very soon found out in the steamer that the rope was gone. She gave a loud blast of her whistle, her lights were seen sweeping in a wide circle, she came up ranging close along-side, and stopped. We were all in a tight group on the poop looking at her. Every man had saved a little bundle or a bag. Suddenly a conical flame with a twisted top shot up forward and threw upon the black sea a circle of light, with the two vessels side by side and heaving gently in its center. Captain Beard had been sitting on the gratings still and mute for hours, but now he rose slowly and advanced in front of us, to the mizzen-shrouds. Captain Nash hailed: 'Come along! Look sharp. I have mail-bags on board. I will take you and your boats to Singapore.'

" 'Thank you! No!' said our skipper. 'We mus* see the last of the ship.'

" 'I can't stand by any longer,' shouted the other. 'Mails—you know.'

" 'Ay! ay! We are all right.'

" 'Very well! I'll report you in Singapore. . . . Good-bye!'

"He waved his hand. Our men dropped their bundles quietly. The steamer moved ahead, and passing out of the circle of light, vanished at once from our sight, dazzled by the fire which burned fiercely. And then I knew that I would see the East first as commander of a small boat. I thought it fine; and the fidelity to the old ship was fine. We should see the last of her. Oh, the glamor of youth! Oh, the fire of it, more dazzling than the flames of the burning ship, throwing a magic light on the wide earth, leaping audaciously to the sky, presently to be quenched by time, more cruel, more pitiless, more bitter than the sea—and like the flames of the burning ship surrounded by an impenetrable night.

* * * * * * *

"The old man warned us in his gentle and inflexible way that it was part of our duty to save for the underwriters as much as we could of the ship's gear. Accordingly we went to work aft, while she blazed forward to give us plenty of light. We lugged out a lot of rubbish. What didn't we save? An old barometer fixed with an absurd quantity of screws nearly cost me my life: a sudden rush of smoke came upon me, and I just got away in time. There were various stores, bolts of canvas, coils of rope; the poop looked like a marine bazaar, and the boats were lumbered to the gunwales. One would have thought the old man wanted to take as much as he could of his first command with him. He was very, very quiet, but off his balance evidently. Would you believe it? He wanted to take a length of old stream-cable and a kedge-anchor with him in the long-boat. We said, 'Ay, ay, sir,' deferentially, and on the quiet let the things slip overboard. The heavy medicine-chest went that way, two bags of green coffee, tins of paint—fancy, paint!— a whole lot of things. Then I was ordered with two hands into the boats to make a stowage and get them ready against the time it would be proper for us to leave the ship.

"We put everything straight, stepped the long-boat's mast for our skipper, who was to take charge of her, and I was not sorry to sit down for a moment. My face felt raw, every limb ached as if broken, I was aware of all my ribs, and would have sworn to a twist in the backbone. The boats, fast astern, lay in a deep shadow, and all around I could see the circle of the sea lighted by the fire. A gigantic flame arose forward straight and clear. It flared fierce, with noises like the whirr of wings, with rumbles as of thunder. There were cracks, detonations, and from the cone of flame the sparks flew upwards, as man is born to trouble, to leaky ships, and to ships that burn.

"What bothered me was that the ship, lying broad-

side to the swell and to such wind as there was—a
mere breath—the boats would not keep astern where
they were safe, but persisted, in a pig-headed way
boats have, in getting under the counter and then
swinging alongside. They were knocking about danger-
ously and coming near the flame, while the ship rolled
on them, and, of course, there was always the danger
of the masts going over the side at any moment. I
and my two boat-keepers kept them off as best we
could, with oars and boat-hooks; but to be constantly
at it became exasperating, since there was no reason
why we should not leave at once. We could not see
those on board, nor could we imagine what caused the
delay. The boat-keepers were swearing feebly, and I
had not only my share of the work but also had to
keep at it two men who showed a constant inclination
to lay themselves down and let things slide.

"At last I hailed, 'On deck there,' and someone
looked over. 'We're ready here.' I said. The head
disappeared, and very soon popped up again. 'The
captain says, All right, sir, and to keep the boats well
clear of the ship.'

"Half an hour passed. Suddenly there was a frightful racket, rattle, clanking of chain, hiss of water, and
millions of sparks flew up into the shivering column
of smoke that stood leaning slightly above the ship.
The cat-heads had burned away, and the two red-
hot anchors had gone to the bottom, tearing out
after them two hundred fathom of red-hot chain.
The ship trembled, the mass of flame swayed as
if ready to collapse, and the fore top-gallant-mast
fell. It darted down like an arrow of fire, shot under,
and instantly leaping up within an oar's-length of the
boats, floated quietly, very black on the luminous

sea. I hailed the deck again. After some time a man
in an unexpectedly cheerful but also muffled tone, as
tho he had been trying to speak with his mouth
shut, informed me, 'Coming directly, sir,' and vanished.
For a long time I heard nothing but the whirr and roar
of the fire. There were also whistling sounds. The
boats jumped, tugged at the painters, ran at each other
playfully, knocked their sides together, or, do what
we would, swung in a bunch against the ship's side.
I couldn't stand it any longer, and swarming up a rope,
clambered aboard over the stern.

"It was as bright as day. Coming up like this, the
sheet of fire facing me was a terrifying sight, and the
heat seemed hardly bearable at first. On a settee
cushion dragged out of the cabin Captain Beard, his
legs drawn up and one arm under his head, slept with
the light playing on him. Do you know what the rest
were busy about? They were sitting on deck right aft,
round an open case, eating bread and cheese and drink-
ing bottled stout.

"On the background of flames twisting in fierce
tongues above their heads they seemed at home like
salamanders, and looked like a band of desparate
pirates. The fire sparkled in the whites of their eyes,
gleamed on patches of white skin seen through the torn
shirts. Each had the marks as of a battle about him—
bandaged heads, tied-up arms, a strip of dirty rag round
a knee—and each man had a bottle between his legs and
a chunk of cheese in his hand. Mahon got up. With
his handsome and disreputable head, his hooked profile,
his long white beard, and with an uncorked bottle in
his hand, he resembled one of those reckless sea-
robbers of old making merry amidst violence and dis-
asters. 'The last meal on board,' he explained solemn-

ly. 'We had nothing to eat all day, and it was no use
leaving all this.' He flourished the bottle and indicated the sleeping skipper. 'He said he couldn't
swallow anything, so I got him to lie down,' he went
on; and as I stared, 'I don't know whether you are
aware, young fellow, the man had no sleep to speak
of for days—and there will be dam' little sleep in the
boats.' 'There will be no boats by-and-by if you fool
about much longer,' I said, indignantly. I walked up
to the skipper and shook him by the shoulder. At last
he opened his eyes, but did not move. 'Time to leave
her, sir,' I said quietly.

"He got up painfully, looked at the flames, at the
sea sparkling round the ship, and black, black as ink
farther away; he looked at the stars shining dim through
a thin veil of smoke in a sky black, black as Erebus.

" ' Youngest first,' he said.

"And the ordinary seaman, wiping his mouth with
the back of his hand, got up, clambered over the taff-
rail, and vanished. Others followed. One, on the point
of going over, stopped short to drain his bottle, and
with a great swing of his arm flung it at the fire.
'Take this!' he cried.

"The skipper lingered disconsolately, and we left him
to commune alone for a while with his first command.
Then I went up again and brought him away at last.
It was time. The ironwork on the poop was hot to the
touch.

"Then the painter of the long-boat was cut, and the
three boats, tied together, drifted clear of the ship. It
was just sixteen hours after the explosion when we
abandoned her. Mahon had charge of the second boat,
and I had the smallest—the 14-foot thing. The long-
boat would have taken the lot of us; but the skipper

said we must save as much property as we could—for the underwriters—and so I got my first command. I had two men with me, a bag of biscuits, a few tins of meat, and a breaker of water. I was ordered to keep close to the long-boat, that in case of bad weather we might be taken into her.

"And do you know what I thought? I thought I would part company as soon as I could. I wanted to have my first command all to myself. I wasn't going to sail in a squadron if there were a chance for independent cruising. I would make land by myself. I would beat the other boats. Youth! All youth! The silly charming, beautiful youth.

"But we did not make a start at once. We must see the last of the ship. And so the boats drifted about that night, heaving and setting on the swell. The men dozed, waked, sighed, groaned. I looked at the burning ship.

"Between the darkness of earth and heaven she was burning fiercely upon a disc of purple sea shot by the blood-red play of gleams; upon a disc of water glittering and sinister. A high, clear flame, an immense and lonely flame, ascended from the ocean, and from its summit the black smoke poured continuously at the sky. She burned furiously; mournful and imposing like a funeral pile kindled in the night, surrounded by the sea, watched over by the stars. A magnificent death had come like a grace, like a gift, like a reward to that old ship at the end of her laborious days. The surrender of her weary ghost to the keeping of stars and sea was stirring like the sight of a glorious triumph. The mast fell just before daybreak, and for a moment there was a burst and turmoil of sparks that seemed to fill with flying fire the night patient and watchful, the vast night lying silent upon the sea. At daylight she was only a charred shell floating still under a cloud of smoke and bearing a glowing mass of coal within.

"Then the oars were got out, and the boats forming in a line moved round her remains as if in procession —the long-boat leading. As we pulled across her stern a slim dart of fire shot out viciously at us, and suddenly she went down, head first, in a great hiss of steam. The unconsumed stern was the last to sink; but the paint had gone, had cracked, had peeled off, and there were no letters, there was no word, no stubborn device that was like her soul, to flash at the rising sun her creed and her name.

"We made our way north. A breeze sprang up, and about noon all the boats came together for the last time. I had no mast or sail in mine, but I made a mast out of a spare oar and hoisted a boat-awning for a sail, with a boat-hook for a yard. She was certainly over-masted, but I had the satisfaction of knowing that with the wind aft I could beat the other two. I had to wait for them. Then we all had a look at the captains' chart, and, after a sociable meal of hard bread and water, got our last instructions. These were simple: steer north, and keep together as much as possible. 'Be careful with that jury-rig, Marlow,' said the captain; and Mahon, as I sailed proudly past his boat, wrinkled his curved nose and hailed, 'You will sail that ship of yours under water, if you don't look out, young fellow.' He was a malicious old man—and may the deep sea where he sleeps now rock him gently, rock him tenderly to the end of time!

"Before sunset a thick rain-squall passed over the two boats, which were far astern, and that was the last

I saw of them for a time. Next day I sat steering my cockle-shell—my first command—with nothing but water and sky around me. I did sight in the afternoon the upper sails of a ship far away, but said nothing, and my men did not notice her. You see I was afraid she might be homeward bound, and I had no mind to turn back from the portals of the East. I was steering for Java—another blessed name—like Bankok, you know. I steered many days.

"I need not tell you what it is to be knocking about in an open boat. I remember nights and days of calm, when we pulled, we pulled, and the boat seemed to stand still, as if bewitched within the circle of the sea horizon. I remember the heat, the deluge of rain-squalls that kept us baling for dear life (but filled our water-cask), and I remember sixteen hours on end with a mouth dry as a cinder and a steering-oar over the stern to keep my first command head on to a breaking sea. I did not know how good a man I was till then. I remember the drawn faces, the dejected figures of my two men, and I remember my youth and the feeling that will never come back any more—the feeling that I could last for ever, outlast the sea, the earth, and all men; the deceitful feeling that lures us on to joys, to perils, to love, to vain effort—to death; the triumphant conviction of strength, the heat of life in the handful of dust, the glow in the heart that with every year grows dim, grows cold, grows small, and expires—and expires, too soon, too soon—before life itself.

"And this is how I see the East. I have seen its secret places and have looked into its very soul; but now I see it always from a small boat, a high outline of mountains, blue and afar in the morning; like faint

mist at noon; a jagged wall of purple at sunset. I have
the feel of the oar in my hand, the vision of a scorching blue sea in my eyes. And I see a bay, a wide bay,
smooth as glass and polished like ice, shimmering in
the dark. A red light burns far off upon the gloom of
the land, and the night is soft and warm. We drag at
the oars with aching arms, and suddenly a puff of wind,
a puff faint and tepid and laden with strange odors of
blossoms, of aromatic wood, comes out of the still
night—the first sigh of the East on my face. That I
can never forget. It was impalpable and enslaving,
like a charm, like a whispered promise of mysterious
delight.

"We had been pulling this finishing spell for eleven
hours. Two pulled, and he whose turn it was to rest
sat at the tiller. We had made out the red light in that
bay and steered for it, guessing it must mark some
small coasting port. We passed two vessels, outlandish
and high-sterned, sleeping at anchor, and, approaching
the light, now very dim, ran the boat's nose against
the end of a jutting wharf. We were blind with
fatigue. My men dropped the oars and fell off the
thwarts as if dead. I made fast to a pile. A current
rippled softly. The scented obscurity of the shore
was grouped into vast masses, a density of colossal
clumps of vegetation, probably—mute and fantastic
shapes. And at their foot the semicircle of a beach
gleamed faintly, like an illusion. There was not a light,
not a stir, not a sound. The mysterious East faced
me, perfumed like a flower, silent like death, dark
like a grave.

"And I sat weary beyond expression, exulting like
a conqueror, sleepless and entranced as if before a profound, a fateful enigma.

"A splashing of oars, a measured dip reverberating on the level of water, intensified by the silence of the shore into loud claps, made me jump up. A boat, a European boat, was coming in. I invoked the name of the dead; I hailed: *Judea* ahoy! A thin shout answered.

"It was the captain. I had beaten the flagship by three hours, and I was glad to hear the old man's voice again, tremulous and tired. 'Is it you, Marlow?' 'Mind the end of that jetty, sir,' I cried.

"He approached cautiously, and brought up with the deep-sea lead-line which we had saved—for the underwriters. I eased my painter and fell alongside. He sat, a broken figure at the stern, wet with dew, his hands clasped in his lap. His men were asleep already. 'I had a terrible time of it,' he murmured. 'Mahon is behind—not very far,' We conversed in whispers, in low whispers, as if afraid to wake up the land. Guns, thunder, earthquakes would not have awakened the men just then.

"Looking round as we talked, I saw away at sea a bright light travelling in the night. 'There's a steamer passing the bay,' I said. She was not passing, she was entering, and she even came close and anchored. 'I wish,' said the old man, 'you would find out whether she is English. Perhaps they could give us a passage somewhere.' He seemed nervously anxious. So by dint of punching and kicking I started one of my men into a state of somnambulism, and giving him an oar, took another and pulled towards the lights of the steamer.

"There was a murmur of voices in her, metallic hollow clangs of the engine-room, footsteps on the deck. Her ports shone, round like dilated eyes. Shapes moved about, and there was a shadowy man high up on the bridge. He heard my oars.

"And then, before I could open my lips, the East spoke to me, but it was in a Western voice. A torrent of words was poured into the enigmatical, the fateful silence! outlandish, angry words, mixed with words and even whole sentences of good English, less strange but even more surprising. The voices swore and cursed violently; it riddled the solemn peace of the bay by a volley of abuse. It began by calling me Pig, and from that went crescendo into unmentionable adjectives—in English. The man up there raged aloud in two languages, and with a sincerity in his fury that almost convinced me I had, in some way, sinned against the harmony of the universe. I could hardly see him, but began to think he would work himself into a fit.

"Suddenly he ceased, and I could hear him snorting and blowing like a porpoise. I said—

" 'What steamer is this, pray?'

" 'Eh? What's this? And who are you?'

" 'Castaway crew of an English bark burnt at sea. We came here to-night. I am the second mate. The captain is in the long-boat, and wishes to know if you would give us a passage somewhere.'

" 'Oh, my goodness! I say. . . . This is the *Celestial* from Singapore on her return trip. I'll arrange with your captain in the morning, . . . and, . . . I say, . . . did you hear me just now?'

" 'I should think the whole bay heard you.'

" 'I thought you were a shore-boat. Now, look here—this infernal lazy scoundrel of a caretaker has gone to sleep again—curse him. The light is out, and I nearly ran foul of the end of this damned jetty. This is the third time he plays me this trick. Now, I ask you, can anybody stand this kind of thing? It's enough to drive a man out of his mind. I'll report him. . . . I'll get the Assistant Resident to give him the sack, by . . . ! See—there's no light. It's out, isn't it? I take you to witness the light's out. There should be a light, you know. A red light on the——'

" 'There was a light,' I said, mildly.

" 'But it's out, man! What's the use of talking like this? You can see for yourself it's out—don't you? If you had to take a valuable steamer along this God-forsaken coast you would want a light, too. I'll kick him from end to end of his miserable wharf. You'll see if I don't. I will——'

" 'So I may tell my captain you'll take us?' I broke in.

" 'Yes, I'll take you. Good-night,' he said, bruskly.

"I pulled back, made fast again to the jetty, and then went to sleep at last. I had faced the silence of the East. I had heard some of its language. But when I opened my eyes again the silence was as complete as tho it had never been broken. I was lying in a flood of light, and the sky had never looked so far, so high, before. I opened my eyes and lay without moving.

"And then I saw the men of the East—they were looking at me. The whole length of the jetty was full of people. I saw brown, bronze, yellow faces, the black eyes, the glitter, the color of an Eastern crowd. And all these beings stared without a murmur, without a sigh, without a movement. They stared down at the boats, at the sleeping men who at night had come to

them from the sea. Nothing moved. The fronds of
palms stood still against the sky. Not a branch stirred
along the shore, and the brown roofs of hidden houses
peeped through the green foliage, through the big
leaves that hung shining and still like leaves forged of
heavy metal. This was the East of the ancient
navigators, so old, so mysterious, resplendent and
somber, living and unchanged, full of danger and
promise. And these were the men. I sat up suddenly. A wave of movement passed through the
crowd from end to end, passed along the head, swayed
the bodies, ran along the jetty like a ripple on the
water, like a breath of wind on a field—and all was still
again. I see it now—the wide sweep of the bay, the
glittering sands, the wealth of green infinite and varied,
the sea of a dream, the crowd of attentive faces, the
blaze of vivid color—the water reflecting it all, the
curve of the shore, the jetty, the high-sterned outlandish craft floating still, and the three boats with the
tired men from the West sleeping, unconscious of the
land and the people and of the violence of sunshine.
They slept thrown across the thwarts, curled on bot-
tom-boards, in the careless attitudes of death. The
head of the old skipper, leaning back in the stern of the
long-boat, had fallen on his breast, and he looked as
tho he would never wake. Farther out old Mahon's
face was upturned to the sky, with the long white
beard spread out on his breast, as tho he had been
shot where he sat at the tiller; and a man, all in a
heap in the bows of the boat, slept with both arms
embracing the stem-head and with his cheek laid on
the gunwale. The East looked at them without a
sound.

"I have known its fascination since; I have seen the mysterious shores, the still water, the lands of brown nations, where a stealthy Nemesis lies in wait, pursues, overtakes so many of the conquering race, who are proud of their wisdom, of their knowledge, of their strength. But for me all the East is contained in that vision of my youth. It is all in that moment when I opened my young eyes on it. I came upon it from a tussle with the sea—and I was young—and I saw it looking at me. And this is all that is left of it! Only a moment; a moment of strength, of romance, of glamor—of youth! . . . A flick of sunshine upon a strange shore, the time to remember, the time for a sigh, and—good-bye!—Night—Good-bye . . . !"

He drank.

"Ah! The good old time—the good old time. Youth and the sea. Glamor and the sea! The good, strong sea, the salt, bitter sea, that could whisper to you and roar at you and knock your breath out of you."

He drank again.

"By all that's wonderful it is the sea, I believe, the sea itself—or is it youth alone? Who can tell? But you here—you all had something out of life: money, love—whatever one gets on shore—and, tell me, wasn't that the best time, that time when we were young at sea; young and had nothing, on the sea that gives nothing, except hard knocks—and sometimes a chance to feel your strength—that only—what you all regret?" And we all nodded at him: the man of finance, the man of accounts, the man of law, we all nodded at him over the polished table that like a still sheet of brown water reflected our faces, lined, wrinkled; our faces marked by toil, by deceptions, by success, by love; our weary eyes looking still, looking always, looking anxiously for something out of life, that while it is expected is already gone—has passed unseen, in a sigh, in a flash—together with the youth, with the strength, with the romance of illusions.

THE BEAUTY SPOT

By Alfred Louis Charles De Musset

Chapter I

In 1756, when Louis XV, wearied with the quarrels
between the magistrature and the grand council, about
the "two sous tax,"[1] determined upon holding a special
lit de justice, the members of Parliament resigned.
Sixteen of these resignations were accepted, and as
many exiles decreed. "But," said Madame de Pompadour to one of the presidents, "could you calmly
stand by and see a handful of men resist the au-
thority of the King of France? Would you not have
a very bad opinion of such a policy? Throw off the
cloak of petty pretense, M. le President, and you will
see the situation just as I see it myself."

It was not only the exiles that had to pay the
penalty of their want of compliance, but also their
relatives and friends. The violation of mail-secrets
was one of the King's amusements. To relieve the
monotony of his other pleasures, it pleased him to
hear his favorite read all the curious things that were
to be found in his subjects' private correspondence.
Of course, under the fallacious pretext of doing his
own detective work, he reaped a large harvest of
enjoyment from the thousand little intrigues which

[1] Two sous per livre from the tenth of the revenue.

thus passed under his eyes; but whoever was connected, whether closely or in a remote degree, with
the leaders of the factions, was almost invariably
ruined.

Every one knows that Louis XV, with all his mani-
fold weaknesses, had one, and only one, strong point;
he was inexorable.

One evening, as he sat before the fire with his feet
on the mantelpiece, melancholy as was his wont, the
marquise, looking through a packet of letters, suddenly burst into a laugh and shrugged her shoulders.
The King wished to know what was the matter.

"Why, I have found here," answered she, "a letter,
without a grain of common sense in it, but a very
touching thing for all that—quite pitiable in fact."

"Whose is the signature?" said the King.

"There is none, it is a love-letter."

"And what is the address?"

"That is just the point. It is addressed to Mademoiselle d'Annebault, the niece of my good friend,
Madame d'Estrades. Apparently it has been put in
among these papers on purpose for me to see."

"And what is there in it?" the King persisted.

"Why, I tell you it is all about love. There is
mention also of Vauvert and of Neauflette. Are there
any gentlemen in those parts? Does your Majesty
know of any?"

The King always prided himself upon knowing
France by heart, that is, the nobility of France. The
etiquette of his court, which he had studied thoroughly,
was not more familiar to him than the armorial bear-
ings of his realm. Not a very wide range of learning;
still nothing beyond it did he reckon worthy the study;
and it was a point of vanity with him, the social

hierarchy being, in his eyes, something like the marble staircase of his palace; he must set foot on it as sole lord and master. After having pondered a few moments, he knitted his brow, as though struck by an unwelcome remembrance; then, with a sign to the marquise to read, he threw himself back in his easy chair, saying with a smile:

"Read on—she is a pretty girl."

Madame de Pompadour assumed her sweetest tone of raillery and began to read a long letter, which, from beginning to end, was one rhapsody of love.

"Just see," said the writer, "how the fates persecute me! At first everything seemed to work for the fulfilment of my wishes, and you yourself, my sweet one, had you not given me reason to hope for happiness? I must, however, renounce this heavenly dream, and that for no fault of mine. Is it not an excess of cruelty to have let me catch a glimpse of paradise, only to dash me into the abyss? When some unfortunate wretch is doomed to death, do they take a barbarous pleasure in placing before his eyes all that would make him love life and regret leaving it? Such is, however, my fate: I have no other refuge, no other hope, than the tomb, for, in my dire misfortune, I can no longer dream of winning your hand. When fate smiled on me, all my hopes were that you should be mine; to-day, a poor man, I should abhor myself if I dared still to think of such blessedness, and, now that I can no longer make you happy, though dying of love for you, I forbid you to love me—"

The Marquise smiled at these last words.

"Madame," said the King, "this is an honorable man. But what prevents him from marrying his lady-love?"

"Permit me, sire, to continue."

"—This overwhelming injustice from the best of kings surprises me. You know that my father asked for me a commission as cornet or ensign in the Guards, and that on this appointment depended the happiness of my life, since it would give me the right to offer myself to you. The Duc de Biron proposed my name; but the King rejected me in a manner the memory of which is very bitter to me. If my father has his own way of looking at things (admitting that it is a wrong one) must I suffer for it? My devotion to the King is as true, as unbounded, as my love for you. How gladly would I give proof of both these sentiments, could I but draw the sword! Assuredly I feel deeply distressed at my request being refused; but that I should be thus disgraced without good reason is a thing opposed to the well-known kindness of his Majesty."

"Aha!" said the King, "I am becoming interested."

"—If you knew how very dull we are! Ah! my friend! This estate of Neauflette, this country-house of Vauvert, these wooded glades!—I wander about them all day long. I have forbidden a rake to be used; the sacrilegious gardener came yesterday with his iron-shod besom. He was about to touch the sand. But the trace of your steps, lighter than the wind, was not effaced. The prints of your little feet and of your red satin heels were still upon the path; they seemed to walk before me, as I followed your beautiful image, and that charging fantom took shape at times as tho it were treading in the fugitive prints. It was there, while conversing with you by the flower-beds, that it was granted me to know you, to appreciate you. A brilliant education joined to the spirit of an angel, the dignity of a queen with the grace of a nymph, thoughts worthy of Leibnitz expressed in language so simple, Plato's bee on the lips of Diana, all this enfolded me as in a veil of adoration. And, during those delicious moments, the darling flowers were blooming about us, I inhaled their breath while listening to you, in their perfume your memory lived. They droop their heads now; they present to me the semblance of death!"

"This is all Rousseau and water," said the King. "Why do you read such stuff to me?"

"Because your Majesty commanded me to do so, for the sake of Mademoiselle d'Annebault's beautiful eyes."

"It is true, she has beautiful eyes."

"—And when I return from these walks, I find my father alone, in the great drawing-room, near the lighted candle, leaning on his elbow, amid the faded gildings which cover our moldy wainscot. It is with pain that he sees me enter. My grief disturbs his. Athénaïs! At the back of that drawing-room, near the window, is the harpsichord over which flitted those sweet fingers that my lips have touched but once— once, while yours opened softly to harmonies of celestial music—opened with such dainty art that your songs were but a smile. How happy are they— Rameau, Lulli, Duni, and so many more! Yes, yes, you love them—they are in your memory—their breath has passed through your lips. I too seat myself at that harpsichord, I strive to play one of those airs that you love;—how cold, how monotonous they seem to me! I leave them and listen to their dying accents while the echo loses itself beneath that lugubrious vault. My father turns to me and sees me dis-

tressed—what can he do? Some boudoir gossip, some
report from the servants' hall has closed upon us the
gates that lead into the world. He sees me young,
ardent, full of life, asking only to live in this world,
he is my father, and can do nothing for me."

"One would think," said the King, "that this fellow
was starting for the hunt, and that his falcon had been
killed on his wrist. Against whom is he inveighing,
may I ask?"

"—It is quite true," continued the Marquise, reading in a lower tone. "It is quite true that we are
near neighbors, and distant relatives, of the Abbé
Chauvelin. . . ."

"That is what it is, is it?" said Louis XV, yawning.
"Another nephew of the *enquêtes et requêtes*. My
Parliament abuses my bounty; it really has too large a
family."

"But if it is only a *distant* relative!"

"Enough; all these people are good for nothing.
This Abbé Chauvelin is a Jansenist! not a bad sort of
fellow, in his way; but he has dared to resign. Please
throw the letter into the fire, and let me hear no
more about it."

Chapter II

If these last words of the King were not exactly a
death-warrant, they were something like a refusal of
permission to live. What could a young man without fortune do, in 1756, whose King would not hear
his name mentioned? He might have looked for a
clerkship, or tried to turn philosopher, or poet, perhaps; but without official dedication, the trade was
worth nothing.

And besides, such was not, by any means, the vocation of the Chevalier Vauvert, who had written, with tears, the letter which made the King laugh. At this very moment, alone with his father, in the old château of Neauflette, his look was desperate and gloomy, even to frenzy, as he paced to and fro.

"I must go to Versailles," he said.

"And what will you do there?"

"I know not; but what am I doing here?"

"You keep me company. It certainly can not be very amusing for you, and I will not in any way seek to detain you. But do you forget that your mother is dead?"

"No, sir. I promised her to consecrate to you the life that you gave me. I will come back, but I must go. I really can not stay in this place any longer."

"And why, if I may ask?"

"My desperate love is the only reason. I love Mademoiselle d'Annebault madly."

"But you know that it is useless. It is only Molière who contrives successful matches without dowries. Do you forget too the disfavor with which I am regarded?"

"Ah! sir, that disfavor! Might I be allowed, without deviating from the profound respect I owe you, to ask what caused it? We do not belong to the Parliament. We pay the tax; we do not order it. If the Parliament stints the King's purse, it is his affair, not ours. Why should M. l'Abbé Chauvelin drag us into his ruin?"

"Monsieur l'Abbé Chauvelin acts as an honest man. He refuses to approve the 'dixième' tax because he is disgusted at the prodigality of the court. Nothing of this kind would have taken place in the days of

Madame de Chateauroux! She was beautiful, at least, that woman, and did not cost us anything, not even what she so generously gave. She was sovereign mistress, and declared that she would be satisfied if the King did not send her to rot in some dungeon when he should be pleased to withdraw his good graces from her. But this Étioles, this le Normand, this insatiable Poisson!"

"What does it matter?"

"What does it matter! say you? More than you think. Do you know that now, at this very time, while the King is plundering us, the fortune of this griset is incalculable? She began by contriving to get an annuity of a hundred and eighty thousand livres —but that was a mere bagatel, it counts for nothing now; you can form no idea of the startling sums that the King showers upon her; three months of the year can not pass without her picking up, as tho by chance, some five or six hundred thousand livres— yesterday out of the salt-tax, to-day out of the increase in the appropriation for the Royal mews. Although she has her own quarters in the royal residences, she buys La Selle, Cressy, Aulnay, Brimborion, Marigny, Saint-Remy, Bellevue, and a number of other estates—mansions in Paris, in Fontainebleau, Versailles, Compiègne—without counting secret hoards in all the banks of Europe, to be used in case of her own disgrace or a demise of the crown. And who pays for all this, if you please?"

"That I do not know, sir, but, certainly, not I."

"It *is* you, as well as everybody else. It is France, it is the people who toil and moil, who riot in the streets, who insult the statue of Pigalle. But Parliament will endure it no longer, it will have no more new imposts. As long as there was question of defraying the cost of the war, our last crown was ready; we had no thought of bargaining. The victorious King could see clearly that he was beloved by the whole kingdom, still more so when he was at the point of death. Then all dissensions, all faction, all ill-feeling ceased. All France knelt before the sick-bed of the King, and prayed for him. But if we pay, without counting, for his soldiers and his doctors, we will no longer pay for his mistresses; we have other things to do with our money than to support Madame de Pompadour."

"I do not defend her, sir. I could not pretend to say either that she was in the wrong or in the right. I have never seen her."

"Doubtless; and you would not be sorry to see her —is it not so?—in order to have an opinion on the subject? For, at your age, the head judges through the eyes. Try it then, if the fancy takes you. But the satisfaction will be denied you."

"Why, sir?"

"Because such an attempt is pure folly; because this marquise is as invisible in her little boudoir at Brimborion as the Grand Turk in his seraglio; because every door will be shut in your face. What are you going to do? Attempt an impossibility? Court fortune like an adventurer?"

"By no means, but like a lover. I do not intend to supplicate, sir, but to protest against an injustice. I had a well-founded hope, almost a promise, from M. de Biron; I was on the eve of possessing the object of my love, and this love is not unreasonable; you have not disapproved of it. Let me venture, then, to plead my own cause. Whether I shall appeal to the King or to Madame de Pompadour I know not, but I wish to set out."

"You do not know what the court is, and you wish to present yourself there."

"I may perhaps be the more easily received for the very reason that I am unknown there."

"You unknown, Chevalier. What are you thinking about? With such a name as yours! We are gentlemen of an old stock, Monsieur; you could not be unknown."

"Well, then, the King will listen to me."

"He will not even hear you. You see Versailles in your dreams, and you will think yourself there when your postilion stops his horses at the city gates. Suppose you get as far as the antechamber—the gallery, the Oeil de Bœuf; perhaps there may be nothing between his Majesty and yourself but the thickness of a door; there will still be an abyss for you to cross. You will look about you, you will seek expedients, protection, and you will find nothing. We are relatives of M. de Chauvelin, and how do you think the King takes vengeance on such as we? The rack for Damiens, exile for the Parliament, but for us a word is enough, or, worse still—silence. Do you know what the silence of the King is, when, instead of replying to you, he mutely stares at you, as he passes, and annihilates you? After the Grève, and the Bastille, this is a degree of torture which, tho less cruel in appearance, leaves its mark as plainly as the hand of the executioner. The condemned man, it is true, remains free, but he must no longer think of approaching woman or courtier, drawing-room, abbey, or barrack. As he moves about every door closes upon him, every one

who is anybody turns away, and thus he walks this
way and that, in an invisible prison."

"But I will so bestir myself in my prison that I
shall get out of it."

"No more than any one else! The son of M. de
Meynières was no more to blame than you. Like you,
he had received promises, he entertained most legiti-
mate hopes. His father, a devoted subject of his
Majesty, an upright man if there is one in the kingdom, repulsed by his sovereign, bowed his gray head
before the *griset*, not in prayer, but in ardent pleading. Do you know what she replied? Here are her
very words, which M. de Meynières sends me in a
letter: 'The King is the master, he does not deem it
appropriate to signify his displeasure to you personally; he is content to make you aware of it by de-
priving your son of a calling. To punish you otherwise would be to begin an unpleasantness, and he
wishes for none; we must respect his will. I pity
you, however; I realize your troubles. I have been
a mother; I know what it must cost you to leave your
son without a profession!' This is how the creature
expresses herself; and you wish to put yourself at her
feet!"

"They say they are charming, sir."

"Of course they say so. She is not pretty, and the
King does not love her, as every one knows. He
yields, he bends before this woman. She *must* have
something else than that wooden head of hers to main-
tain her strange power."

"But they say she has so much wit."

"And no heart!—Much to her credit, no doubt."

"No heart! She who knows so well how to declaim
the lines of Voltaire, how to sing the music of Rous-

seau! She who plays Alzire and Colette! No heart.
Oh, that can not be! I will never believe it."

"Go then and see, since you wish it. I advise, I
do not command, but you will only be at the expense
of a useless journey.—You love this D'Annebault
young lady very much then?"

"More than my life."

"*Alors*, be off!"

Chapter III

It has been said that journeys injure love, because
they distract the mind; it has also been said that they
strengthen love, because they give one time to dream
over it. The chevalier was too young to make such
nice distinctions. Weary of the carriage, when half-
way on his journey, he had taken a saddle-hack and
thus arrived toward five o'clock in the evening at the
"Sun" Inn—a sign then out of fashion, since it dated
back to the time of Louis XIV.

There was, at Versailles, an old priest who had
been rector of a church near Neauflette; the chevalier
knew him and loved him. This curé, poor and simple
himself, had a nephew, who held a benefice, a court
abbé, who might therefore be useful. So the chevalier
went to this nephew who—man of importance as he
was—his chin ensconced in his "rabat," received the
newcomer civilly, and condescended to listen to his
request.

"Come!" said he, "you arrive at a fortunate moment.
This is to be an opera-night at the court, some sort
of fête or other. I am not going, because I am sulking
so as to get something out of the marquise; but here
I happen to have a note from the Duc d'Aumont; I

asked for it for some one else, but never mind, you can have it. Go to the fête; you have not yet been presented, it is true, but, for this entertainment, that is not necessary. Try to be in the King's way when he goes into the little *foyer*. One look, and your fortune is made."

The chevalier thanked the abbé, and, worn out by a disturbed night and a day on horse-back, he made his toilet at the inn in that negligent manner which so well becomes a lover. A maid-servant, whose experience had been decidedly limited, dressed his wig as best she could, covering his spangled coat with powder. Thus he turned his steps toward his luck with the hopeful courage of twenty summers.

The night was falling when he arrived at the château. He timidly advanced to the gate and asked his way of a sentry. He was shown the grand staircase. There he was informed by the tall Swiss that the opera had just commenced, and that the King, that is to say, everybody, was in the hall.[2]

"If Monsieur le Marquis will cross the court," added the doorkeeper (he conferred the title of "Marquis" at a venture), "he will be at the play in an instant. If he prefers to go through the apartments—"

The chevalier was not acquainted with the palace. Curiosity prompted him, at first, to reply that he would cross the apartments; then, as a lackey offered to follow as a guide, an impulse of vanity made him add that he needed no escort. He, therefore, went

[2] This does not refer to the present theater, built by Louis XV, or rather by Madame de Pompadour, but only completed in 1769 and inaugurated in 1770, for the marriage of the Duc de Berri (Louis XVI) with Marie Antoinette. The "hall" in question was a sort of portable theater, that was moved into this or that gallery or apartment, after the manner in vogue in the days of Louis XIV.

forward alone, but not without a certain emotion of timidity.

Versailles was resplendent with light. From the ground-floor to the roof there glittered and blazed lusters, chandeliers, gilded furniture, marbles. With the exception of the Queen's apartments, the doors were everywhere thrown open. As the chevalier walked on he was struck with an astonishment and an admiration better imagined than described, for the wonder of the spectacle that offered itself to his gaze was not only the beauty, the sparkle of the display itself, but the absolute solitude which surrounded him in his enchanted wilderness.

To find one's self alone in a vast enclosure, be it temple, cloister, or castle, produces a strange, even a weird feeling. The movement—whatever it be—seems to weigh upon the solitary individual; its walls gaze at him! its echoes are listening to him; the noise of his steps breaks in upon a silence so deep that he is impressed by an involuntary fear and dares not advance without a feeling akin to awe. Such were the chevalier's first impressions, but curiosity soon got the upper hand and drew him on. The candelabra of the Gallery of Mirrors, looking into the polished surfaces, saw their flames redoubled in them. Every one knows what countless thousands of cherubs, nymphs, and shepherdesses disport themselves on the panelings, flutter about on the ceilings, and seem to encircle the entire palace as with an immense garland. Here, vast halls, with canopies of velvet shot with gold and chairs of state still impressed with the stiff majesty of the "great King"; there, creased and disordered ottomans, chairs in confusion around a card-table; a never-ending succession of empty salons, where all this

magnificence shone out the more that it seemed entirely
useless. At intervals were half-concealed doors opening upon corridors that extended as far as the eye
could reach, a thousand staircases, a thousand passages
crossing each other as in a labyrinth; colonnades,
raised platforms built for giants, boudoirs ensconced
in corners like children's hiding-places, an enormous
painting of Vanloo near a mantel of porphyry; a
forgotten patch-box, lying beside a piece of grotesque
Chinese workmanship; here a crushing grandeur, there
an effeminate grace; and everywhere, in the midst of
luxury, of prodigality, and of indolence, a thousand
intoxicating odors, strange and diverse, mingle perfumes of flowers and women, an enervating warmth,
the very material and sensible atmosphere of pleasure
itself.

To be in such a place, amid such marvels, at twenty,
and to be there alone, is surely quite sufficient cause
for temporary intoxication. The chevalier advanced
at haphazard, as in a dream.

"A very palace of fairies," he murmured, and, indeed, he seemed to behold, unfolding itself before
him, one of those tales in which wandering knights
discover enchanted castles. Were they indeed mortal
creatures that inhabited this matchless abode? Were
they real women who came and sat on these chairs
and whose graceful outlines had left on those cushions that slight impress, so suggestive, even yet, of
indolence? Who knows but that, behind those thick
curtains, at the end of some long dazzling gallery,
there may perhaps soon appear a princess asleep for
the last hundred years, a fairy in hoops, an Armida
in spangles, or some court hamadryad that shall issue

forth from this marble column, or burst from out of
that gilded panel?

Bewildered, almost overpowered, at the sight of all
these novel objects, the young chevalier, in order the
better to indulge his reverie, had thrown himself on
a sofa, and would doubtless have forgotten himself
there for some time had he not remembered that he
was in love. What, at this hour, was Mademoiselle
d'Annebault, his beloved, doing—left behind in her old
château?

"Athénaïs!" he exclaimed suddenly, "why do I
thus waste my time here? Is my mind wandering?
Great heavens! Where am I? And what is going on
within me?"

He soon rose and continued his travels through this
terra incognita, and of course lost his way. Two or
three lackeys, speaking in a low voice, stood before
him at the end of a gallery. He walked toward them
and asked how he should find his way to the play.

"If M. le Marquis," he was answered (the same title
being still benevolently granted him), "will give himself the trouble to go down that staircase and follow
the gallery on the right, he will find at the end of it
three steps going up; he will then turn to the left, go
through the Diana salon, that of Apollo, that of the
Muses, and that of Spring; he will go down six steps
more, then, leaving the Guards' Hall on his right and
crossing over to the Ministers' staircase, he will not fail
to meet there other ushers who will show him the
way."

"Much obliged," said the chevalier, "with such
excellent instruction, it will certainly be my fault if
I do not find my way."

He set off again boldly, constantly stopping, how-

ever, in spite of himself, to look from side to side, then
once more remembering his love. At last, at the end
of a full quarter of an hour, he once more found, as
he had been told, a group of lackeys.

"M. le Marquis is mistaken," they informed him;
"it is through the other wing of the château that he
should have gone, but nothing is easier for him than
to retrace his steps. M. le Marquis has but to go
down this staircase, then he will cross the salon of the
Nymphs, that of Summer, that of——"

"I thank you," said the chevalier, proceeding on his
way. "How foolish I am," he thought, "to go on
asking people in this fashion like a rustic. I am
making myself ridiculous to no purpose, and even
supposing—tho it is not likely—that they are not
laughing at me, of what use is their list of names,
and the pompous sobriquets of these salons, not one of
which I know?"

He made up his mind to go straight before him as
far as possible. "For, after all," said he to himself, "this place is very beautiful and prodigiously vast
but it is not boundless, and, were it three times as
large as our rabbit enclosure, I must at last reach the
end of it."

But it is not easy in Versailles to walk on for a long
time in one direction, and this rustic comparison of
the royal dwelling to a rabbit enclosure doubtless dis-
pleased the nymphs of the place, for they at once set
about leading the poor lover astray more than ever,
and, doubtless, to punish him, took pleasure in making him retrace his steps over and over again, constantly bringing him back to the same place, like a
countryman lost in a thicket of quickset; thus did they

shut him in in this Cretan labyrinth of marble and gold.

In the "Antiquities of Rome," by Piranesi, there is a series of engravings which the artist calls "his dreams," and which are supposed to reproduce his own visions during a fit of delirious fever. These engravings represent vast Gothic halls; on the flagstones are strewn all sorts of engines and machines, wheels, cables, pulleys, levers, catapults, the expression of enormous power and formidable resistance. Along the walls you perceive a staircase, and upon this staircase, climbing, not without trouble, Piranesi himself. Follow the steps a little higher and they suddenly come to an end before an abyss. Whatever has happened to poor Piranesi, you think that he has, at any rate, reached the end of his labors, for he can not take another step without falling; but lift your eyes and you will see a second staircase rising in the air, and upon these stairs Piranesi again, again on the brink of a precipice.

Look now still higher, and another staircase still rises before you, and again poor Piranesi continuing his ascent, and so on, until the everlasting staircase and the everlasting Piranesi disappear together in the skies; that is to say, in the border of the engraving.

This allegory, offspring of a nightmare, represents with a high degree of accuracy the tedium of useless labor and the species of vertigo which is brought on by impatience. The chevalier, wandering incessantly from salon to salon and from gallery to gallery, was at last seized with a fit of downright exasperation.

"Parbleu," said he, "but this is cruel! After having been so charmed, so enraptured, so enthralled, to find myself alone in this cursed palace." (It was no longer a palace of fairies!) "I shall never be able to get out it! A plague upon the infatuation which inspired me with the idea of entering this place, like Prince Fortunatus with his boots of solid gold, instead of simply getting the first lackey I came across to take me to the play at once!"

The chevalier experienced this tardy feeling of repentance for his rashness at a moment when, like Piranesi, he was half-way up a staircase, on a landing between three doors. Behind the middle one, he thought he heard a murmur so sweet, so light, so voluptuous, that he could not help listening. At the very instant when he was tremblingly advancing with the indiscreet intention of eavesdropping, this door swung open. A breath of air, balmy with a thousand perfumes, a torrent of light that rendered the very mirrors of the gallery lusterless struck him so suddenly that he perforce stepped back.

"Does Monsieur le Marquis wish to enter?" asked the usher who had opened the door.

"I wish to go to the play," replied the chevalier.

"It is just this moment over."

At the same time, a bevy of beautiful ladies, their complexions delicately tinted with white and carmine, escorted by lords, old and young, who led them, not by the arm, nor by the hand, but by the tips of their fingers, began filing out from the Palace Theater, taking care to walk sidewise, in order not to disarrange their hoops.

All of these brilliant people spoke in a low voice, with an air half grave, half gay, a mixture of awe and respect.

"What can this be?" said the Chevalier, not guessing that chance had luckily brought him to the little *foyer*.

"The King is about to pass," replied the usher.

There is a kind of intrepidity which hesitates at nothing; it comes but too easily, it is the courage of vulgar people. Our young provincial, altho he was reasonably brave, did not possess this faculty. At the mere words, "The King is about to pass," he stood motionless and almost terror-stricken.

King Louis XV, who when out hunting would ride on horseback a dozen leagues with ease, was, in other respects, as is known, royally indolent. He boasted, not without reason, that he was the first gentleman of France, and his mistresses used to tell him, not without truth, that he was the best built and the most handsome. It was something to remember to see him leave his chair, and deign to walk in person. When he crossed the *foyer*, with one arm laid, or rather stretched, on the shoulder of Monsieur d'Argenson, while his red heel glided over the polished floor (he had made his laziness the fashion), all whisperings ceased; the courtiers lowered their heads, not daring to bow outright, and the fine ladies, gently bending their knees within the depths of their immense furbelows, ventured that coquettish good-night which our grandmothers called a courtesy, and which our century has replaced by the brutal English shake of the hand.

But the King paid attention to nothing, and saw only what pleased him. Alfieri, perhaps, was there, and it is he who thus describes, in his memoirs, his presentation at Versailles:

"I well knew that the king never spoke to strangers who were not of striking appearance; all the same I could not brook the impassible and frowning demeanor of Louis XV. He scanned from head to foot the man who was being presented to him, and it looked as if he received no impression by so doing. It seems to me, however, that if one were to say to a giant, 'Here is an ant I present to you,' he would smile on looking at it, or perhaps say, 'Oh! what a little creature.' "

The taciturn monarch thus passed among these flowers of feminine loveliness, and all this court, alone in spite of the crowd. It did not require of the chevalier much reflection to understand that he had nothing to hope from the King, and that the recital of his love would obtain no success in that quarter.

"Unfortunate that I am!" thought he. "My father was but too well informed when he told me that within two steps of the king I should see an abyss between him and me. Were I to venture to ask for an audience, who would be my patron? Who would present me? There he is—the absolute master, who can by a word change my destiny, assure my fortune, fulfil my desires. He is there before me; were I to stretch out my hand I could touch his embroidered coat—and I feel myself farther from him than if I were still buried in the depths of my native province! Oh! If I could only speak to him! Only approach him! Who will come to my help?"

While the chevalier was in this unhappy state of mind he saw entering with an air of the utmost grace and delicacy a young and attractive woman, clad very simply in a white gown, without diamonds or embroideries and with a single rose in her hair. She gave her hand to a lord *tout à l'ambre*, as Voltaire expresses it, and spoke softly to him behind her fan. Now chance willed it that, in chatting, laughing, and gesticulating, this fan should slip from her and fall beneath a chair, immediately in front of the chevalier. He at once hurried to pick it up, and as in doing so he had set one knee on the floor, the young lady appeared to

him so charming that he presented her the fan without
rising. She stopped, smiled, and passed on, thanking
him with a slight movement of the head, but at the
look she had given the chevalier he felt his heart beat
without knowing why. He was right. This young lady
was *la petite d'Étioles*, as the malcontents still called
her, while others in speaking of her said "la Marquise"
in that reverent tone in which one says "The Queen."

Chapter IV

"She will protect me! She will come to my rescue!
Ah! how truly the abbé spoke when he said that one
look might decide my life. Yes, those eyes, so soft
and gentle, that little mouth, both merry and sweet,
that little foot almost hidden under the *pompon*—
Yes, here is my good fairy!"

Thus thought the chevalier, almost aloud, as he returned to the inn. Whence came this sudden hope?
Did his youth alone speak, or had the eyes of the
marquise told a tale?

He passed the greater part of the night writing to
Mademoiselle d'Annebault such a letter as we heard
read by Madame de Pompadour to her lord.

To reproduce this letter would be a vain task. Excepting idiots, lovers alone find no monotony in repeating the same thing over and over again.

At daybreak the chevalier went out and began roam-
ing about, carrying his dreams through the streets. It
did not occur to him to have recourse once more to
the protecting abbé, and it would not be easy to tell
the reason which prevented his doing so. It was like
a blending of timidity and audacity, of false shame and
romantic honor. And, indeed, what would the abbé

have replied to him, if he had told his story of the night before? "You had the unique good fortune to pick up this fan; did you know how to profit by it? What did the marquise say to you?"

"Nothing."

"You should have spoken to her."

"I was confused; I had lost my head."

"That was wrong; one must know how to seize an opportunity; but this can be repaired. Would you like me to present you to Monsieur So-and-so, one of my friends; or perhaps to Madame Such-a-one? That would be still better. We will try and secure for you access to this marquise who frightened you so, and then"—and so forth.

Now the chevalier little relished anything of this kind. It seemed to him that, in telling his adventure, he would, so to speak, soil and mar it. He said to himself that chance had done for him something unheard of, incredible, and that it should remain a secret between himself and Fortune. To confide this secret to the first comer was, to his thinking, to rob it of its value, and to show himself unworthy of it. "I went alone yesterday to the castle at Versailles," thought he, "I can surely go alone to Trianon?" This was, at the time, the abode of the favorite.

Such a way of thinking might, and even should, appear extravagant to calculating minds, who neglect no detail, and leave as little as possible to chance; but colder mortals, if they were ever young, and not everybody is so, even in youth, have known that strange sentiment, both weak and bold, dangerous and seductive, which drags us to our fate. One feels one's self blind, and wishes to be so; one does not know where one is going and yet walks on. The charm of the thing consists in this recklessness and this very ignorance; it is the pleasure of the artist in his dreams, of the lover spending the night beneath the windows of his mistress; it is instinct of the soldier; it is, above all, that of the gamester.

The chevalier, almost without knowing it, had thus taken his way to Trianon. Without being very *paré*, as they said in those days, he lacked neither elegance nor that indescribable air which forbids a chance lackey, meeting one, from daring to ask where one is going. It was, therefore, not difficult for him, thanks to information he had obtained at the inn, to reach the gate of the château—if one can so call that marble *bon-bonnière*, which has seen so many pleasures and pains in bygone days. Unfortunately, the gate was closed, and a stout Swiss wearing a plain coat was walking about, his hands behind his back, in the inner avenue, like a person who is not expecting any one.

"The King is here!" said the chevalier to himself, "or else the marquise is away. Evidently, when the doors are closed, and valets stroll about, the masters are either shut in or gone out."

What was to be done? Full as he had been, a moment earlier, of courage and confidence, he now felt, all at once, confused and disappointed. The mere thought, "The King is here!" alone gave him more alarm than those few words, on the night before: "The King is about to pass!" For then he was but facing the unknown, and now he knew that icy stare, that implacable, impassible majesty.

"Ah! Bon Dieu! What a figure I should cut if I were to be so mad as to try and penetrate this garden, and find myself face to face with this superb monarch, sipping his coffee beside a rivulet."

At once the sinister shadow of the Bastille seemed to fall before the poor lover; instead of the charming image that he had retained of the marquise and her smile, he saw dungeons, cells, black bread, questionable water; he knew the story of Latude, thirty years an inmate of the Bastille. Little by little his hope seemed to be taking to itself wings.

"And yet," he again said to himself, "I am doing no harm, nor the King either. I protest against an injustice; but I never wrote or sang scurrilous songs. I was so well received at Versailles yesterday, and the lackeys were so polite. What am I afraid of? Of committing a blunder? I shall make many more which will repair this one."

He approached the gate and touched it with his finger. It was not quite closed. He opened it, and resolutely entered.

The gatekeeper turned round with a look of annoyance.

"What are you looking for? Where are you going?"

"I am going to Madame de Pompadour."

"Have you an audience?"

"Yes."

"Where is your letter?"

He was no longer the "marquis" of the night before, and, this time, there was no Duc d'Aumont. The chevalier lowered his eyes sadly, and noticed that his white stockings and Rhinestone buckles were covered with dust. He had made the mistake of coming on foot, in a region where no one walked. The gatekeeper also bent his eyes, and scanned him, not from head to foot, but from foot to head. The dress seemed neat enough, but the hat was rather askew, and the hair lacked powder.

"You have no letter. What do you wish?"

"I wish to speak to Madame de Pompadour."

"Really! And you think this is the way it is done?"

"I know nothing about it. Is the King here?"

"Perhaps. Go about your business and leave me alone."

The chevalier did not wish to lose his temper, but, in spite of himself, this insolence made him turn pale.

"I sometimes have told a lackey to go away," he replied, "but a lackey never said so to me."

"Lackey! I a lackey?" exclaimed the enraged gate-keeper.

"Lackey, doorkeeper, valet, or menial, I care not, and it matters little."

The gatekeeper made a step toward the chevalier with clenched fists and face aflame. The chevalier, brought to himself by the appearance of a threat, lifted the handle of his sword slightly.

"Take care, fellow," said he, "I am a gentleman, and it would cost me but thirty-six livres to put a boor like you under ground."

"If you are a nobleman, monsieur, I belong to the King; I am only doing my duty; so do not think—"

At this moment the flourish of a hunting-horn sounding from the Bois de Satory was heard afar, and lost itself in the echo. The chevalier allowed his sword to drop into its scabbard, no longer thinking of the interrupted quarrel.

"I declare," said he, "it is the King starting for the hunt! Why did you not tell me that before?"

"That has nothing to do with me, nor with you either."

"Listen to me, my good man. The King is not here;

I have no letter, I have no audience. Here is some money for you; let me in."

He drew from his pocket several pieces of gold. The gatekeeper scanned him anew with a superb contempt.

"What is that?" said he, disdainfully. "Is it thus you seek to penetrate into a royal dwelling? Instead of making you go out, take care I don't lock you in."

"*You*—you valet!" said the chevalier, getting angry again and once more seizing his sword.

"Yes, I," repeated the big man. But during this conversation, in which the historian regrets to have compromised his hero, thick clouds had darkened the sky; a storm was brewing. A flash of lightning burst forth, followed by a violent peal of thunder, and the rain began to fall heavily. The chevalier, who still held his gold, saw a drop of water on his dusty shoe as large as a crown piece.

"Peste!" said he, "let us find shelter. It would never do to get wet."

He turned nimbly toward the den of Cerberus, or, if you please, the gatekeeper's lodge.

Once in there, he threw himself unceremoniously into the big armchair of the gatekeeper himself.

"Heavens! How you annoy me!" said he, "and how unfortunate I am! You take me for a conspirator, and you do not understand that I have in my pocket a petition for his Majesty! If I am from the country, you are nothing but a dolt."

The gatekeeper, for answer, went to a corner to fetch his halberd, and remained standing thus with the weapon in his fist.

"When are you going away?" he cried out in a stentorian voice.

The quarrel, in turn forgotten and taken up again,

seemed this time to be becoming quite serious, and
already the gatekeeper's two big hands trembled
strangely on his pike;—what was to happen? I do
not know. But, suddenly turning his head—"Ah!" said
the chevalier, "who comes here?"

A young page mounted on a splendid horse (not an
English one;—at that time thin legs were not the
fashion) came up at full speed. The road was soaked
with rain; the gate was but half open. There was a
pause; the keeper advanced and opened the gate. The
page spurred his horse, which had stopped for the
space of an instant; it tried to resume its gait, but
missed its footing, and, slipping on the damp ground,
fell.

It is very awkward, almost dangerous, to raise a
fallen horse. A riding-whip is of no use. The kicking
of the beast, which is doing its best, is extremely dis-
agreeable, especially when one's own leg is caught under
the saddle.

The chevalier, however, came to the rescue without
thinking of these inconveniences, and set about it so
cleverly that the horse was soon raised and the rider
freed. But the latter was covered with mud and could
scarcely limp along.

Carried as well as might be to the gatekeeper's lodge
and seated in his turn in the big armchair, "Sir," said
he to the chevalier, "you are certainly a nobleman.
You have rendered me a great service, but you can
render me a still greater one. Here is a message from
the King for Madame la Marquise, and this message is
very urgent, as you see, since my horse and I, in order
to go faster, almost broke our necks. You understand
that, wounded as I am, with a lame leg, I could not
deliver this paper. I should have, in order to do so,

to be carried myself. Will you go there in my stead?"

At the same time he drew from his pocket a large envelop ornamented with gilt arabesques and fastened with the royal seal.

"Very willingly, sir," replied the chevalier, taking the envelop.

And, nimble and light as a feather, he set out at a run and on the tips of his toes.

Chapter V

When the chevalier arrived at the château he found another doorkeeper in front of the peristyle:

"By the King's order," said the young man, who this time no longer feared halberds, and, showing his letter, he passed gaily between half a dozen lackeys.

A tall usher, planted in the middle of the vestibule, seeing the order and the royal seal, gravely inclined himself, like a poplar bent by the wind—then, smiling, he touched with one of his bony fingers the corner of a piece of paneling.

A little swinging door, masked by tapestry, at once opened as if of its own accord. The bony man made an obsequious sign, the chevalier entered, and the tapestry, which had been drawn apart, fell softly behind him.

A silent valet introduced him into a drawing-room, then into a corridor, in which there were two or three closed doors, then at last into a second drawing-room, and begged him to wait a moment.

"Am I here again in the château of Versailles?" the chevalier asked himself. "Are we going to begin another game of hide-and-seek?"

Trianon was, at that time, neither what it is now

nor what it had been. It has been said that Madame
de Maintenon had made of Versailles an oratory, and
Madame de Pompadour a boudoir. It has also been
said of Trianon that *ce petit château de porcelaine*
was the boudoir of Madame de Montespan. Be that
as it may, concerning these boudoirs, it appears that
Louis XV put them everywhere. This or that gallery,
which his ancestor walked majestically, was then
divided oddly into an infinity of apartments. There
were some of every color, and the King went flutter-
ing about in all these gardens of silk and velvet.

"Do you think my little furnished apartments are
in good taste?" he one day asked the beautiful Com-
tesse de Sérrant.

"No," said she, "I would have them in blue."

As blue was the King's color, this answer flattered
him.

At their next meeting, Madame de Sérrant found
the salon upholstered in blue, as she had wished it.

That in which the chevalier now found himself alone
was neither blue nor pink, it was all mirrors. We
know how much a pretty woman with a lovely figure
gains by letting her image repeat itself in a thousand
aspects. She bewilders, she envelops, so to speak,
him whom she desires to please. To whatever side he
turns, he sees her. How can he avoid being charmed?
He must either take to flight or own himself con-
quered.

The chevalier looked at the garden, too. There,
behind, the bushes and labyrinths, the statues and the
marble vases, that pastoral style which the marquise
was about to introduce, and which, later on, Madame
Du Barry and Marie Antoinette were to push to such
a high degree of perfection, was beginning to show

itself. Already there appeared the rural fantasies
where the *blasé* conceits were disappearing. Already
the puffing tritons, the grave goddesses, and the
learned nymphs, the busts with flowing wigs, frozen
with horror in their wealth of verdure, beheld an
English garden rise from the ground, amid the wondering trees. Little lawns, little streams, little bridges,
were soon to dethrone Olympus to replace it by a
dairy, strange parody of nature, which the English
copy without understanding—very child's play, for
the nonce the pastime of an indolent master who tried
in vain to escape the ennui of Versailles while remaining at Versailles itself.

But the chevalier was too charmed, too enraptured
at finding himself there for a critical thought to
present itself to his mind. He was, on the contrary,
ready to admire everything, and was indeed admiring,
twirling his missive between his fingers as a rustic
does his hat, when a pretty waiting-maid opened the
door, and said to him softly:

"Come, monsieur."

He had followed her, and after having once more
passed through several corridors which were more or
less mysterious, she ushered him into a large apartment where the shutters were half-closed. Here she
stopped and seemed to listen.

"Still at hide-and-seek!" said the chevalier to himself. However, at the end of a few moments, yet
another waiting-maid, who seemed to be even prettier
than the first, repeated to him in the same tone the
same words:

"Come, monsieur."

If he had been the victim of one kind of emotion at
Versailles, he was subject to another, and still deeper

feeling now, for he stood on the threshold of the
temple in which the divinity dwelt. He advanced
with a palpitating heart. A soft light, slightly veiled
by thin, gauze curtains, succeeded obscurity; a delicious perfume, almost imperceptible, pervaded the air
around him; the waiting-maid timidly drew back the
corner of a silk portière, and, at the end of a large
chamber furnished with elegant simplicity, he beheld
the lady of the fan—the all-powerful marquise.

She was alone, seated before a table, wrapped in a
dressing gown, her head resting on her hand, and,
seemingly, deeply preoccupied. On seeing the chevalier enter, she rose with a sudden and apparently
involuntary movement.

"You come on behalf of the King?"

The chevalier might have answered, but he could
think of nothing better than to bow profoundly while
presenting to the marquise the letter which he brought
her. She took it, or rather seized upon it, with extreme
eagerness. Her hands trembled on the envelop as
she broke the seal.

This letter, written by the King's hand, was rather
long. She devoured it at first, so to speak, with a
glance, then she read it greedily, with profound attention, with wrinkled brow and tightened lips. She was
not beautiful thus, and no longer resembled the magic
apparition of the *petit foyer*. When she reached the
end, she seemed to reflect. Little by little her face,
which had turned pale, assumed a faint color (at this
hour she did not wear rouge), and not only did she
regain that graceful air which habitually belonged to
her, but a gleam of real beauty illumined her delicate
features; one might have taken her cheeks for two
rose-leaves. She heaved a sigh, allowed the letter to

fall upon the table, and, turning toward the chevalier, said, with the most charming smile:

"I kept you waiting, monsieur, but I was not yet dressed, and, indeed, am hardly so even now. That is why I was forced to get you to come through the private rooms, for I am almost as much besieged here as tho I were at home. I would like to answer the King's note. Would it be too much trouble to you to do an errand for me?"

This time he *must* speak; the chevalier had had time to regain a little courage:

"Alas! madame," said he, sadly, "you confer a great favor on me, but, unfortunately, I can not profit by it."

"Why not?"

"I have not the honor to belong to his Majesty."

"How, then, did you come here?"

"By chance; I met on my way a page who had been thrown and who begged me—"

"How 'thrown'?" repeated the marquise, bursting out laughing. She seemed so happy at this moment that gaiety came to her without an effort.

"Yes, madame, he fell from his horse at the gate. I luckily found myself there to help him to rise, and, as his dress was very much disordered, he begged me to take charge of his message."

"And by what chance did you find yourself there?"

"Madame, it was because I had a petition to present to his Majesty."

"His Majesty lives at Versailles."

"Yes, but you live here."

"Oh! So it is you who wished to entrust me with a message."

"Madame, I beg you to believe—"

"Do not trouble yourself, you are not the first. But why do you address yourself to me? I am but a woman—like any other."

As she uttered these words with a somewhat ironical air, the marquise threw a triumphant look upon the letter she had just read.

"Madame," continued the chevalier, "I have always heard that men exercise power, and that women—"

"Guide it, eh? Well, monsieur, there is a queen of France."

"I know it, madame; that is how it happened that I found myself *here* this morning."

The marquise was more than accustomed to such compliments, tho they were generally made in a whisper; but, in the present circumstances, this appeared to be quite singularly gratifying to her.

"And on what faith," said she, "on what assurance, did you believe yourself able to penetrate as far as this? For you did not count, I suppose, upon a horse's falling on the way."

"Madame, I believed—I hoped— "

"What did you hope?"

"I hoped that chance—might make—"

"Chance again! Chance is apparently one of your friends; but I warn you that if you have no other, it is a sad recommendation."

Perhaps offended Chance wished to avenge herself for this irreverence, for the chevalier, whom these few questions had more and more troubled, suddenly perceived, on the corner of the table, the identical fan that he had picked up the night before. He took it, and, as on the night before, presented it to the marquise, bending the knee before her.

"Here, madame," he said to her, "is the only friend that could plead for me—"

The marquise seemed at first astonished, and hesitated a moment, looking now at the fan, now at the chevalier.

"Ah! you are right," she said at last, "it is you, monsieur! I recognize you. It is you whom I saw yesterday, after the play, as I went by with M. de Richelieu. I let my fan drop, and you 'found yourself there,' as you were saying."

"Yes, madame."

"And very gallantly, as a true chevalier, you returned it to me. I did not thank you, but I was sure all the same, that he who knows how to pick up a fan with such grace would also know, at the right time, how to pick up the glove. And we are not ill-pleased at that, we women."

"And it is but true, madame; for, on reaching here just now, I almost had a duel with the gatekeeper."

"Mercy on us!" said the marquise, once more seized with a fit of gaiety. "With the gatekeeper! And what about?"

"He would not let me come in."

"That would have been a pity! But who are you, monsieur? And what is your request?"

"Madame, I am called the Chevalier de Vauvert. M. de Biron had asked in my behalf for a cornetcy in the Guards."

"Oh! I remember now. You come from Neauflette; you are in love with Mademoiselle d'Annebault—"

"Madame, who could have told you?"

"Oh! I warn you that I am much to be feared. When memory fails me, I guess. You are a relative of the Abbé de Chauvelin, and were refused on that account; is not that so? Where is your petition?"

"Here it is, madame; but indeed I can not understand—"

"Why need you undertsand? Rise and lay your paper on the table. I am going to answer the King's letter; you will take him, at the same time, your request and my letter."

"But, madame, I thought I had mentioned to you—"

"You will go. You entered here on the business of the King, is not that true? Well, then, you will enter there in the business of the Marquise de Pompadour, lady of the palace to the Queen."

The chevalier bowed without a word, seized with a sort of stupefaction. The world had long known how much talk, how many ruses and intrigues, the favorite had brought to bear, and what obstinacy she had shown to obtain this title, which in reality brought her nothing but a cruel affront from the Dauphin. She had longed for it for ten years; she willed it, and she had succeeded. So M. de Vauvert, whom she did not know, altho she knew of his love, pleased her as a bearer of happy news.

Immovable, standing behind her, the chevalier watched the marquise as she wrote, first, with all her heart—with passion—then with reflection, stopping, passing her hand under her little nose, delicate as amber. She grew impatient: the presence of a witness disturbed her. At last she made up her mind and drew her pen through something; it must be owned that after all it was but a rough draft.

Opposite the chevalier, on the other side of the table, there glittered a fine Venetian mirror. This timid messenger hardly dared raise his eyes. It would, however, have been difficult not to see in this mirror, over the head of the marquise, the anxious and charming face of the new lady of the palace.

"How pretty she is!" thought he; "it is a pity that I am in love with somebody else; but Athénaïs is more beautiful, and moreover it would be on my part such horrible disloyalty."

"What are you talking about?" said the marquise. The chevalier, as was his wont, had thought aloud without knowing it. "What are you saying?"

"I madame? I am waiting."

"There; that is done," the marquise went on, taking another sheet of paper; but at the slight movement she had made in turning around the dressing-gown had slipped on her shoulder.

Fashion is a strange thing. Our grandmothers thought nothing of going to court in immense robes exposing almost the entire bosom, and it was by no means considered indecent; but they carefully hid the back of their necks, which the fine ladies of to-day expose so freely in the balcony of the opera. This is a newly invented beauty.

On the frail, white, dainty shoulder of Madame de Pompadour there was a little black mark that looked like a fly floating in milk. The chevalier, serious as a giddy boy who is trying to keep his countenance, looked at the mark, and the marquise, holding her pen in the air, looked at the chevalier in the mirror.

In that mirror a rapid glance was exchanged, which meant to say on the one side, "You are charming," and on the other, "I am not sorry for it."

However, the marquise readjusted her dressing-gown.

"You are looking at my beauty spot?"

"I am not looking, madame; I see and I admire."

"Here is my letter; take it to the King with your petition."

"But, madame—"

"Well?"

"His Majesty is hunting; I have just heard the horn in the wood of Satory."

"That is true. I did not think of it. Well, to-morrow. The day after; it matters little. No, immediately. Go. You will give that to Lebel. Good-by, monsieur. Try and remember the beauty spot you have just seen; the King alone in the whole kingdom has seen it; and as for your friend, Chance, tell her, I beg of you, to take care and not chatter to herself so loud, as she did just now. Farewell, chevalier."

She touched a little bell, then, lifting a flood of laces upon her sleeve, held out to the young man her bare arm. He once more bent low, and with the tips of his lips scarcely brushed the rosy nails of the marquise. She saw no impoliteness in it—far from it—but, perhaps, a little too much modesty.

At once the little waiting-maids reappeared (the big ones were not yet up), and, standing behind them, like a steeple in the middle of a flock of sheep, the bony man, still smiling, was pointing the way.

Chapter VI

Alone, ensconced in an old armchair in the back of his little room at the sign of "the Sun," the chevalier waited the next day, then the next, and no news!

"Singular woman! Gentle and imperious, good and bad, the most frivolous of women, and the most obstinate! She has forgotten me. What misery! She is right;—she is all-powerful, and I am nothing."

He had risen, and was walking about the room.

"Nothing!—no, I am but a poor devil. How truly my father spoke! The marquise was mocking me; that is all; while I was looking at her, it was only the reflection in that mirror, and in my eyes, of her own charms—which are, certainly, incomparable—that made her look so pleased! Yes, her eyes are small, but what grace! And Latour, before Diderot, has taken the dust from a butterfly's wing to paint her portrait. She is not very tall, but her figure is perfectly exquisite. Ah! Mademoiselle d'Annebault! Ah! my beloved friend, is it possible that I, too, should forget?"

Two or three sharp raps at the door awoke him from his grief.

"Who is there?"

The bony man, clad all in black, with a splendid pair of silk stockings, which simulated calves that were lacking, entered, and made a deep bow.

"This evening, Monsieur le Chevalier, there is to be a masked ball at the court, and Madame la Marquise sends me to say that you are invited."

"That is enough, monsieur. Many thanks."

As soon as the bony man had retired, the chevalier ran to the bell; the same maid-servant who, three days before, had done her best to be of service to him, assisted him to put on the same spangled coat, striving to acquit herself even better than before.

And then the young man took his way toward the palace, invited this time, and more quiet outwardly, but more anxious and less bold than when he had made his first steps in that, to him, still unknown world.

Chapter VII

Bewildered, almost as much as on the former occasion, by all the splendors of Versailles, which this evening was not empty, the chevalier walked in the great gallery, looking on every side and doing all he could to learn why he was there; but nobody seemed to think of accosting him. At the end of an hour he became wearied and was about to leave, when two masks, exactly alike, seated on a bench, stopped him on his way. One of them took aim at him with her finger as if with a pistol; the other rose and went to him:

"It appears, monsieur," said the mask, carelessly taking his arm, "that you are on very good terms with our marquise."

"I beg your pardon, madame, but of whom are you speaking?"

"You know well enough."

"Not the least in the world."

"Oh! but indeed you do."

"Not at all."

"All the court knows it."

"I do not belong to the court."

"You are playing the child. I tell you it is well known!"

"That may be, madame, but I am ignorant of it."

"You are not ignorant, however, of the fact that the day before yesterday a page fell from his horse at the gate of Trianon. Were you not there by chance?"

"Yes, madame."

"Did you not help him to rise?"

"Yes, madame."

"And did not you enter the château?"

"Certainly."

"And was not a paper given to you?"

"Yes, madame."

"And did you not take it to the King?"

"Assuredly."

"The King was not at Trianon; he was hunting; the marquise was alone—is not that so?"

"Yes, madame."

"She had just risen; she was scarcely clad, excepting, as it is rumored, in a wide dressing-gown."

"People whom one can not prevent from speaking tell all that runs through their heads."

"That is all well enough, but it appears that there passed between your eyes and hers a look which did not offend her."

"What do you mean by that, madame?"

"That you did not displease her."

"I know nothing about that, and I should be distressed that such sweet and rare good-will, which I did not expect, and which touched me to the bottom of my heart, should give occasion to any idle speeches."

"You take fire too quickly, chevalier; one would think you were challenging the whole court; you would never succeed in killing so many people."

"But, madame, if the page fell, and if I carried his message—allow me to ask why I am interrogated."

The mask pressed his arm and said to him:

"Listen, monsieur."

"As much as you please, madame."

"This is what we are thinking about now: The King no longer loves the marquise, and nobody believes that he ever loved her. She has just committed an imprudence; she has set the whole Parliament against her with her "two sous" tax, and to-day she dares

attack a far greater power—the Society of Jesuits.
She will fail, but she has weapons, and, before perishing, she will defend herself."

"Well, madame, what can I do?"

"I will tell you. M. de Choiseul has half quarreled
with M. de Bernis; neither of them is sure what it is
he would like to attempt. Bernis is going away;
Choiseul will take his place. A word from you can
decide it."

"In what way, madame, pray?"

"By allowing your story of the other day to be
told."

"What earthly connection can there be between my
visit, the Jesuits, and the Parliament?"

"Write me one word and the marquise is lost. And
do not doubt that the warmest interest, the most complete gratitude—"

"I humbly beg your pardon again, madame, but
what you are asking of me would be an act of cowardice."

"Is there any honor in politics?"

"I know nothing of all that. Madame de Pompadour let her fan fall before me; I picked it up; I
gave it back to her; she thanked me; she permitted
me with that peculiar grace of hers to thank her in
my turn."

"A truce to ceremonies: time flies; my name is the
Countess d'Estrades; you love Mademoiselle d'Annebault, my niece; do not say no, it is useless. You
are seeking a cornetcy; you shall have it to-morrow,
and if you care for Athénaïs you will soon be my
nephew."

"Ah! madame, what excess of goodness!"

"But you must speak."

"No, madame."

"I have been told that you love that little girl."

"As much as it is possible to love; but if ever my love is to declare itself in her presence my honor must also be there."

"You are very obstinate chevalier! Is that your final reply?"

"It is the last, as it was the first."

"You refuse to enter the Guards? You refuse the hand of my niece?"

"Yes, madame, if that be the price."

Madame d'Estrades cast upon the chevalier a piercing look, full of curiosity; then seeing in his face no sign of hesitation she slowly walked away, losing herself in the crowd.

The chevalier, unable to make anything of this singular adventure, went and sat down in a corner of the gallery.

"What does that woman mean to do?" said he to himself. "She must be a little mad. She wishes to upset the state by means of a silly calumny, and she proposes to me that in order to merit the hand of her niece I should dishonor myself. But Athénaïs would no longer care for me, or, if she lent herself to such an intrigue, I would no longer care for her. What! Strive to harm this good marquise, to defame her, to blacken her character. Never! no, never!"

Always intent upon his own thoughts, the chevalier very probably would have risen and spoken aloud, but just then a small rosy finger touched him on the shoulder.

He raised his eyes and saw before him the pair of masks who had stopped him.

"You do not wish to help us a little then?" said one

of the masks, disguising her voice. But altho the
two costumes were exactly alike, and all seemed calculated to mislead, the chevalier was not deceived.
Neither the look nor the tone was the same.

"Will you answer, sir?"

"No, madame."

"Will you write."

"Neither will I write."

"It is true that you are obstinate. Good-night,
lieutenant."

"What do you say, madame?"

"There is your commission and your marriage contract." And she threw the fan to him.

It was the one which the chevalier had already twice
picked up. The little cupids of Boucher sported on
the parchment of the gilded mother-of-pearl master-
piece. There was no longer any doubt; it was the fan
of Madame de Pompadour.

"Heavens! Marquise, is it possible?"

"Very possible," said she, raising the little piece of
black veil on her chin.

"I know, madame, how to answer—"

"It is not necessary. You are a loyal gentleman,
and we shall see each other again, for we are to be in
the same house. The King has placed you in the
'cornette blanche.' Remember that for a petitioner
there is no greater eloquence than to know how to be
silent if need be—"

"And forgive us," added she, laughing as she ran
away, "if before bestowing upon you our niece's hand,
we thought it expedient to find out your true worth."[3]

<hr/>

[3] Madame d'Estrades not long after was disgraced together
with M. d'Argenson, for having conspired, this time seriously,
against Madame de Pompadour.

THE TOKEN

By Joseph Hergesheimer

What Epes Calef principally thought, walking
sharply away from his discharged responsibility at the
Custom House, through the thin icy light of the late
afternoon, was that he was glad that was finally done
with. It was, he assured himself again, with articu-
lating lips. The next time he went to sea, to the
East, to Patagonia and Canton and the Falklands, or
lay in the Macao Roads with the Brahminy kites
perched high on the rigging, he would be first mate,
perhaps even master, of the *Triton*, and no longer a
mere supercargo. No words could adequately express
how much he hated that position of barterer. Very
privately—in view of his father's special characteristic—he hadn't considered it at all a necessary part
of his training for the commanding of Calef ships;
others of his acquaintance, making like him toward
such a superlative destiny, had worked their way progressively aft with no pause over kegs of Spanish
dollars and the ridiculous merchants of Co-Hongs and
countinghouses. They had always, from the first, been
seamen, while he—But he need bother no longer, his
seemingly endless wearisome apprenticeship, the tire-
some dickering, was over; and in the coming spring,
before the lilacs had bloomed in Salem, he would per-

(From "The Saturday Evening Post," copyright, 1921, by the
  Curtis Publishing Co.; copyright, 1923, by Joseph Herges-
  heimer.)

sonally, individually, order the last fast holding the
Triton to earth cast off.

He swore a little, in a manner at once of the sea
and of vainglorious youth. Epes Calef was not yet
twenty, and his breath congealed in a sparkling mist.
He was, he reminded himself with a lifting pleasure,
home; the *Triton* had docked at noon, but he had been
so busy with the infernal accounts and manifest, the
wharfinger and harbor master, that he had hardly dwelt
upon his safe and happy return. Neither, he suddenly
realized, had he yet seen any member of his family;
even Snelling Pingre, their head clerk, had been able
only to wave briefly from a distance. His, Epes',
father
was more often than not at Derby Wharf on the return
of one of his ships; either Ira Calef, or Bartlett, the
elder son. Now Bartlett, his thoughts ran on, had always been splendidly suited to his appointed activity—
an application to the purely financial side of the Calefs'
wide trading voyages.

With Bartlett in Salem gradually taking the place of
their father, and Epes a master on the sea, the fortunes
and prestige of the family would increase in the next
generation and the next. But this reflection, or rather
its implication, suddenly changed the substance of his
thoughts. They settled on Annice Balavan—with an
unaccountable, an unreasonable sensation of amazement. Epes recognized that he was about to marry
her. He had made this a possibility, no, inevitable,
just before he had left on this last voyage. He was
in for it, he told himself, in a phrase not wholly
gracious, since he had given her the Calef token.

It was remarkable about that—it was an obang,
really; a thin gold coin of the East, almost as broad
as his palm and stamped with angular signs—because

there could be no doubt that when a Calef gave it to a woman, no matter who she was or what the circumstances, he married her. It had come to Salem in the reticule of a ridiculous Dutch girl to whom the obang had been given in the hotel of the Dutch East Indian Company at Batavia by the first adventurous Calef. And after that its tradition, its power, had fast animated it. Epes' attitude toward this, and to Annice Balavan, was consequently fatalistic. Now, after nearly two years on the islands and continents and wide waters of the world, he didn't see how he had come to give the token to Annice. He had, all at once, no great desire for marriage, except to the *Triton;* but with a youthfully philosophical sigh he accepted the impending consequences of his gift as inevitable to life.

There was some consolation in the reflection that Annice was, it was practically admitted, the prettiest girl in Salem and there was a permissible question if there were any better looking in Boston. Her considerable part of the Balavan money, too, would be a material assistance to the not inconsiderable Calef funds and ambitions. It was, after all, Epes decided, a very sensible and advantageous arrangement; the more so because he knew beforehand that Annice would not insist on going to sea with him; everyone, in fact, connected with a ship hated a woman, the master's wife, on board. She didn't like the sea, and made no secret of her feeling; the air from it, drawing in through Salem Harbor, took the crispness out of her muslins and made her hair, she declared, look like strings. But that was nonsense; her ashen-gold hair, even in its net, had the softest and most delicate beauty imaginable. Very different it was from Sumatra's; but then, everything about Sumatra, the younger sister, was unlike

Annice; particularly the former's exaggerated—Epes
called it that—passion for ships and the sea. She
carried this to a most unbecoming extent; positively
her questions were a nuisance.

He passed the Essex House on the right, and then
the Marine Store. The light faded rapidly and it was
growing noticeably colder, frigid and still; the sky
was a clear pale yellow that flickered in the patches of
metallic ice along the gutters, and footfalls, voices,
carried surprisingly. Unaccustomed, for a comparatively long period, to winter, he was at once aware
of its sting and yet found a gratification, without specially heavy clothes, in disregarding it. He had been
hardened to both danger and exposure, and he accepted
them with a sense of challenge and victory. How little
Salem, the land, compared with the shifting sea,
changed; here there was no making or taking in of sail;
it didn't matter what happened in the way of weather.
the houses, the stone-laid streets, even commonly the
trees, were always placidly, monotonously the same
The life in them, as well, went always over the old
charted and recharted course, every morning resembled
every other morning, each night all the others. Why,
take this latter voyage, twenty-five days from Bombay
to Liverpool——

He had reached Summer Street, and turned again
past Mechanics Hall; soon he would be on Chestnut,
and then wholly home. Where, he wondered, after he
was married to Annice, would he live? Maybe on Bath
Street, overlooking Washington Square, or close to the
Ammidons. Annice, he thought, would rather prefer
that; there was at last a movement away from Chestnut Street toward the square. It made no difference
to him; his home primarily—yes, his heart—would be

on the quarter-deck of his ship. His wife might arrange all the details on shore. She would do it very well, too; Annice, in addition to her beauty, was capable; she had a direct, positive mind.

He would get the preliminaries of that business over with as soon as possible, and then, late in April, or in May—Where, he speculated already, would he set sail for? There were so many alternatives, so many diverse cargoes to load and progressively discharge. Abruptly he was swinging in between the hand-wrought iron fencing across the Calef dwelling. It was an imposing square house of brick with a square-looking classic portico, a tall elaborate Palladian window above, and four great chimneys at the corners of the white-railed captain's walk that crowned the flattened roof. Epes found the front door unsecured, and entered, calling in a voice that echoed in the bare, dignified hall.

Instantly, from the floor above, his mother replied, but in a voice strangely, almost unrecognizably emotional, and he heard her equally disturbed and hurried approach. The darkly paneled and carved stairway, bending above his head at the tall window over the portico, hid her until she had almost reached him; and then with an involuntary painful contraction of his heart he saw that she was in deep mourning, and that her face was heavy, sodden with tears. Before he could question her, her arms were about his shoulders and she was sobbing again.

"Epes, Epes, I was afraid you weren't coming back either."

"What is it?" he stammered. "Is father——"

She drew slightly away from him, gazing with streaming eyes into his questioning face. "Why,

haven't you—But that is incredible!" She was close
to him again. "Bartlett is dead. It—it happened in
New York, from a torn finger and blood poisoning. In
two days, Epes; we hardly got there, saw him. Your
father had to go to Boston, and is just back; but he'll
see you almost at once, in the music room, he said."

How like his father that insistent formality was,
Epes thought; nothing, it seemed, was to shake the
dignity, the aloofness of Ira Calef. His manner positively carried with it a chill as palpable as that now
in the streets. He was, of course, both to the world at
large and to his family, the perfect shape of integrity;
but that, with his rigidly correct deportment, appeared to be his only conception of what was owing,
through him, to exterior circumstance and people. All
people—Clia, his wife, his two sons—had been exterior
to Ira Calef; it was always evident that he viewed,
weighed every possible development of living solely in
the light of his own unalterable convictions and wishes.
They were, it was true, always carefully studied,
logical; nor were his decisions quickly formed, in any
heat, generous or bitter; it was the inflexible manner,
the finality and detachment of their announcement
which made them appear so unbearably arbitrary.

The music room, like the stair wall, was entirely
paneled, walls and ceiling in dark wood, and the mahogany in it, the waxed floor, even the windows with
their multiplicity of small panes, held in replica the
withdrawn, almost morose effect given by Ira Calef
himself. He came presently, in a gait neither slow
nor fast, into the music room, where, without his
mother, Epes was waiting. The other's show of welcome was, for him, unusual; he held Epes' hand for
more than the strictly necessary moment, and at once

indicated a chair and the fact that Epes might sit. He was a big man, past sixty, handsomely proportioned, with a handsome face evenly pallid except for the discolorations hanging under eyes themselves almost without a perceptible shading. They were, of course, gray, yet they were so pale that but for their domineering focus they rather resembled clear water slightly crystallized with ice. He made an adequate but brief reference to Bartlett's death, dwelling for a little on the collapse of the boy's mother; and then leaning back and deliberately, for the time, shifting the conversation, asked Epes Calef for a detailed account of what on his voyage as supercargo he had accomplished.

This Epes, to his considerable relief of mind, was able to explain satisfactorily. The master of the *Triton,* Whalen Dove, had come on board the ship at Gravesend, twenty miles down river from London, and after they had been wind-bound for two weeks at Ramsgate they had proceeded to Madeira for wine, put into Colombo after twenty days, and had gone on almost immediately to the Coromandel Coast, Pondicherry and Madras, where the cargo had been disposed of through Lyss, Saturi & Demonte. Yes, the ship had come home by way of Rotterdam. Lost Teneriffe above the clouds five degrees west. They had made seventeen knots with the main skysail set, when a British ship was under double-reefed topsails. But in a three-quarters gale, west southwest, they carried away a mizzen topsail and the foresail burst.

Ira Calef listened to this in an admirable silence that at the same time conveyed the impression that he was exercising an unnecessary amount of patience in the waiting for details of more importance. Epes

quickly recalled himself from his enthusiasm in the
mere fact of seamanship. There were close to two
hundred cases of indigo in the *Triton's* hold—186, to be
precise; about a million pounds of Madras sugar; 460
pieces of redwood; 709 bags of ginger; 830 bags of
pepper; 22 chests of tea—The duty, the elder decided,
would be over twenty thousand dollars.

"You didn't like this," he said unexpectedly to his
son.

Epes met his cold gaze fairly. "No, sir," he replied.
"Always the taste for mere ships."

To this there was no permissible answer.

"I am sorry for that," the other proceeded, "for,
now that Bartlett is dead, it will be needful for you
to give up the sea as a career; I shall require you to
stay in Salem. There are plenty of good, even faith-
ful masters of ships; but after me you are the only remaining Calef; and it won't do for you to be knocking
around the windy reaches of the globe." He stopped,
entirely inattentive of Epes' strained lips, his half-
lifted hand.

A choking emotion, partly made up of incredulity
and in part a burning resentment, fast-rising rebellion,
filled Epes Calef. This—this wasn't right, it wasn't
fair, it wasn't possible. They couldn't take and, for
all his past life, fix his every ambition and hope and
standard on the sea, and then in a sentence or two de-
stroy him, ruin everything he was and might be; for
what his father had just said amounted to no less.
It was inhuman. It couldn't be! Evidently Ira Calef
expected him to speak, to acquiesce, for his regular
eyebrows mounted ever so slightly. But the thing, the
only safety, for Epes now was to remain silent.

"I am not even, completely, certain of Salem," the

elder went on in his level voice, after what had almost
become an unbearable pause. "I personally shall never
live anywhere else; but it may be necessary for you
to move into Boston—for a number of years anyhow.
I am getting more and more absorbed in marine insurance; and the opportunities for the study of that are
moving away from us here. I have spoken to Annice
about all this, and since she is a sensible girl with no
fancy for a husband eternally below the horizon she is
delighted."

"I see," Epes said uncertainly.

Annice Balavan would be delighted with all that his
father had just said, especially with the Boston part,
the larger society there. She was a natural part of this
new, incredibly horrible plan; instantly he identified her
with it, saw her moving radiant and content over its
monotonous bricks and floors and earth. Something
within him, automatic, brought him to his feet. The
other glanced up, once.

"You are, of course, upset by the suddenness of the
news of your brother's death," he conceded. "If you
like you may go to your room with no further discussion at present. There isn't a great deal left to be
said—more movements than words. The most advantageous arrangements will be made for Annice and you;
her mother has already promised to furnish a Boston
house for her in the new style. I am pleased with the
manner in which you appear to have accomplished your
duties on the *Triton*."

In his room a fire of coals was burning in the grate,
with a faintly audible splitting and small rushes of
gaseous flame. It cast a perceptible ruddiness on the
immediate oak flooring, while the rest of the room was
rapidly dimming; the windows, beyond which the

familiar limbs of the elms on the street were sharp and black, showed only rectangles of cold gray; the yellow light had faded from the sky. Epes stood irresolutely, with his gaze lowered, his brow drawn with lines. He could just see his blue sea chest, sent up from the ship earlier in the afternoon; and the brass disks of a nocturnal, his chiefest treasure, hung, he knew, above the chest on the wall. That old instrument of navigation, for finding at night, through the North Star, the hour, seemed to challenge and mock his wretchedness and impotence. That latter word most perfectly held the essence of his tragic situation.

He could do nothing!

Epes slipped into a chair and attempted to combat this. A daring resolution hovered about him, reckless, and yet, he told himself fiercely, entirely justified; he might run away to sea; the sea, the service, he loved. He could ship any day, from any port, as third, probably second mate, and after a single voyage become first officer. That was the reasonable thing to do. He understood that an appeal to his father was worse than useless; the opening of any protest, a difference of opinion, determination, would close Ira Calef to both sympathy and attention. He would be simply, remotely unbending—the eyebrows would climb, his mouth harden, a cutting phrase end the conversation. His father, Epes had realized, was different from the other pleasant fathers he knew; he had always been, well—inhuman. That term in such a connection was new, presumptuous, but Epes in his present mood defiantly allowed it. However, not until now had he acutely suffered from the elder Calef's disposition. Outside he had heard the words "an India liver" applied to his father; yet even Salem was cautious, deferential in its attitude there; Epes could never remember an occasion when his father had been balked in a decision, or even seriously contradicted.

He felt actually as though he hated that frozen parental figure; and he almost blamed Bartlett for dying. That recalled the fact that his brother was dead, that his emotion was neither appropriate nor decent; but the threatened, overpowering wrong to him persisted in dominating every other response. Yes, Epes repeated, he would run away; that—very successfully—had been done before. He'd leave everything, go with only the clothes in which he stood, leaving, out of the sum due him from the *Triton*, payment for them. That act, he recognized, must take him forever from his family, from, as long as Ira Calef lived, his home, Salem. The other would never relent. He thought for a moment of his mother's helpless position; never had he heard her raise her voice, oppose in any particular her husband. He was not, it was true, unkind or discourteous to her, he merely ignored the possibility of her having a single independent desire, a fraction of personality or will. And during Epes' life she had shown no indication that he was wrong. What, Epes now wondered, was the actuality beneath her calm demeanor; maybe she hated, detested Ira Calef. This amazing speculation redirected his thoughts to Annice Balavan.

Or rather, it drew his mind back to the token, the gage of the Calef men. Its reputed, its proved force exerted a species of numbing magic on him; his superstitious regard for it held his imagination as though in chains. Epes had given the obang to Annice, and therefore he was going to marry her; there was no escape from the girl who possessed it. This instinct

was so strong that it struck at all his vague planning—
Annice, if he knew her, would never consent to marry
a runaway sailor, third mate or first or master. No
matter what he might project, an unforeseen circumstance, accident, would betray him and marry him to
Annice Balavan.

He tried to throw this conviction off, to laugh it
away for nonsense; he derided himself unsparingly;
rising, he told himself that he would tramp down
through the house and out at once; but instead he sank
back into his chair. Yet it might be that he could get
away, come back successful, rich, in a very few years—
one good voyage would secure that—and find Annice
waiting for him. This seemed to him an inspiration,
and a hard, active spirit welled up within him. After
no more than one voyage to China. But again a dis-
ability, as gray as the dusk without, flooded him; he
couldn't, when the moment came, walk away in that
manner from responsibility. No matter what his father
was like, he was incontrovertibly his father; already
Epes Calef saw his world as the deck of a ship, and
the high order, the discipline of that plane was the
base of his being. There was, of course, injustice on
the sea; tyrannical captains; but the injustice and
tyranny could not be met with mutiny. For example,
if as a subordinate he were directed to take his ship
onto rocks that he could clearly see, what was there for
him to do but that? How could he question or penetrate the superior, the totally responsible position?

There had been cases when a master, obviously
insane or incapacitated, had been restrained, held in his
cabin against the next port inquiry, by his principal
officers; but even at the height of his desire Epes
couldn't call his father insane. Still seeing his fate as

a part of the obsessing sea he told himself that figuratively he had been set ashore on a sterile and deserted beach while his ship, having swung about with her sails filling gloriously, left him for the rush of free water. Accustomed to the open, to hour after hour, day after day, month on month, on deck, he felt all at once that he couldn't breathe in his closed room the confined heat of the coals. Epes, for a little, suffered acutely, in a constriction of nerves. His whole life was to be like this!

A knock sounded at the door, and a servant entered with fresh candles, which he proceeded to fix on the dressing stand, the overmantel, and light. The illumination, at first uncertain, wan, gained in steady brightness. It was time to dress for dinner. There had been no opportunity for him to procure mourning, but he put on his darkest, most formal clothes, and tied a severe black neckcloth.

The candelabra on the dining table showed his mother's place to be empty—she was not yet able to manage the casual—and the chair that had been Bartlett's was pushed against the wall. Ira Calef, seen to extreme advantage at the ceremony of dinner, hardly spoke; he was intent upon his codfish, with a green sauce; and he tasted critically the brown sherry before him in a large goblet of fragile glass flecked with gold. With this, it developed, he was dissatisfied; the wine had, he said curtly, withered; sherry, upon opening, could not withstand delay. He sent out the entire decanter with the order to replace it with another bottling—the Tio Pepe of the *Saragon*. He listed his cellar by the names of the vessels in which the various importations had been made. During this process he maintained an inflexible silence colored with his familiar suggestion of a restraint that no immoderate cause could break. To Epes the sherry, when it arrived, had no more warmth or flavor than was probable in the celebrated muddiness of the Hugli River.

Selecting a cheroot blindly from the box held at his elbow, and lighting it at the tendered spill, he retired mentally in the thin veil of smoke that rose across his face.

"You will, of course, stop in at the Balavans' this evening," his father said presently. Everything he uttered, Epes thought, took subconsciously the form of a direction. Still he must, he supposed, see Annice, if only for the announcement of his return.

The Balavans lived on the north edge of town, their terraced lawn descended to navigable water—to the anchorage, in fact, of the now vanished Balavan merchant fleet, and a deserted warehouse. And, shown through the hall to a drawing-room against the dark, bare garden, Epes found not Annice, as he had expected, but Sumatra. She was glad to see him. She was an indifferent girl, and this was specially noticeable; but he returned, inwardly and visibly, little if any of her pleasure.

"Tell me every shift of the wheel," she demanded, facing him from the long stool of the spinet. "Be a human log."

"I thought Annice was here," he replied.

"She will be soon enough. Did the *Triton* do anything really stirring, outsail seven ships or part both chains in Table Bay? I hope you came into Derby Wharf with the sheer poles coach-whipped and cross-pointed Turks'-heads with double-rose props."

"I assure you, Sumatra," he told her stiffly, "that I haven't any idea of what you are talking about. And,

what is more, I don't think you have." With this he
half turned from her.

He could still see her, tho, a thickly set girl—was
she sixteen yet?—with a rosy, impertinent face and
hair loosely confined in a ribbon. Her name had been
given her from the fact that a Balavan, a master of
ships, had in the eighteenth century discovered pepper
growing wild on the coast of Sumatra. But there was
now, Epes told himself, a far better reason—heaven
knew she was peppery. Rather a detestable child.

Far from being disconcerted by the brevity of his
retort she replied that she had heard it didn't matter
what he understood or didn't understand about the sea
—"Now that you are to be a clerk."

After the stress, the difficulty of his homecoming,
and from Sumatra, this was positively too much; and
all the bitterness banked up by his father's unassailable
situation fell upon her.

"All your life," he asserted, "you have been a joke,
with your language like a crazy ship chandler. You
have never been in the least feminine or attractive, and
you never can be, not by the width of a finger nail.
Part of it—being built like a sampan—you can't help;
but that won't help you, will it? But you might, at
least, get a vocabulary that ought to suit you better.
All I say is, you'll notice, that it ought to. What suits
you I shouldn't try to guess. That's mostly what I
think about you; but on this other subject, where my
private affairs, perhaps sorrows, are concerned, shut
up."

This ill-tempered, rasped conclusion came so abruptly
that it surprised even him. He glanced at her a shade
regretfully, and saw with a feeling of satisfaction that
once, anyhow, he had impressed, silenced her. Her

head was bent, her face obscured by her forward-swung hair; her slippers were very rigidly together.

"I suppose you are right," she admitted after a long breath. "Probably you won't believe it, but I have never thought much about myself or how I affected people. Yes, a lot of them—and you, too—must think I am a joke. So few care for anything as I do for the sea. It used to seem to me that perhaps you did; I was wrong tho."

"Didn't I tell you to let me alone?" he cried, again furious. "How do you know what I care for? What do you mean by daring to judge me, you—you—"

"Aren't you leaving the sea for your father's counting-house?" Sumatra calmly demanded of him.

"If I am it's because my duty is there," he replied miserably.

"You are the hell of a sailor," she commented.

Ever since she could walk Sumatra had, on occasion, sworn; at times it had amused Epes Calef, but now it only added to his dislike, his condemnation of her. She should not, he told her severely, have been encouraged to continue it. Her answer was the expressed reflection that he might do better on shore; his delicacy was much too great for salt water.

"Do you honestly hate me?" she asked unaccountably. "I mean, when you are not in a rage."

"No, I don't hate you, in a rage or out of it," he said coldly. "Often you go beyond your years, and you presume a good deal; but after a while you'll make a good wife for the captain of a West India lugger or some fellow trading with Bermuda Hundred."

This was an adroit insult, and pleasurably he watched her flush. She became so unhappy that he was magnanimously touched with remorse, and said with a

kindly condescension that it was too bad she hadn't
been born a boy.

At that he had it swiftly proven to him that attitudes, interests, vocabularies were misleading, for logical and wholly feminine tears actually streamed over
her healthy cheeks. It grew worse, for she rose and
came close to him, with clasped desperate hands.

"Don't listen to him!" she begged. "He's a horrid
man of snow, even if he is your father; and if you let
him he'll spoil your life. Tell him that you have made
up your mind to go to sea, and that nothing can
change it. You won't be struck dead. He isn't God
with a stick of lightning."

"You don't understand," he stammered, backing
away from her, intolerably embarrassed. "I am not,
as you seem to think, afraid of my father. I have
been over and over it all in my head. No, it's something different. You couldn't understand," he repeated.
"No girl could."

"You are wrong," she replied slowly. "I see all that
you mean, and—yes—I suppose I admire you for it.
You can't mutiny"—she echoed his own phrase—
"others could, but not a Calef. Yet you make me
furious, you are so helpless, so stupid. You will marry
Annice and grow fat and near-sighted, that's what'll
happen to you."

Annice, in the doorway, asked: "Well, why not?"

Disregarding Sumatra, Epes went forward to meet
the girl who possessed the Calef token. He had, in
spite of his assertions, forgotten how lovely she was,
slender and palely gold; her gray-gold hair was like a
cloud in sifted sunlight, her skin had an even, warm
pallor that remotely suggested oranges, and her eyes
were a cool autumnal brown.

"Epes," she continued, "how burned and well you look."

She took his vigorous hands in hers, held them lightly for a second, and then relinquished him.

"There is an ocean of things for us to talk about and arrange," she proceeded, from a divan; and her glance at Sumatra was a dismissal.

The younger girl made a profound curtsy to them both, surprisingly graceful for her solidity of waist, and disappeared. Epes realized that he ought to kiss Annice, but he felt awkward in the extreme. She held her face delicately to him; it was like a tea rose. He was, he supposed, fortunate; but no sensation of gladness accompanied that supposition. It was so sad about Bartlett, she went on; and how enormously his death had affected them. Wasn't it unexpectedly sweet of her mother to furnish their house—"in miraculous brocades and hangings, with a French boudoir"?

Walking slowly home, the stars, very high above him, were like a powdering of dry, luminous snow on the polished night. The cold was so intense that his exposed face ached. What an odorous heat there would be over the mooring at the Prince's Ghat in Calcutta! He remembered the firm, light pressure of the northeast trades, the perpetual fleecy trades clouds about the horizon, the bonitos and albacore in the deeply blue, sunny water. Lovely sailing.

Was it true that all that, for him, was already a thing of the past? Epes couldn't believe it, and yet— what other conclusion was possible? Turning his thoughts to the past hour with Annice he tried, in her, to find a recompense for what he was losing, but without success. He was proud of her; in her way she was fine and beautiful. Perhaps what he understood love to be came later; it might be unreasonable to expect the whole measure of joy at once. Annice was cool enough; indeed they had acted as though they had been married for a year or more, as though they had been continuously together instead of having been so lately separated by the diameter of the world.

There was a light in the small room at the rear of the hall, used by his father as an office; and as he laid aside his wraps the elder appeared in the doorway, obviously desiring speech.

"I have seen Mr. Dove," Ira Calef told his son; "and he corroborates your report, with some added praise. I am very well pleased, Epes. Your conduct this evening, too, was admirable. I did not quite expect, at once, such a full comprehension of my intentions. The fact is," he proceeded in a general discursive manner, "that the country is changing very rapidly. A great many men are blind to this, and as a result they will have to suffer. It is not so with me. The days of the colony are at last definitely at an end; from now on not adventure but finance will be the ruling spirit. That is one of the reasons why I am withdrawing you from the sea. Let other paid men—good men, but essentially subordinate—undertake the gales and half gales; it is important for you, a Calef, to be at the center of affairs and safe."

Epes' expression was dull, unrevealing; everything that was being said contradicted and outraged his every fiber. Safe! Good men, but subordinate! He longed to shout—for all sailors, before and aft the mast—a contradiction of his father's cold patronizing periods. He loathed the money sharks who on land, in houses, traded on the courage and endurance and fidelity of ships' masters and crews. If Ira Calef was right, and they had grown unimportant, if their greatness was doomed to vanish—why, then he wanted to go too.

All this filled his brain and throat, clamored for expression; but not a word, not a protesting sound came from him. Suddenly he was tired; Epes felt as tho the leaden weight of his future already rested on him. The other made an approving reference to Annice Balavan; and perversely, for no discoverable reason, in place of the golden vision of Annice he saw Sumatra, square, like a sampan—and defiant.

When, for the time, Ira Calef had quite finished the expression of his balanced judgments Epes rose with the shadow of an instinctive bow.

"Very good, sir." The sea phrase was spoken in a voice without animation.

Above, close by his room, he was mildly surprised to find his mother. It was evident that she had been waiting for him, and followed, carefully closing the door behind them.

"How did you find Annice?" she asked.

But to his reply that Annice had seemed well enough she paid no attention. With a quick, nervous gesture she pressed her handkerchief against her eyes.

"And your father——"

Epes said nothing.

"Epes," she cried, in a sudden realization of all that, it was now clear, she wanted to say to him, "no matter how hard and unreasonable he may seem, you mustn't contradict him. It isn't as tho he were going to do you harm. What he plans is right; he can see so much farther than we can. And you will be very happy, I am sure, with Annice. You'll forget the sea?" her voice rose in inquiry.

"Never," Epes answered.

Clia Calef shivered momentarily. "I was afraid of something like that," she admitted. "And that is why it is necessary for me to speak to you. You must do what your father wants."

This was, he thought, in view of his restraint, all unnecessary. He regarded his mother, seated with her head blurred against the candlelight, with a mature, unsympathetic attention. Women—the characteristic feminine world—were very far outside the scope of his interests and being. Even to his mother he could not explain, seek to justify himself; his inner being had grown obdurate, solitary; life, which had once, in the form of blue water, everywhere surrounded and touched him, had retreated, flowed away, leaving him on that sandy, meaningless beach. Why did she talk and talk?

"You have been wonderfully quiet," she still went emotionally on; "I could tell that from Ira's manner. But I wasn't sure. I'm not yet; and for that reason, to save hideous trouble, I made up my mind to tell you. There is a little strangeness about your father, and it comes out when he is contradicted. Except for that he is splendid. I don't just know what it is, but contradiction makes him wretched; he—he loses control of himself." She was speaking faster, with an obvious increasing difficulty. "I did it, once. We hadn't been married long, and it was in the garden. He had just come back from the counting-house, and he was carrying a light cane, a wanghee. And, Epes, he struck me with it. Oh, not very hard; not, really, too hard. I didn't say a word. I stood for a second, quite frozen, and then I turned to walk out of the garden, to leave him, forever. I intended to go, but it did hurt. I was confused, and instead of finding the gate I walked into the geraniums and fainted. So, you see, I stayed."

Epes Calef drew in an audible harsh breath.

"You mustn't judge him!" she exclaimed eagerly. "I am sure it spoiled a large part of his life. He carried me into the house, and neither of us have referred to it since. Yes, it hurt him beyond speech; for weeks he slept hardly at all. Epes, Epes, I can't have it happen to him again. He is your father and you must help. You love him, too, I am certain; and what he arranges is always, always best."

She was so tremulous, so self-effacing, that he felt he couldn't bear to hear another word. It was terrible, and as wrong as possible.

"He ought to be denied," Epes said in a strong voice. "Now that you have told me this I think it might be what he, what we all need; perhaps I shall have to."

"That is not for you to judge," Clia Calef told him with a resumption of dignity. "You would be very wicked indeed, and not only, perhaps, harm Ira permanently, but me as well. I have to live with him, and not you. Epes, you have the ignorance of youth; but if I can help it I won't have you upsetting our life."

He was, he saw, literally nothing before her love for the man who had struck her with his wanghee.

"It would spoil everything," she half whispered to herself. "I have tried hard, so long."

Epes rose sharply. "You must go to bed," he directed. "If you are not careful you will be sick." He was deathly sick. She clung to him.

"Promise me, promise you will do as he says."

"I have already decided that," he answered in his weary, dead voice.

Epes, with his hand under her arm, conducted her to her room. A wave of warmth flowed into the hall as the door opened and shut, like the soiled enervating breath of a hidden corruption.

It was a physical impossibility, in the temporarily empty days following immediately Epes' arrival home, for his spiritual darkness to stay at its intensest; at least his state of mourning made it unnecessary for him to go to the meaningless parties being then crowded into the heart of the winter season. It was uncomfortable for him at home, and he fell into the habit of lounging through the afternoons in the more informal of the Balavans' drawing-rooms. There, in his special position and license, he was permitted to smoke his cheroots and listen to the light easy run of Annice's voice, so much like the easy light tripping of her fingers over the keyboard of the spinet. He was engaged in exactly this manner an hour or so before Annice's departure for one of the principal cotillons of the year, at Hamilton Hall; and Annice, who had dressed early so that she could be with him, was sitting erectly by an opposite wall. Sumatra was present, too; a fact to which her elder sister repeatedly called attention by urging the necessity of Sumatra's changing for the ball. Sumatra, Epes had learned, had been half permitted and half coerced into going.

"I can get ready in twelve minutes," she announced.

"I don't doubt that," Annice retorted; "but what will you look like when it is done? In the first place your hair is like wire and takes the longest while to be really possible—"

"It won't matter," said Sumatra; "Epes told me I couldn't make myself attractive, no matter how much we all tried."

"Did you say that, Epes?" Annice asked. "It was rather tactless of you, because, tho you'd never guess it, Sumatra is crazy about you. It might even be more than I am."

Epes Calef gazed at Sumatra with a brutal indifference. She met his eyes courageously, and in an even voice replied to her sister.

"I was once," she corrected the other, "when I thought that Epes belonged to the sea. But now he's on land——" She made a gesture of dismissal. "Epes, while I suspect he's very good, is my great disappointment. I don't like good people."

"What experience have you had with bad?" he asked cuttingly. "As usual, you are just talking words. You are a regular sea lawyer."

"Do get dressed, Sumatra," Annice said.

"Something light and feminine," Epes added; "with wreaths of flowers for you to put your feet through."

He couldn't understand why, whenever he talked to Sumatra, he became so vindictive. He had no particular desire to be nasty; it came up in spite of him.

"Perhaps no one will ask me to dance."

"If they do," he advised her, "and it is near supper, don't let go or you'll get no oysters."

"Sumatra, get dressed," Annice commanded.

"Maybe I won't at all."

"Do you mean you'll go like you are?"

"It wouldn't kill anyone, would it? I shouldn't come home and cry if I didn't get an armful of favors; I can get along, for a few minutes anyhow, by myself."

This, Epes thought, promised to be amusing. Peppery Sumatra! Annice glanced at him hastily.

"Please, Sumatra," she entreated; "we simply can't

be late. I'll give you my white-ribbed Spanish stockings."

The other serenely answered, "The feet would be too big."

He had never noticed her feet, and to his considerable surprize they were smaller, narrower than Annice's.

"You are a lumpish, impossible child," the elder said acrimoniously. "Why I begged mother to let you start the cotillons I can't imagine. And when we get there you are not to hang about me."

"I won't; you're not seaworthy. You are cut away too much through the middle; you would go over in a good blow."

Epes incautiously laughed.

"Be still," Annice directed him; "she must not be encouraged in such conduct."

"Well," he said pacifically, "you wouldn't, Trinidad." He often substituted the West India island for that from which she was named, reminding her of his matrimonial prediction.

"Yes, sampan," Annice echoed him. "Will you or will you not get dressed?"

"I will, when I have twelve minutes. It doesn't, you know, take me three hours." Nevertheless, she rose. "You haven't been specially nice to me, have you?" she said slowly, carefully avoiding Epes Calef. "You made pretty clear all you thought. I don't believe I could·be like that."

Suddenly she gazed full at Epes. "It might be your father in you," she concluded; "if I were you I shouldn't encourage that—for Annice's sake. It would be so hard on her."

"Thank you, but I can take care of myself," Annice

assured her brightly; "and it would be nicer to omit
the personal history."

"All I say is wrong!" Sumatra declared.

"All," Epes echoed her.

"I must be a sampan."

"Must."

"Square bowed, and only fit for rivers."

"For rivers."

"But even that is better than a desk," she reminded
him. She was beside the door, and paused with a hand
upon the frame, looking over her shoulder. "What
Annice told you was true," she reiterated. "I had a
little picture hidden in a drawer, which I am now going
up to tear into bits."

When she had gone Annice turned to him in a
conciliatory manner.

"There is something I meant to tell you at once, this
afternoon, but it slipped from my mind. I hope you
won't be angry and I can't imagine how it happened.
But the whole thing, of course, is exaggerated; it must
be all nonsense at bottom. Still I am sorrier than
words can say. Epes, somehow I've lost the token."

He gazed, startled at her, with a stirring of the old
Calef superstition within him. However, he con-
cealed it.

"That is too bad. We think it's rather valuable, you
know. Perhaps it will turn up; there are so many
places you might have left it."

No, she replied; she knew how they felt about it, and
she had left it, she was certain, in the lacquer box on
her dressing-case. It was very mysterious and uncertain.

"Now," she said with a smile, "you won't have to
marry me. The spell, the charm is broken."

This he repudiated in a form correct and stiff. The influence that absurd East Indian coin exerted upon his thoughts was amazing. He repeated, silently, her words —"Now you won't have to marry me." But certainly they had no force, no reality. He was bound to her not by an obang, but by honor. At the same time his feeling was undeniably different; he regarded her from a more detached position. What was that Sumatra had hinted—about crying over a scarcity of favors, and taking three hours to dress? It didn't matter to him, nothing did; it only added to the general weariness, waste of existence. Epes recalled the promised French boudoir in the threatened Boston house. That was it— his life hereafter was to be passed in a little scented room choked with brocade and hangings.

A maid appeared, enveloped Annice in a long cloak luxuriously lined with sables, twisted a silvery veiling over her netted hair, over her lovely regular features, her face with its indefinite suggestion of golden oranges.

"I thought Sumatra would be late," she declared in an abstracted exasperation. Then through the veiling she gave him a metallic and masked kiss. From the hall her voice sounded, fretful about her carriage boots.

The carriage with Annice and Sumatra departed; he must go, too; where, he didn't know, it no longer mattered; home, he supposed. There was a second stamping of hoofs before the Balavan dwelling, and Mrs. Balavan, in street wraps, passed the drawing-room door. Epes remembered that he had heard his mother speak of going to a ballad soirée with her. Still he remained seated, after the hour of dinner, and it was nearly nine before he left.

The light in his father's office was, as usual, turned

up, a thin haze of tobacco smoke perceptible. Without the desire to go up to his room Epes sat in a lower chamber. Snatches of the conversation—the quarrel, really—between Sumatra and Annice returned to him. How essentially different they were. Annice was far, far the lovelier. She made a business of being beautiful. But at least that, in a wife, was something; the majority of wives had far less. What a curious double life it would be—two separate people with one name, in one house. She could never, he was sure, mean more to him than she did now. And it was clear that for her part her demand was no greater.

Sumatra would be the opposite—there was no end to what she expected, fought for, insisted upon. Strangely enough, he couldn't see her as a wife—even for that coastwise figure he had so often pictured—at all. He was unable to discover what sort of man would suit her, but certainly one armed with a belaying pin. He became conscious of a clamor faintly heard from another part of Salem; it grew more distinct, and he recognized that it was the confused alarms and uproar of a fire. The fire evidently lay in the direction of Marlboro Street; the noise increased rather than subsided; but even this didn't stir him until his father appeared.

"I shall have to neglect my duty this evening," he explained; "there are some questions of foreign exchange. But perhaps you will take my place."

Epes went silently out to the hall, where two leather buckets, painted with the name Active Fire Club, were hanging. He secured them, and a wool scarf, and went unexcitedly in search of the fire. It was, as he had thought, in the vicinity of Marlboro Street, the Baptist Church. The Fire Engine Exchange, he saw, to which

generally the men of the Calef family belonged, had secured the place of honor, directly at the conflagration. Its reservoir was connected by hose to another engine, and that latter to a third, which drew from the source of their water. A pandemonium rose about Epes—the hoarse, jeering shouts of the competing companies, authoritative voices magnified by trumpets, the clatter of the hand pump, and the dull roar of the unconquerable flames. A curtain of black smoke, ruddy at its base and, above, poured with live cinders, rolled up across the immaculate green sky and frosty stars.

The members of the Active Fire Club had formed their line for the rapid orderly passing of buckets, and Epes had taken his place at the end, when he saw a short, familiar feminine shape standing alone. It was Sumatra, and it was extremely wrong of her to be there, like that, so late.

He left his position hurriedly and laid a hand on her arm. How, he demanded, had she got there, and why was she by herself?

"Oh, Epes!" she exclaimed with pleasure. "The cotillon nearly killed me, it was so stupid; and then I heard the alarms, and James Saltonstall wanted to come; and so, you see, here we—here I am."

"Where is he? Why did he leave you?"

Before she could answer there was a louder opposed shouting of voices:

"Suck him dry, Exchange!"

"Overwash them, Adams. Drown the damned silk stockings!"

Sumatra clutched his hand excitedly. "Don't you see—they are trying to burst the Exchange engine; we haven't enough men to pump, because some didn't leave

Hamilton Hall, and James is at the sweep. You must go, too, Epes. Quick, quick, or it will be too late!"

His negative attitude settled into an active perversity; Epes Calef made up his mind that he wouldn't pump; they could knock the silly engines into painted fragments for all him. Sumatra gave him a strong impatient shove forward, but he resisted her.

"The fire will be over in a few more minutes," he observed.

She damned the fire excitedly; it was the engine she cared about. "I'll pump, myself!" Sumatra cried.

He turned to her with a smile, but that was immediately lost as he saw that she had every intention of fulfilling her threat. Sumatra had started toward the profane companies of men when he caught her by the shoulder.

He said coldly, "You're crazy. Nobody ever heard of such a thing—a girl pumping at a fire! You'd be talked about, insulted in songs all over the country. Come home at once."

She wrenched herself from his hold, and Epes was obliged to stand in front of her with his arms outspread. Sumatra's face grew crimson with rage.

"Get out of my way!" she commanded him. "Do you think everyone is a coward and a ninny like you? I'll pump if I want to, and it doesn't matter who sings about it. I don't care what the other fools of women do."

"No, you won't," he told her grimly.

She gave him a shove, and she was so strong that, unprepared, he staggered. She nearly succeeded in evading him, but he caught her with an arm around her vigorous waist. In an instant they were fighting. Braced, with her hand crushing into his face, she tried

to break his hold; then Sumatra struck him in the eye.
Infuriated, he wanted to knock her head off, but he had
to restrain himself to a negative attack.

"I'll throw you down and sit on you," he gasped;
"here, on the street."

By way of reply she kicked his shins until, through
the hurt, he could feel the blood sliding into his shoes.
Shouts, which now, in his rage, he heard but dimly,
derisive and encouraging calls, surrounded him. The
girl, the little Amazon, was implored to crack his coco;
there were protesting cries of shame, but these were
lost in the larger approval and entertainment. By
Jupiter, but she was finishing him! This, Epes desperately told himself, was horrible beyond words.

"Stop it!" he said savagely, again and again.

But through set teeth Sumatra replied that she'd
pump if she chose, and no—no l-l-land shark could stop
her. At this there was a hurrah. Her strength was
amazing, and entirely wrong; she was like a maniac.
Then with a free arm he punched her directly and
rudely in the stomach. Sumatra settled against him
limply; and holding her up, dragging her with him past
threatening faces wavering in the dark, he succeeded in
getting her around a corner to a deserted street.

She was still limp, struggling for breath; her face
was pale and her hair in torn disorder. Sumatra slowly
recovered, and—amazingly—she smiled. Epes' anger,
too, fled; he gazed at her, examining in dismay her
clothes with a feeling which might almost have been
called admiration. Yet he spoke severely.

"You ought to be in a cage," he told her; "you're
just wild."

However was she to fix her clothes, she replied;

where could she go? "I ought to go back to Hamilton Hall."

To this he agreed, the Balavan house was far, inconveniently situated; and they decided, since the Calefs and Balavans were now practically one family, to stop at his dwelling for the repairing of her clothes and spirit. He secured his buckets and they hurried back, through a serene air like liquid ice, over Summer Street to Chestnut. The light was still burning in Ira Calef's office, and noiselessly they turned into an opposite room.

Epes went on into the dining room, opening darkly beyond, leaving Sumatra with candles on the floor before a tall mirror. There, bearing a high silver candlestick and a following indeterminate illumination, he discovered a bottle of champagne, tagged the ship *Nautilus* and the year, and gathered two high glasses and some ice. He was tingling with excitement, a disturbance deeper than physical. He felt oddly detached from his late life, the commonplace and irresponsible; his mind was without images, thought—it was like a whirling of crackling colored lights. He found his situation—the uncorked champagne, the two glasses, the unsuspecting near presence of his father, Sumatra, rearranged, entering the dining room—extraordinary and invigorating. The wine foamed whitely through the ice, turning into a silky clear amber that stung his lips. Sumatra observed, sitting down, that she ought to go on to the cotillon at once.

"What," she demanded, "will James Saltonstall think?"

That, Epes replied, was of singularly small importance.

The rose flush had returned to her cheeks, her eyes

were shining; she was decidedly more attractive than he had admitted. But that, he made up his mind, he'd never tell her. She sipped and sipped from her glass; that in itself was unusual, startling. No, he corrected his impression, it would have been in any other girl of Sumatra's age, but not in her. The most unexpected, inappropriate things seemed to become her perfectly.

"I don't want to go," she added, so long after her other phrase that he almost lost the connection. "We are so different," Sumatra pointed out; "I hardly ever do what I don't want to. It's a good thing for your father I'm not you."

"It wouldn't make any difference," he said, listlessness again falling over him; "in the end it would be the same; you'd stay or go as he said."

"I would not."

"Oh, yes, but you would."

"He couldn't make me," she insisted; "not about that. It's too terribly important."

Epes became annoyed. "Can't you understand that, to my father, nothing is important except what he wants?"

"Why argue?" she decided. "After all, I am not you. And yet, even as it is, I believe if I were concerned, which I'm not, I could do what I decided with him."

He laughed. "Try, and if you are successful, why— why, I'd marry you instead of Annice."

The flush deepened painfully in her countenance; she regarded him with startled eyes. For a moment there was a ridiculously tense silence; and then, relaxing, she shook her head negatively.

"It wouldn't be any good; you'd have no regard for me."

"Regard for you!" he exclaimed. "If you did that I'd think more of you than anything else on earth; more than I did of—of the *Triton*." His voice, his manner darkened. "But you mustn't; there's a lot you don't understand—my father, first of all. He can be very nasty."

"I've told you before, he's only a man," she reminded him. "I shouldn't be afraid." Her direct gaze again challenged him, but Epes shook his head dejectedly. Suddenly she laid a hand over his. "I didn't tear that picture up," she whispered. Then with a sweep of her arm she finished what had been in her glass, and rose. "Come on, he's still in the office."

Epes Calef urged her in careful tones not to be a donkey; he tried, here discreetly, to restrain her; but she went resolutely on, through the front room into the hall. There would be a frightful row, but he couldn't desert Sumatra. However, in the passage she paused, with her lips against his ear.

"Remember, better than the *Triton*, or it would kill me."

Ira Calef looked up from his table, frowning slightly as she entered the office, followed by Epes. The elder's face was as white as marble under the artificial light.

"Why, Sumatra," he greeted her easily.

Epes tried to step between her and his father—disaster—but she held him back, speaking immediately in a voice as level as, but a little faster than, Ira Calef's.

"I suppose you think it's strange to see me here, so late, with Epes; but it is stranger even than you imagine." She put a hand over Epes Calef's mouth. "No," she protested, "you promised to let me speak. Mr. Calef," said the incredible Sumatra, "perhaps I

ought to apologize to Mrs. Calef and you—Epes and
I are married."

Epes' amazement, which he barely restrained, was no
greater than his father's, but the latter's was given, for
him, full expression.

"Married!" he repeated in a voice slightly and sig-
nificantly louder than usual. "Why, that is outrageous!
Nothing, nothing at all was said to me. My plan was
wholly different."

He rose, beyond the table, with one hand resting
beside a paper weight of greenish glass. Epes' eyes
fastened upon this.

"It was, as you might guess, in a hurry," Sumatra
went on; "we decided only today. You must remember
that I am as much a Balavan as Annice, and I suit
Epes far better; I understand and agree with his ambition."

The man's manner was colder than the night.

"What ambition?" he demanded.

"To go to sea, of course."

"Epes isn't going to sea," he instructed her.

"He wasn't, as your son," she corrected him; "but
married to me, yes."

"No," Ira Calef answered in a restrained, bitter
temper that yet had the effect of a shout.

"But he is," Sumatra Balavan retorted. "He is, and
now you can't stop him. It doesn't matter what you
want, I won't have a husband fastened like a sponge to
the earth, and as soft as a sponge." Her anger, equal
with Ira Calef's, rose.

The room grew quiet. Epes' attention was still con-
centrated on the heavy rectangle of glass close by his
father's hand. With a sensation like an enveloping
breath of winter air he saw the other's fingers reach out

and close about the paper weight. He hadn't a second
to spare; but Sumatra, too, had seen the instinctive
movement on the table.

"I wish you would," she told the man facing her with
a set, icy glare. "I'd have you dropped off the end of
Derby Wharf. I'm not your wife or son; there would
be no reason for my protecting you, hiding your beast-
liness from the world. Nothing could be better than
having you throw a paper weight at me."

The shadows under Ira Calef's eyes, on the deathly
pallor of his face, were like black smudges; a shiver
passed over his rigidity. His hand drooped; both hands
held the edge of the table before him. Epes, in a swift
insight brushed with compassion, saw what was in his
father's mind—the huddled light figure crushing the
geranium border.

"Get out of here," the elder said to Sumatra in
strained, dry tones. "Go, and take him with you."

"To sea?" she insisted.

"If there is any .alt water in hell."

But, once more in the hall, she was pitiably shaken.
"What can we do?" she implored Epes, against him.

He reassured her that that was easy enough; a far
different, apparently trivial and ill-timed question occupied him.

"Sumatra," he proceeded, "tonight Annice told me
that she had lost the obang, the Calef token. Did you
find it?"

"No, Epes," she replied, "I didn't find it." Her
voice sank, died. "I didn't find it, Epes," she repeated
with difficulty. "I couldn't, very well. could I, when I
had stolen it?"

PURPLE AND FINE LINEN

By May Edginton

The woman with the black hair, that had a kind of blue bloom upon it like the bloom on grapes, watched everyone who went by. She watched intently. She was walking up one side of the Haymarket and down the other, and then along Piccadilly, and then cutting down into Pall Mall and clubland, most of the dull, dark afternoon.

Her clothes, which had probably once been good, were now hopeless ruins, and over the bloomy black hair was pulled a lusterless black hat. But her eyes were not lusterless. They were alive and burning, tho her face was tired and dim and vague and her lips were more blue than red. She had a naturally lithe and beautiful figure at which, had her clothes not been such wrecks, every passing man would have looked, yet she dragged her feet. Her feet were heavy like the feet of a very tired person.

She was begging.

She was begging cautiously, surreptitiously, with an eye sharply open for the police. For she was begging in a manner contrary to the manner ordained by law. She held no tray of trumpery or box of matches or dying flowers in her hands.

She was just begging.

She begged mostly of men, especially when she saun-

tered in the heart of rich clubland. It was a cold day,
and the men who went by looked mostly so warm and
well-fed. Sometimes someone paused and gave her
something.

She observed them carefully, telling them different
stories.

Opposite two big clubs, to the doors of which cars
and taxicabs drove incessantly, she paused and looked
across the street. She crossed the street, braving the
club commissionaires, very watchful for the likes of
her, and accosted a fat member who was waddling in,
warmly coated.

On the steps of the same famous club a man stood
observing the famous street. He was fairly tall and
very broad and there was no doubt about his prosperity.
He had been standing there for quite a minute, observing London, observing the traffic, the cars, the cabs,
the pedestrians, the police and the woman who begged.

He saw her raven hair and white face and drab
condition and lithe figure and manner of begging, just
as he saw and noted any other incidents of the streets
of the great city. For he was a visitor to London and
a temporary member of the ancient and honorable club
on whose steps he stood on that dull, dark afternoon.

"No, I don't want a taxi," he answered the commissionaire.

He glanced after the woman who begged, until she
turned back, retracing her steps slowly. She looked
about her stealthily, wistfully, desperately, seeking the
next probable almsgiver, and her eyes lighted on him,
standing there.

She said to herself: "A Colonial, most likely, and
rich."

For she was used to summing up men at a glance and taking her chances.

The man came down the steps, walking with the free swing of the athlete and open-air man, his overcoat slung over his arm, and began to walk leisurely toward the Carlton.

The woman quickened her steps and came alongside.

She spoke: "Please, sir, help me with a trifle—it's my birthday."

Her birthday, poor drab!

"Go away!" he said in a hard voice. "Don't come troubling me."

As he answered her it happened that he glanced round, and he caught the queerest look in her eyes as they flashed at him under the black hat. Almost he put his hand in his pocket to find a coin to reward her for that flash of the eyes. For they were beautiful eyes. In fact, his hand hovered in the edge of his pocket for an appreciable second, but he withdrew it again.

Big and burly, masterfully he went on. He arrived on the fringe of a crowd, gathered about the victim of a street accident. Policemen were hurrying to the spot to disperse the crowd. He was in no haste. He paused interestedly to observe the demeanor of all these strangers, and the methods of the police—to draw comparisons between the Old World and the New. Pausing there on the edge of the inquisitive crowd, he lighted a cigaret.

He began to elbow his way through—a rough business, for traffic filed up along the street—and the ghoulish sightseers, profiting by the difficulties of the police, pushed forward. But he made his way masterfully. He gained the farther edge of the swaying crowd and freed a hand to pat at the left side of his coat.

His leather note case no longer bulged the inside breast pocket.

"Hell! What a darn fool!" he exclaimed. "Now," he thought, "do I go to the nearest police station or this Scotland Yard place they admire so?"

Then, hesitating a second, he saw, walking along the pavement before him, free from the crowd as he was, the woman who had begged.

She walked so swiftly.

As swiftly he went after her. She slipped between the bonnets of cars and cabs and omnibuses across the street, and he dived through them in pursuit. She turned to the left and was in the Haymarket, signaling to a crawling taxicab. Just as he rounded the corner of the Carlton restaurant, he saw her jump in.

He signaled a second cab from the rank, and leaped into it.

"Follow that taxi, there, see! That one! Hang on to it, and don't lose sight, or—"

They were off. His driver had an intelligent face. The man inside the cab thought: "He'll do it. And who knows? I may be going to see something really worth seeing this afternoon. I may be going into some den of crime—get among some crooks who'll show me more of London than I've seen already. I'd like to see the underworld of this old city. And I'll bet I'll get my money back at the end too."

He loved money because he had sweated to make it. He had toiled and fought and suffered to make it. He had the number of his notes duly checked. He reverenced money and guarded it, even while he spent it freely.

The cab slowed, drew to the curb, and stopped. He saw the blazing lighted windows of a fashionable women's shop. He leaned out of the window and saw another cab that had drawn up immediately before them, and as he looked he saw the lithe figure of a woman in sorry clothes alight from it. She hurried into the shop.

Her taxicab drew off slowly to the adjacent rank and waited, flag still down. She was keeping it. Her driver alighted and stood beside his cab, watchful gaze fixed upon the shop door.

"Doesn't trust her not to bilk him," said the man in the second cab sardonically to himself. "And if he knew what I know he'd know himself right." Aloud he asked his driver, "You saw that? Wait as near him as you can. I'm waiting at this door."

For a full half hour or more he stood near the lighted windows, slightly drawn aside from them, waiting. He had nothing else to do, after all, in these idle hours that stretched between him and a good dinner somewhere, save to hunt his quarry down. And he was a stolid man, patient in pursuit of what he wanted. He had never yet tired in hunting down either man or woman who had injured him.

There emerged, among other women, a woman. Any man's eyes would have flown to her. She wore a slim outfit of black satin, fur-edged. Her shoes were of black satin, with sparkling straps; her stockings were of sheerest silk, the color of flesh. First of all, it was only by her old hat, pulled low over her black hair, that he recognized her.

She was *the* woman.

She had a natural flush like geranium petals in her white cheeks, and her murky eyes shone like the street lamps out of the fog.

"My Lord!" said the watcher, with a grim, twisted smile. But he did not lay a hand on her arm and threaten her with the nearest policeman; he followed her quietly across to the taxicab rank, where their two vehicles waited.

She entered hers first, not observing him, and gave her instructions.

"I bet I'll see some fun before I've finished to-night," he said to himself as his cab moved away, following hers. "Where next?"

He looked at his wrist watch. Five o'clock. . . .

Her cab curved down Conduit Street, entered Bond Street and drew up before a jeweler's. She went in.

She came out again.

The chase went on, to a beauty parlor higher up. Here she paid off her taxicab before she went in. And after she had gone in he sat and thought a moment and then paid off his. He was not altogether ignorant of the ways of women in beauty parlors. This would take time, possibly. And he went into the ground-floor department of the shop and looked around, and could not see her. But he was in time to see the gilded elevator vanishing upward and the glimpse of black satin shoes strapped with sparkling fire.

"Sir?" murmured an engaging attendant.

He looked around.

He saw in the background a cushioned seat or two beyond all the perfumes and powders and creams and the pretty women buying them. "Thanks," he replied urbanely, "I'm waiting for a lady who has just gone upstairs."

So he sat down, and no one troubled him more.

He thought about her.

"Why didn't she buy a hat too?" he thought. "A whole-hogger like her—why not the hat too?"

And he thought: "I wonder whom she hoped she was going to mash to-night?"

The full hour, as he had expected, he sat in that dreamy, odorous atmosphere, and then the elevator bell, which had sounded many times for many clients, tinkled again. The elevator shot upward and came down.

She stepped out.

Now he saw why she hadn't bought a hat and why she had left the hat she had somewhere upstairs, behind her. She was in evening dress. The long satin coat, thickly fur-edged, was slightly open, and he caught the gleam of a diamond earring between the upstanding collar and her neck. Her raven hair bloomed blue-black. The gray-white of her tired face was now the cream-white of skillfully laid cosmetics. The hectic geranium flush had merged into the faintest painting of rouge. Her lips were no longer bluish, but richly red. And while they had massaged her face and dressed her hair, evidently a manicurist had been at work. The hand that held her slim coat round her slim figure had received its toilet too. She was a beautiful woman.

For a moment he sat forward, hands on knees, feet planted square, staring. It seemed a pity—what a pity! A woman like that! But he was not soft-hearted, and he jumped up and followed her over the threshold.

"Cab, sir?" said the commissionaire of the beauty shop, seeing him in such close attendance.

He nodded; the commissionaire whistled; a taxicab came up. And then, with a sardonic smile, as she stood slightly in front of him, a woman in a dream, waiting her turn to be served, he took her arm very firmly in his hand.

She started and shuddered so violently that he felt her heart beating as his hand pressed between her arm and her side.

She turned and saw him, the man who had stood on the steps of the rich club a while before; from whom she had begged. If she had screamed, bluffed, argued, protested, complained or pleaded it would have seemed natural to him. But, as if life had taken from her the faculty of surprise, she just stood there dumb, resigned; looked at him.

"Spent it all?" he smiled.

There was a rasp to his voice, a bitter hardness to his smile.

She gave a long sigh, and for a moment faltered against his hand as if all strength went out of her. He looked at her sharply. Her face, overlaid with that cream-white and rose tinting, might have showed the gray of starvation. . . . But his look remained grim. He was not sorry for her, nor for anyone. He had fought the world himself and come within sight, a few times, of the ultimate wall against which sank the beaten and the weary; but he had not fallen exhausted under the shadow of that wall. If she did so, it was her affair.

He was not soft. "Well?" he asked.

The taxicab waited, with the commissionaire holding open the door.

"Give me a little time," she gasped.

"Get in," he said.

He seemed to be helping her in, with that hard hand

on her arm. He got in closely after her. The commissionaire paused for orders at the open door.

The rich man looked at the beggar woman, sidelong. "I'll tell him the nearest police station," he whispered. "Have you anything to say against that?"

She looked full in his eyes. "God!" he said to himself, "she's desperate." She answered him in a swift whisper:

"Yes. I have. Give me a little time."

It might be interesting; amusing even. One lived and one could always learn.

Scowling slightly, he ordered the commissionaire, "Oh, tell him to drive through the park, and then we'll see."

He felt in his pocket, and handed the commissionaire a shilling. With his other hand he retained his grip of the woman's arm. She was a beautiful woman. It might have been affection that made him hold her so.

The taxicab started. They drove through intersecting streets toward Park Lane.

"Well," he said, "I've watched you. I've followed you for more than an hour and a half since you stole my note case in that crowd. How did you do it? Come along! Out with it! I'd like to know."

She was looking intently into his face.

"It would amuse you?"

"It would amuse me."

She started: "When you refused me, I followed you—"

"Knowing I was a stranger and prosperous—"

"Yes; knowing that. I'd put you down as South African; or—or perhaps Australian—"

"I'm Australian."

"I was right, then," she said in a voice extraordinarily even, the voice of one who does not so much think of what she is saying as talk to gain time. "Well, I followed you, hoping for some sort of development, hoping that I'd get something out of you. Then—that heaven-sent accident, and the crowd. I pushed in close to you. I was at your shoulder the whole time, but you never saw me. Once in the crowd you patted your left inside breast pocket. You weren't wearing your overcoat. You were pushing about. You're a big man —rather fat. Your coat bulged a little as you struggled. You put your arm up and held your hat for quite half a minute. It was foggy. I put my arm under yours, across your chest; I—I had the pocketbook out in a minute. It was wonderful!"

"But you've done it so often that the thrill's surely gone."

"It was the first time."

He burst out laughing, coarsely.

She sat there taut, listening to the tune of his laughter, glad that he laughed. The taxicab entered the park at the Hyde Park corner gates.

Now solitude and dusk encompassed them.

"I'll tell him now, the nearest police station."

Then suddenly that tense, withheld woman woke up. She was across his breast, in his arms, her mouth close to his; pleading. "No! No! Mercy! Give me three hours. Three hours. And then, what you like. I beg you, just as one human creature to another, for three hours!"

He put her back forcibly into her corner. There was some scent they had sprayed on her hair. . . .

He held her back in her corner.

"I won't let you off."

"No! No! Anything you like—after three hours. Please—"

She sobbed.

"You'll spoil that fine make-up on your face."

She stopped.

"If I gave you three hours, I'd want to keep you in sight all the time. For I won't let you go. And that'd spoil your game, eh?"

"You can keep me in sight all the time."

"Eh?"

"I will be your prisoner. But please, three hours. . . ."

"You want till nine o'clock?"

"Nine-thirty, please. Please!"

"I've a dull evening before me," he remarked thoughtfully. "Very well. I'll give you three hours and not let you out of my sight. What do you want to do with your last minutes, eh?"

"At nine o'clock I want to go to a house in Chesham Crescent and see—someone. That is all. I must—I must see someone at nine o'clock at Chesham Crescent. I'm so near—so near now! After all these years! Fate couldn't be so cruel as to prevent me!"

"Nine o'clock. At nine o'clock you have to be in Chesham Crescent. Very well, if I take you there. And listen! You'll dine with me first. This is a bully fine evening, giving dinner to a thief who's just pinched my wallet with two hundred pounds. It may make me laugh."

Then for a teeming minute they sat in silence, while the taxicab sped on, approaching the Bayswater side of the great park.

"If I'm to take you out to dinner," he said suddenly,

with a hint of mockery in his tone, "I must change my clothes. I don't always. I'm a rough man. But since you're got up regardless"—his sidelong look in the half dark added "at my expense"—"why, I must do you credit." And, taking her hand in a firm grip, as if to assure himself that she should not escape while his head was turned, he leaned from the window.

"Fourteen Cheylesmore Mansions," he called to the taxi man.

"Where's that?" she asked apprehensively, when his head came in again.

"My flat. The place I've taken temporarily while I'm in London. You can wait there while I change."

She did not reply, but sat in total silence, submissive, shrinking in repugnance, but resigned. He saw what she thought. It was a natural thought. But he did not undeceive her. She had put herself into this position, hadn't she? She deserved her loathing anticipations.

The taxicab drew up.

It was the first time the man from Australia had ushered a woman of such appearance into that flat. When he opened the door with his latchkey she walked in before him with a natural air of expecting amenities at least, whatever was to follow.

A manservant appeared in the background beyond them.

"Show this lady into the sitting-room, William," said the man from Australia, "and bring her a cocktail while she waits for me. My things are ready?"

"All ready, sir."

The manservant opened the door of a warm red room, and the woman walked in. As if a sense of her tiredness were upon her under the expectations that buoyed her up, she sank, wilted, into a couch by the fire. She seemed to lose herself by the fire in the warm red room. Instantly she traveled to another land than the land where he had met her. For a moment the man from Australia stood gazing in upon her, puzzled again; and then he went out sturdily, shut the door, and spoke to the servant.

"William. That lady. She's to stay where she is until I'm ready. No hanky-panky. Savvy?"

"Very good, sir."

In a quarter of an hour he was with her again. He opened the sitting-room door quickly and quietly, hovering, observant, before he went in. But she was still lost by the fire, inanimate upon the red couch. The only movement she had made was to take off the coat and lay it aside. He saw the grace of her thin white throat and arms.

Beside her was an untouched cocktail.

"Don't you like your cocktail?"

She looked up at him. She was at bay, looking him over swiftly, wondering just when the kill would be made. His masculinity could have made him tender, tho his worldly sense kept him hard. He picked up the glass and offered it to her.

"Got a little warm, perhaps. That fellow shall make another!"

"I daren't drink it; thank you."

"Daren't drink it?"

"I haven't eaten to-day."

She was a liar, of course.

"I should have thought, with two hundred pounds on you, you'd have made a bee line for the nearest ham-and-beef, at least."

"I forgot."

"Forgot?" He ruminated. She was a liar. He smiled.

"Well," he said in a tone of raillery, "you must do justice to your dinner. If you won't drink this—"

He tossed it off.

"Come along."

She rose with a languor that made him a trifle dubious. Suppose she really hadn't eaten that day? He had known what it was to go a day without food.

Anyhow, that would soon be remedied.

They went down, side by side, in the elevator, and out into the vestibule. This time, when she came into the street again, she saw that a limousine waited.

"My man rang up for it while I was dressing," her escort explained. "When one takes a lady to dine—"

His hand at her elbow—lightly touching it, yet ready to grip firm, she knew—she got in. She took the right-hand corner as one accustomed to drive in such cars. The chauffeur spread over them a supple rug of sleek skin, and they were off again.

He darted hard, curious looks at her.

"You look in your right place, somehow."

She smiled. "It is many years since I had a car like this."

"Played your cards badly then, with a figure like yours. Where were your wits?"

"I suppose you are right," she said. "I played my cards very badly. I always have. I hate—selling."

"Woman's business, isn't it?" he returned gruffly.

"Very few women think so."

She looked out of her window at the passing throngs. London was alive and blazing. There was a look of peace and a great expectancy in her face, almost as if she didn't think or care about him and what he could do to her. It was strange. She might have been unafraid; and yet that a woman should be unafraid in such conditions was nearly impossible. While she looked out of the window on her side, he remained turned toward her, looking at her.

"Lord, you're a cool customer!"

Now she smiled.

"No. I am not cool."

"You don't even ask where I'm taking you."

"It doesn't matter, so that the time passes."

"Doesn't it, indeed? Well, madam, we are going to the Ritz. You're a nice-looking woman, and I'm going to show you off. I'm a lonely stranger here, and my female acquaintance so far isn't the kind I boast about."

And they drew up before the vast pillared portico.

She stood a moment just inside the vestibule, looking about her like a woman awaked from a long sleep.

"See many friends?" he asked sardonically at her elbow.

"Not friends," she answered; "not friends now. But I see the faces of people who used to be my friends. There—oh! there—that must be Cicely Gloucester! There's her husband. Can that be her baby daughter—that tall thing? Isn't she lovely? Oh! I wonder. . . ."

"Go and recall yourself to their memory," he suggested.

She shrank. "Impossible! They wouldn't. . . . I've been on the Continent for more than seventeen years; wandering from place to place."

"What places?"

"Nice, Cannes, Rome, Paris, Vienna, Budapest. . . ."

S. S. II-7

"You're a good actress, madam. I'll pay you all the compliments you deserve."

Hardly listening, she walked with him into the dining-room. Their table was at the side, near a corner.

The Australian seemed disappointed.

"I'd have liked to show you off in the very middle of the room."

She shrank.

"This is better. Please!"

"We've got to have it, I suppose. The darn place is full."

So they sat down at the little table, in the intimacy of a dinner à deux, and she dropped her coat back over her chair, and looked about her, sitting very still.

"Always feed the condemned," he said to her under his breath when he had ordered Russian caviar, bortsch, sole, turkey—"because I expect you'll get pretty hard tack where you're going, and tough at that," he explained pleasantly—salad à l'Américaine, omelet en surpris, and champagne, and they were waiting the first course.

It was as if she tore her attention from the sea of tables spread beyond them.

"The condemned?"

"You're going to a police station in"—he glanced at the watch on his wrist—"two hours and a half."

"So I am!" she laughed.

"Light-headed?" he thought. "Here," he said aloud, "was that true about having eaten nothing to-day? Feel a bit light-headed, eh?"

"It was true, but I'm not light-headed, altho I well might be."

"At least you're not morbid. Don't meet your troubles till you come to 'em, anyway."

All the same he marveled. She was cool!

"Frightened?" he whispered with a smile.

The omelet en surpris had just been served to them. Her cheeks had taken on a beautiful flush under the cleverly slight make-up; her eyes glistened; she talked; she was making herself a fine companion; yet was it possible that she was at ease; careless, reckless of what was going to happen to her? Her attention, through all her attractive conversation, was not really focused on him; he felt that. And yet it was not focused on the looming calamity either. Her soul seemed away on wings in a country of its own. He was mystified and hated it, for he liked to feel that he understood people in and out. He prided himself on it. He filled up her glass and his own. She had not tried to tempt him to excess, but had drunk glass for glass with him. His mystification grew.

"Frightened?"

"Of what?" she asked, bringing her happy eyes to rest on him.

Yes, her eyes were happy. They had been wretched, anxious, earlier in the afternoon, but now they were happy.

What did she hope for from him?

"Prison."

"Oh, no," she said calmly, almost as if she brushed the word aside. "What happens to me after my three hours' grace is up does not matter."

"Here," he said carefully, "what *is* all this about three hours' grace? What do you want to do?"

"In half an hour I want to be at Chesham Crescent; Number 10 Chesham Crescent."

"Yes, Chesham Crescent, Mayfair. Now tell me, what for?"

"To visit someone."

"Front door or kitchen entrance?" he inquired with a twist of the lip.

"Front door. It is my old home. I went there as a bride."

"Where you go, I go."

She sighed. "I suppose it must be so."

"Look," he said, "tell me a story. It'll be all lies, no doubt, but I shan't object so long as you make it a good one. Tell me what you want me to believe you're going to do at 10 Chesham Crescent."

"Something I've waited and longed for for seventeen years."

"Why, how old are you?"

"Thirty-six."

"That might be true," he commented. "Go on."

She asked timorously, "What do you want to know?"

"Who lives there?"

"My ex-husband."

"Ex-husband?"

"Lord Malvern. He divorced me seventeen years ago."

"Go on. That's a very pretty beginning."

She made a little gesture of resignation. "There's no reason why you shouldn't know what everyone knows—and has forgotten—if it will placate you. I'm in your power. I ran away with a man. I was miserable with my husband, or thought I was—"

"You were a mere kid, as they usually say in these cases."

"I was even peculiarly childish. I thought my lover was a god and a Galahad rolled into one."

"You married him?"

"Oh, no! Thank Heaven, not that!"

"Then what—?"

"I told you, I've been living on the Continent, as best I could, sometimes living softly, sometimes half starving, for years. I hadn't an old friend left. My family repudiated me. Lately I've tried to pull myself together; tried to remember that tho the law separates us I still have someone to live for—"

"Who?"

Her eyes gleamed with tears, but her mouth, now red and fuller-lipped after food and drink, tried to laugh.

"I've had bad luck; been very ill; lost my looks; was literally stranded in Paris, hardly hoping, when the letter came."

"Be explicit."

"Lord Malvern's letter."

"He's written to you? Provision? Reconciliation? Eh?"

The man laughed. He disbelieved every word she said, but mockingly displayed his interest in the progress of her story. She answered gravely:

"No. To grant my request. I'd made it every year just before my birthday. I'd written every year and begged and begged him to let me see my little girl for five minutes; just because it is my birthday, I used to say, every year. He never answered once, till this year. And this year he telegraphed to me quite suddenly; he must have telegraphed as soon as he had my letter. I am to see her for five minutes to-night at 9:30."

"You managed to scrape up your fare across?"

"Just managed. That was yesterday. I got the first train, the big boat, after I had that wire. I begged in the streets all to-day trying to get enough to 'make me presentable to my daughter."

"Well, madam," he said with a hard smile, "you certainly look presentable."

"Thanks to your forbearance, your patience. I will bless you all my life for these three hours."

He stared at her, all doubting. She was a fine actress.

"I'll see you through to the end," he stated. "I daresay you can explain me somehow to his lordship—"

"Oh, must you—"

"I'll love to see you extricate yourself from the position you've described to me so feelingly."

"You don't believe a word I say."

"That doesn't prevent my appreciation of your story. You've got a brain like a fiction writer."

She was unmoved. She didn't care. "Very well," she said, "come into the house with me if you insist. It doesn't matter. All that matters is that I'm to see my Meggie for a moment; that she'll see her mother looking as I look now; that there'll be no pity and no shock in my baby's mind; oh! I'm happy!"

And suddenly with a catch like a sob in her voice, looking at her little jeweled watch, she begged, "Oh, let us go! Take me away! Don't make me lose one precious moment!"

"What next?" he was debating within himself while they paused for a second outside, waiting for the car.

A thought struck him. Holding her arm, he turned

to the commissionaire. "Do you know Lord Malvern by sight?"

"Oh, yes, sir. He is here frequently."

"Does he—er—live at 10 Chesham Crescent?"

"That's the address, sir."

The car drew up.

"You told the truth there," he soliloquized aloud.

The woman did not trouble to answer. She got in, lifted by his wary hand on her elbow.

"Well, if he really does live there," said the Australian to himself, but aloud, "What next? You're not taking me into any gaming house or any sort of trap. What next?"

But she did not even hear him.

She was talking aloud to herself, in the fashion of the very lonely.

"I wonder if it'll be changed. I wonder if he's still got that Bokhara rug my mummy gave me, in the hall. But I suppose all my own things have gone. That new ballroom has been made, I heard. And the music-room—I should think that is Meggie's. It would be an adorable girl's room. . . . I wonder if . . . I hope the Chinese god is still on the pedestal at the staircase. . . . It'll be queer, seeing all those things . . . the things I used to be able to think of as mine, as a wife can do. . . . There's a lot in being a wife. . . . I've been both, and I know . . . all I don't want to see the same is the servants. . . . I want all new faces; all strange faces. . . . Strange as I'll be to Meggie. Oh! what'll I say first? How explain? What'll she say? . . . He must have prepared her a little; he must have. He couldn't just leave us to meet. . . . I wonder what she's thought all this time?

Girls are kinder, broader-minded nowadays . . . she
may even have excuses for me in her heart. . . . I
pray God she will. . . . Curzon Street. . . . Only
a minute now. Now I must be strong."

The Australian sat upright, listening to her, his mouth
half open. Light, from the lamps they shot by, fell
upon him, revealing to her his rugged face, deep small
straight eyes, pugnacious nose and mouth, had she
cared to look.

She turned to him suddenly.

"I must be strong!" she wailed.

Her hand was all at once in his. How thin! How
hot! How fragile!

He did not reply, but maintained an imperturbable
front, and she recovered herself.

"I *am* strong!" she said exultantly.

Even in the dim light he could see the splendor of
her eyes.

They drew up.

The Australian alighted, helped her out, kept his
hold of her with one hand, sought in his pocket for the
fare with the other.

As they walked up the steps she was still talking—
to herself, to him, to the air.

"I thought he'd never forgive me. He is a revengeful man. Very revengeful. But this is very dear, very
sweet of him. As people get older they should get
kinder, do you not think so? He is not revengeful any
more. He is letting me see my Meggie at last, this
birthday. A birthday of birthdays! . . ."

The Australian pushed the bell with determination,
and the door opened at once, letting out a flood of
light. A youngish butler stood there, who showed no

recognition of her. She hesitated a while over her
name, then gave it decisively:

"Lady Malvern and—"

"Mr. Frampton," said the Australian.

He realized that she had not, of course, known his
name.

"His lordship is expecting you," said the butler,
ushering them in. He was a very pallid man whose
face betrayed nothing, and yet the Australian, in some
remote, keen way, sensed atmospheric storm or stress
or calamity. He sensed that something was about to
happen.

As they stepped into the hall there appeared suddenly, from an open door on the left—as if this
woman's coming had been avidly watched for—a tall
man. His age might have been forty-five or fifty.
His face, hair and bearing were all older. He was slim
and gray and steely; and the Australian, after the
habitually swift glance he flashed upon him, had her
words in his mind like the underline to a picture: "He
is a revengeful man."

This was, indeed, primarily, a most revengeful man.

The woman stepped forward, the epitome of grace
and ease and well-being.

One thin hand clutched around her, in the approved
manner of the temporary fashion, in a sort of delicate,
fastidious way, the black satin coat. The satin was no
glossier than her hair.

"Max," she began, "after all these years. . . ."

Her voice vibrated and faltered, smile as she might,
play-act as she might. On the face of the gray man
appeared also a faint smile, terrible and delighted.

"You are looking wonderful," he said with a little

bow, and his look appraised her, her clothes, and whole ensemble. "And I heard—"

"No wonder she wanted to look well," the Australian was thinking; confounded, shaken almost into belief in spite of himself.

She was answering, on a high hysterical note of expectation: "I am feeling wonderful, thank you. I always have; I always do. Repentance and sackcloth would never suit me, you know, Max. But please, my time is short. Mayn't I at once . . . ?"

"You are not alone," said Lord Malvern. "I expected you to come alone."

"May I introduce Mr. Frampton—Lord Malvern."

The men nodded.

Lord Malvern's look inquired Frampton's status. New husband, new lover? said the look. It was cold as ice and unbearably insulting. The Australian swallowed it reluctantly.

"Is she here?" the woman cried.

Lord Malvern smiled again that faint smile of terrible delight. "Why, of course. I wouldn't bring you here on a fool's errand, after all those marvelously pathetic letters of yours, written year after year, which have melted my heart at last."

She moved forward. "Oh, let me see her!"

"You will find her looking beautiful!" said Lord Malvern.

"But—" he added, frowning toward the intruder.

She glanced at Frampton. His return glance answered stubbornly: "You are my prisoner. Where you go, I go." She pulled herself together and smiled once more.

"Mr. Frampton knows everything. I—I want to

show him Meggie. He can hardly believe I have a grown-up daughter."

"You will hardly believe it yourself when you see her. This way."

"Where—the music-room?"

"Yes. You haven't forgotten your way. But still, give me the pleasure of showing you." He escorted her with an exaggeration of courtesy down a wide tiled passage, and the Australian followed close, still wary, tho confused and confounded.

"Does she know I'm coming? What has she been told of me? Oh, Max!"

"She knows nothing, as you will see for yourself." He now threw open the door of the room they sought.

"Oh, my God!" the Australian thought he said, but his lips did not move. The only sound that tore the air was a dreadful one, a long scream.

The woman turned: "Who screamed? Who screamed? Don't scream!" And she ran forward and fell in a heap, half lying, half on her knees, not knowing, perhaps, that she moaned any more than she knew when her dried lips uttered that barren shriek.

The girl lay on a bier, candles around her; flowers; her hands crossed on her breast. Her mouth half smiled; she had been a pretty child, and in death was lovely.

Now in the great room there fell a complete silence; the mother raised herself and kissed those cold hands, not saying a word, not crying, not trembling. But she was just the ghost of the radiant woman who had come in.

Through the red mist of his sudden rage the Australian heard Lord Malvern speaking very quietly somewhere near him.

"It happened the day before yesterday, the day I received your annual request, dear lady. Under the circumstances I thought I would accede to it. It does no harm now."

He was a most revengeful man.

The Australian ran into the room and lifted the kneeling woman with one arm. She made no resistance, gave not so much as an inquiring look. In one arm he half lifted her to the threshold. And there, standing aside, watching them both with his dreary, implacable smile, was Lord Malvern, like an image. The Australian lifted his free hand and struck the smile from the image's mouth.

He was out on the pavement outside with the silent woman still gripping his arm.

"Time's up," he said in her ear.

"Time? Ah, time? Ah, yes. I forget. I am your prisoner."

He lifted her into the car and got in too. "Drive," he ordered vaguely, yet surely. He bent his face to her cold one. "I won't add one to the revengeful men to-night," he said softly and slowly. "I'll spend my life trying to make you happy! You must be sick of the old world. But there's a new world and I want to show it to you. Let's go."

THE FURY

By Paul Heyse

The day had scarcely dawned. Over Vesuvius
hung one broad gray stripe of mist, stretching across
as far as Naples, and darkening all the small towns
along the coast. The sea lay calm. Along the shore
of the narrow creek that lies beneath the Sorrento
cliffs, fishermen and their wives were at work already,
some with giant cables drawing their boats to land,
with the nets that had been cast the night before,
while others were rigging their craft, trimming the
sails, or fetching out oars and masts from the great
grated vaults that have been built deep into the rocks
for shelter to the tackle overnight. Nowhere an idle
hand; even the very aged, who had long given up
going to sea, fell into the long chain of those who were
hauling in the nets. Here and there, on some flat
housetop, an old woman stood and spun, or busied herself about her grandchildren, whom their mother had
left to help her husband.

"Do you see, Rachela? yonder is our padre curato,"
said one to a little thing of ten, who brandished a
small spindle by her side; "Antonio is to row him over
to Capri. Madre Santissima! but the reverend sig-
nore's eyes are dull with sleep!" and she waved her
hand to a benevolent-looking little priest, who was set-

ting himself in the boat, and spreading out upon the
bench his carefully tucked-up skirts.

The men upon the quay had dropped their work to
see their pastor off, who bowed and nodded kindly,
right and left.

"What for must he go to Capri, granny?" asked the
child. "Have the people there no priest of their own,
that they must borrow ours?"

"Silly thing!" returned the granny. "Priests they
have in plenty—and the most beautiful of churches, and
a hermit too, which is more than we have. But there
lives a great signora, who once lived here; she was so
very ill! Many's the time our padre had to go and
take the Most Holy to her, when they thought she
could not live the night. But with the Blessed Virgin's help she got strong and well, and was able to
bathe every day in the sea. When she went away, she
left a fine heap of ducats behind her for our church,
and for the poor; and she would not go, they say,
until our padre promised to go and see her over there,
that she might confess to him as before. It is quite
wonderful, the store she lays by him! Indeed, and
we have cause to bless ourselves for having a curato
who has gifts enough for an archbishop, and is in such
request with all the great folks. The Madonna be with
him!" she cried, and waved her hand again, as the
boat was about to put from shore.

"Are we to have fair weather, my son?" inquired the
little priest, with an anxious look toward Naples.

"The sun is not yet up," the young man answered;
"when he comes, he will easily do for that small trifle
of mist."

"Off with you, then! that we may arrive before the
heat."

Antonio was just reaching for his long oar to shove away the boat, when suddenly he paused, and fixed his eyes upon the summit of the steep path that leads down from Sorrento to the water. A tall and slender girlish figure had become visible upon the heights, and was now hastily stepping down the stones, waving her handkerchief. She had a small bundle under her arm, and her dress was mean and poor. Yet she had a distinguished if somewhat savage way of throwing back her head, and the dark tress wreathed round it was like a diadem.

"What have we to wait for?" inquired the curato.

"There is someone coming who wants to go to Capri—with your permission, padre. We shall not go a whit the slower. It is a slight young thing, but just eighteen."

And that moment the young girl appeared from behind the wall that bounds the winding path.

"Laurella!" cried the priest. "And what has she to do in Capri?"

Antonio shrugged his shoulders. She came up with hasty steps, her eyes fixed straight before her.

"Ha! l'Arrabiata! good-morning!" shouted one or two of the young boatmen. But for the curato's presence, they might have added more; the look of mute defiance with which the young girl received their welcome appeared to tempt the more mischievous among them.

"Good-day, Laurella!" now said the priest. "How are you? Are you coming with us to Capri?"

"If I may, padre."

"Ask Antonio there; the boat is his. Every man is master of his own, I say, as God is master of us all."

"There is half a carlino, if I may go for that?" said Laurella, without looking at the young boatman.

"You need it more than I," he muttered, and pushed aside some orange-baskets to make room: he was to sell the oranges in Capri, which little isle of rocks has never been able to grow enough for all its visitors.

"I do not choose to go for nothing," said the girl, with a slight frown of her dark eyebrows.

"Come, child," said the priest; "he is a good lad, and had rather not enrich himself with that little morsel of your poverty. Come now, and step in," and he stretched his hand to help her, "and sit you down by me. See, now, he has spread his jacket for you, that you may sit the softer. Young folks are all alike; for one little maiden of eighteen they will do more than for ten of us reverend fathers. Nay, no excuse, Tonino. It is the Lord's own doing, that like and like should hold together."

Meantime Laurella had stepped in, and seated herself beside the padre, first putting away Antonio's jacket without a word. The young fellow let it lie, and, muttering between his teeth, he gave one vigorous push against the pier, and the little boat flew out into the open bay.

"What are you carrying there in that little bundle?" inquired the padre, as they were floating on over a calm sea, now just beginning to be lighted up with the early rays of the rising sun.

"Silk, thread, and a loaf, padre. The silk is to be sold at Anacapri, to a woman who makes ribbons, and the thread to another."

"Spun by yourself?"

"Yes, sir."

"You once learned to weave ribbons yourself, if I remember right?"

"I did, sir; but mother has been much worse, and

I cannot stay so long from home; and a loom to our-selves we are not right enough to buy."

"Worse, is she? Ah! dear, dear! when I was with you last, at Easter, she was up."

"The spring is always her worst time. Ever since those last great storms, and the earthquakes she has been forced to keep her bed from pain."

"Pray, my child. Never slacken your prayers and petitions that the Blessed Virgin may intercede for you; and be industrious and good, that your prayers may find a hearing."

After a pause: "When you were coming toward the shore, I heard them calling after you, 'Good-morning, l'Arrabiata!' they said. What made them call you so? It is not a nice name for a young Christian maiden, who should be meek and mild."

The young girl's brown face glowed all over, while her eyes flashed fire.

"They always mock me so, because I do not dance and sing, and stand about to chatter, as other girls do. I might be left in peace, I think; I do *them* no harm."

"Nay, but you might be civil. Let others dance and sing, on whom this life sits lighter; but a kind word now and then is seemly even from the most afflicted."

Her dark eyes fell, and she drew her eyebrows closer over them, as if she would have hidden them.

They went on a while in silence. The sun now stood resplendent above the mountain chain; only the tip of Mount Vesuvius towered beyond the group of clouds that had gathered about its base; and on the Sorrento plains the houses were gleaming white from the dark green of their orange-gardens.

"Have you heard no more of that painter, Laurella?"

asked the curator—"that Neapolitan, who wished so much to marry you?" She shook her head. "He came to make a picture of you. Why would you not let him?"

"What did he want it for? There are handsomer girls than I. Who knows what he would have done with it? He might have bewitched me with it, or hurt my soul, or even killed me, mother says."

"Never believe such sinful things!" said the little curator very earnestly. "Are not you ever in God's keeping, without whose will not one hair of your head can fall? and is one poor mortal with an image in his hand to prevail against the Lord? Besides, you might have seen that he was fond of you; else why should he want to marry you?"

She said nothing.

"And wherefore did you refuse him? He was an honest man, they say, and comely; and he would have kept you and your mother far better than you ever can yourself, for all your spinning and silk-winding."

"We are so poor!" she said passionately; "and mother has been ill so long, we should have become a burden to him. And then I never should have done for a signora. When his friends came to see him, he would only have been ashamed of me."

"How can you say so? I tell you the man was good and kind; he would even have been willing to settle in Sorrento. It will not be so easy to find another, sent straight from heaven to be the saving of you, as this man, indeed, appeared to be."

"I want no husband—I never shall," she said, very stubbornly, half to herself.

"Is this a vow? or do you mean to be a nun?"

She shook her head.

"The people are not so wrong who call you wilful, although the name they give you is not kind. Have you ever considered that you stand alone in the world, and that your perverseness must make your sick mother's illness worse to bear, her life more bitter? And what sound reason can you have to give for rejecting an honest hand, stretched out to help you and your mother? Answer me, Laurella."

"I have a reason," she said reluctantly, and speaking low; "but it is one I cannot give."

"Not give! not give to me? not to your confessor, whom you surely know to be your friend—or is he not?"

Laurella nodded.

"Then, child, unburden your heart. If your reason be a good one, I shall be the very first to uphold you in it. Only you are young, and know so little of the world. A time may come when you will find cause to regret a chance of happiness thrown away for some foolish fancy now."

Shyly she threw a furtive glance to the other end of the boat, where the young boatman sat, rowing fast. His woolen cap was pulled deep down over his eyes; he was gazing far across the water, with averted head, sunk, as it appeared, in his own meditations.

The priest observed her look, and bent his ear down closer.

"You did not know my father?" she whispered, while a dark look gathered in her eyes.

"Your father, child! Why, your father died when you were ten years old. What can your father (Heaven rest his soul in paradise!) have to do with this present perversity of yours?"

"You did not know him, padre; you did not know that mother's illness was caused by him alone."

"And how?"

"By his ill-treatment of her; he beat her and trampled upon her. I well remember the nights when he came home in his fits of frenzy. She never said a word, and did everything he bade her. Yet he would beat her so, my heart felt ready to break. I used to cover up my head and pretend to be asleep, but I cried all night. And then, when he saw her lying on the floor, quite suddenly he would change, and lift her up and kiss her till she screamed and said he smothered her. Mother forbade me ever to say a word of this; but it wore her out. And in all these long years since father died, she has never been able to get well again. And if she should soon die—which God forbid!—I know who it was that killed her."

The little curato's head wagged slowly to and fro; he seemed uncertain how far to acquiesce in the young girl's reasons. At length he said: "Forgive him, as your mother has forgiven! And turn your thoughts from such distressing pictures, Laurella; there may be better days in store for you, which will make you forget the past."

"Never shall I forget that!" she said, and shuddered. "And you must know, padre, it is the reason why I have resolved to remain unmarried. I never will be subject to a man, who may beat and then caress me. Were a man now to want to beat or kiss me, I could defend myself; but mother could not—neither from his blows nor kisses—because she loved him. Now, I will never so love a man as to be made ill and wretched by him."

"You are but a child, and you talk like one who

knows nothing at all of life. Are all men like that poor
father of yours? Do all ill-treat their wives, and give
vent to every whim and gust of passion? Have you
never seen a good man yet? or known good wives,
who live in peace and harmony with their husbands?"

"But nobody ever knew how father was to mother;
she would have died sooner than complain or tell of
him, and all because she loved him. If this be love—
if love can close our lips when they should cry out
for help—if it is to make us suffer without resistance,
worse than ever our worst enemy could make us suffer—then, I say, I never will be fond of mortal man."

"I tell you you are childish; you know not what you
are saying. When your time comes, you are not likely
to be consulted whether you choose to fall in love or
not." After a pause, he added, "And that painter:
did you think he could have been cruel?"

"He made those eyes I have seen my father make,
when he begged my mother's pardon and took her in
his arms to make it up. I know those eyes. A man
may make such eyes, and yet find it in his heart to
beat a wife who never did a thing to vex him! It
made my flesh creep to see those eyes again."

After this she would not say another word. The
curato also remained silent. He bethought himself of
more than one wise saying, wherewith the maiden might
have been admonished; but he refrained, in consideration of the young boatman, who had been growing
rather restless toward the close of this confession.

When, after two hours' rowing, they reached the
little bay of Capri, Antonio took the padre in his
arms, and carried him through the last few ripples of
shallow water, to set him reverently down upon his
legs on dry land. But Laurella did not wait for him

to wade back and fetch her. Gathering up her little
petticoat, holding in one hand her wooden shoes and
in the other her little bundle, with one splashing step
or two she had reached the shore. "I have some time
to stay at Capri," said the priest. "You need not
wait—I may not perhaps return before to-morrow.
When you get home, Laurella, remember me to your
mother; I will come and see her within the week.
You mean to go back before it gets dark?"

"If I find an opportunity," answered the girl, turning all her attention to her skirts.

"I must return, you know," said Antonio, in a tone
which he believed to be one of great indifference. "I
shall wait here till the Ave Maria. If you should not
come, it is the same to me."

"You must come," interposed the little priest; "you
never can leave your mother all alone at night. Is it
far you have to go?"

"To a vineyard by Anacapri."

"And I to Capri. So now God bless you, child—
and you, my son."

Laurella kissed his hand, and let one farewell drop,
for the padre and Antonio to divide between them.
Antonio, however, appropriated no part of it to himself; he pulled off his cap exclusively to the padre,
without even looking at Laurella. But after they had
turned their backs, he let his eyes travel but a short
way with the padre, as he went toiling over the deep
bed of small, loose stones; he soon sent them after the
maiden, who, turning to the right, had begun to climb
the heights, holding one hand above her eyes to protect them from the scorching sun. Just before the
path disappeared behind high walls, she stopped, as if
to gather breath, and looked behind her. At her feet

lay the marina; the rugged rocks rose high around
her; the sea was shining in the rarest of its deep-blue
splendor. The scene was surely worth a moment's
pause. But, as chance would have it, her eyes, in
glancing past Antonio's boat, met Antonio's own, which
had been following her as she climbed.

Each made a slight movement, as persons do who
would excuse themselves for some mistake; and then,
with her darkest look, the maiden went her way.

Hardly one hour had passed since noon, and yet for
the last two Antonio had been sitting waiting on the
bench before the fishers' tavern. He must have been
very much preoccupied with something, for he jumped
up every moment to step out into the sunshine, and
look carefully up and down the roads, which, parting
right and left, lead to the only two little towns upon
the island. He did not altogether trust the weather,
he then said to the hostess of the osteria; to be sure,
it was clear enough, but he did not quite like that tint
of sea and sky. Just so it had looked, he said, before
the last awful storm, when the English family had
been so nearly lost; surely she must remember it?

No, indeed, she said, she didn't.

Well, if the weather should happen to change before
night, she was to think of him, he said.

"Have you many fine folk over there?" she asked
him, after a while.

"They are only just beginning; as yet, the season
has been bad enough; those who come to bathe, came
late."

"The spring came late. Have you not been earning
more than we at Capri?"

"Not enough to give me macaroni twice a week, if
I had had nothing but the boat—only a letter now

and then to take to Naples, or a gentleman to row out
into the open sea, that he might fish. But you know
I have an uncle who is rich; he owns more than one
fine orange-garden; and, 'Tonino,' says he to me,
'while I live you shall not suffer want; and when I am
gone you will find that I have taken care of you.' And
so, with God's help, I got through the winter."

"Has he children, this uncle who is rich?"

"No, he never married; he was long in foreign parts,
and many a good piastre he has laid together. He is
going to set up a great fishing business, and set me over
it, to see the rights of it."

"Why, then you are a made man, Tonino!"

The young boatman shrugged his shoulders. "Every
man has his own burden," said he, starting up again
to have another look at the weather, turning his eyes
right and left, altho he must have known that there
can be no weather side by one.

"Let me fetch you another bottle," said the hostess;
"your uncle can well afford to pay for it."

"Not more than one glass; it is a fiery wine you
have in Capri, and my head is hot already."

"It does not heat the blood; you may drink as
much of it as you like. And here is my husband coming; so you must sit a while, and talk to him."

And in fact, with his nets over his shoulder, and his
red cap upon his curly head, down came the comely
padrone of the osteria. He had been taking a dish
of fish to that great lady, to set before the little curato.
As soon as he caught sight of the young boatman, he
began waving him a most cordial welcome; and he
came to sit beside him on the bench, chattering and
asking questions. Just as his wife was bringing her
second bottle of pure unadulterated Capri, they heard

the crisp and crunch, and Laurella was seen approaching from the left-hand road to Anacapri. She nodded slightly in salutation; then stopped, and hesitated.

Antonio sprang from his seat. "I must go," he said. "It is a young Sorrento girl, who came over with the signor curato in the morning. She has to get back to her sick mother before night."

"Well, well, time enough yet before night," observed the fisherman; "time enough to take a glass of wine. Wife, I say, another glass!"

"I thank you; I had rather not"; and Laurella kept her distance.

"Fill the glasses, wife; fill them both, I say; she only wants a little pressing."

"Don't," interposed the lad. "It is a wilful head of her own she has; a saint could not persuade her to do what she does not choose." And, taking a hasty leave, he ran down to the boat, loosened the rope, and stood waiting for Laurella. Again she bent her head to the hostess, and slowly approached the water, with lingering steps. She looked around on every side, as if in hopes of seeing some other passenger. But the marina was deserted. The fishermen were asleep, or rowing about the coast with rods or nets; a few women and children sat before their doors, spinning or sleeping; and strangers as had come over in the morning were waiting for the cool of the evening. She had not time to look about her long; before she could prevent him, Antonio had seized her in his arms and carried her to the boat, as if she had been an infant. He leaped in after her, and with a stroke or two of his oar they were in deep water.

She had seated herself at the end of the boat, half turning her back to him, so that he could only see her profile. She wore a sterner look than ever; the low, straight brow was shaded by her hair; the rounded lips were firmly closed; only the delicate nostril occasionally gave a wilful quiver. After they had gone a while in silence, she began to feel the scorching of the sun; and, unloosening her bundle, she threw the handkerchief over her head, and began to make her dinner of the bread; for in Capri she had eaten nothing.

Antonio did not stand this long; he fetched out a couple of the oranges with which the baskets had been filled in the morning. "Here is something to eat to your bread, Laurella," he said. "Don't think I kept them for you; they had rolled out of the basket, and I only found them when I brought the baskets back to the boat."

"Eat them yourself; bread is enough for me."

"They are refreshing in this heat, and you have had to walk so far."

"They gave me a drink of water, and that refreshed me."

"As you please," he said, and let them drop into the basket.

Silence again. The sea was smooth as glass. Not a ripple was heard against the prow. Even the white seabirds that roost among the caves of Capri pursued their prey with soundless flight.

"You might take the oranges to your mother," again commenced Tonino.

"We have oranges at home; and when they are gone, I can go and buy some more."

"Nay, take these to her, and give them to her with my compliments."

"She does not know you."

"You can tell her who I am."

"I do not know you either."

It was not the first time that she had denied him thus. One Sunday of last year, when that painter had first come to Sorrento, Antonio had chanced to be playing *boccia* with some other young fellows in the little piazza by the chief street.

There, for the first time, had the painter caught sight of Laurella, who, with her pitcher on her head, had passed by without taking any notice of him. The Neapolitan, struck by her appearance, stood still and gazed after her, not heeding that he was standing in the very midst of the game, which, with two steps, he might have cleared. A very ungentle ball came knocking against his shins, as a reminder that this was not the spot to choose for meditation. He looked round, as if in expectation of some excuse. But the young boatman who had thrown the ball stood silent among his friends, in such an attitude of defiance that the stranger had found it more advisable to go his ways and avoid discussion. Still, this little encounter had been spoken of, particularly at the time when the painter had been pressing his suit to Laurella. "I do not even know him," she said indignantly, when the painter asked her whether it was for the sake of that uncourteous lad she now refused him. But she had heard that piece of gossip, and known Antonio well enough when she had met him since.

And now they sat together in this boat, like two most deadly enemies, while their hearts were beating fit to kill them. Antonio's usually so good-humored face was heated to scarlet; he struck the oars so sharply that the foam flew over to where Laurella sat, while his lips moved as if muttering angry words. She pretended not to notice, wearing her most unconscious

THE FURY

look, bending over the edge of the boat, and letting
the cool water pass between her fingers. Then she
threw off her handkerchief again, and began to smooth
her hair, as tho she had been alone. Only her
eyebrows twitched, and she held up her wet hands in
vain attempts to cool her burning cheeks.

Now they were well out in the open sea. The island
was far behind, and the coast before them lay yet
distant in the hot haze. Not a sail was within sight,
far or near—not even a passing gull to break the still-
ness. Antonio looked all round, evidently ripening
some hasty resolution. The color faded suddenly
from his cheek, and he dropped his oars. Laurella
looked round involuntarily—fearless, yet attentive.

"I must make an end of this," the young fellow
burst forth. "It has lasted too long already! I only
wonder that it has not killed me! You say you do not
know me? And all this time you must have seen me
pass you like a madman, my whole heart full of what
I had to tell you; and then you only made your cross-
est mouth, and turned your back upon me."

"What had I to say to you?" she curtly replied.
"I may have seen that you were inclined to meddle
with me, but I do not choose to be on people's wicked
tongues for nothing. I do not mean to have you for
a husband—neither you nor any other."

"Nor any other? So you will not always say! You
say so now, because you would not have that painter.
Bah, you were but a child! You will feel lonely
enough yet, some day; and then, wild as you are, you
will take the next best who comes to hand."

"Who knows? which of us can see the future? It
may be that I will change my mind. What is that to
you?"

"What is it to me?" he flew out, starting to his feet, while the small boat leaped and danced. "What is it to me, you say? You know well enough! I tell you, that man shall perish miserably to whom you shall prove kinder than you have been to me!"

"And to you, what did I ever promise? Am I to blame if you be mad? What right have you to me?"

"Ah! I know," he cried, "my right is written nowhere. It has not been put in Latin by any lawyer, nor stamped with any seal. But this I feel: I have just the right to you that I have to heaven, if I die an honest Christian. Do you think I could look on and see you go to church with another man, and see the girls go by and shrug their shoulders at me?"

"You can do as you please. I am not going to let myself be frightened by all those threats. I also mean to do as I please."

"You shall not say so long!" and his whole frame shook with passion. "I am not the man to let my whole life be spoiled by a stubborn wench like you! You are in my power here, remember, and may be made to do my bidding."

She could not repress a start, but her eyes flashed bravely on him.

"You may kill me if you dare," she said slowly.

"I do nothing by halves," he said, and his voice sounded choked and hoarse. "There is room for us both in the sea. I cannot help thee, child"—he spoke the last words dreamily, almost pitifully—"but we must both go down together—both at once—and now!" he shouted, and snatched her in his arms. But at the same moment he drew back his right hand; the blood gushed out; she had bitten him fiercely.

"Ha! can I be made to do your bidding?" she

cried, and thrust him from her, with one sudden movement. "Am I here in your power?" and she leaped
into the sea and sank.

She rose again directly; her scanty skirts clung close;
her long hair, loosened by the waves, hung heavy
about her neck. She struck out valiantly, and, without uttering a sound, she began to swim steadily from
the boat toward the shore.

With senses benumbed by sudden terror, he stood,
with outstretched neck, looking after her, his eyes fixed
as tho they had just been witness to a miracle.
Then, giving himself a shake, he seized his oars, and
began rowing after her with all the strength he had,
while all the time the bottom of the boat was redden-
ing with the blood that kept streaming from his hand.

Rapidly as she swam, he was at her side in a moment.
"For the love of our most Holy Virgin," he cried,
"get into the boat! I have been a madman! God alone
can tell what so suddenly darkened my brain. It came
upon me like a flash of lightning and set me all on fire.
I knew not what I did or said. I do not even ask you
to forgive me, Laurella, only to come into the boat
again and not to risk your life!"

She swam on as tho she had not heard him.

"You can never swim to land. I tell you it is two
miles off. Think of your mother! If you should come
to grief, I should die of horror."

She measured the distance with her eye, and then,
without answering him one word, she swam up to the
boat, and laid her hands upon the edge; he rose to
help her in. As the boat tilted over to one side with
the girl's weight, his jacket that was lying on the bench
slipped into the water. Agile as she was, she swung
herself on board without assistance, and gained her

former seat. As soon as he saw that she was safe, he
took to his oars again, while she began quietly wringing
out her dripping clothes, and shaking the water from
her hair. As her eyes fell upon the bottom of the
boat, and saw the blood, she gave a quick look at the
hand, which held the oar as if it had been unhurt.

"Take this," she said, and held out her handkerchief. He shook his head, and went on rowing. After
a time she rose, and, stepping up to him, bound the
handkerchief firmly round the wound, which was very
deep. Then, heedless of his endeavors to prevent her,
she took an oar, and, seating herself opposite him,
began to row with steady stroke, keeping her eyes from
looking toward him—fixed upon the oar that was scarlet with his blood. Both were pale and silent. As they
drew near land, such fishermen as they met began
shouting after Antonio and gibing at Laurella; but
neither of them moved an eyelid, or spoke one word.

The sun stood yet high over Procida when they
landed at the marina. Laurella shook out her petticoat, now nearly dry, and jumped on shore. The old
spinning woman, who in the morning had seen them
start, was still upon her terrace. She called down,
"What is that upon your hand, Tonino? Jesus Christ!
the boat is full of blood!"

"It is nothing, comare," the young fellow replied.
"I tore my hand against a nail that was sticking out
too far; it will be well to-morrow. It is only this
confounded ready blood of mine, that always makes a
thing look worse than it is."

"Let me come and bind it up, comparello. Stop one
moment; I will go and fetch the herbs, and come to
you directly."

"Never trouble yourself, comare. It has been

dressed already; to-morrow morning it will be all over and forgotten. I have a healthy skin, that heals directly."

"Addio!" said Laurella, turning to the path that goes winding up the cliffs. "Good-night!" he answered, without looking at her; and then taking his oars and baskets from the boat, and climbing up the small stone stairs, he went into his own hut.

He was alone in his two little rooms, and began to pace them up and down. Cooler than upon the dead calm sea, the breeze blew fresh through the small unglazed windows, which could only be closed with wooden shutters. The solitude was soothing to him. He stooped before the little image of the Virgin, devoutly gazing upon the glory round the head (made of stars cut out in silver paper). But he did not want to pray. What reason had he to pray, now that he had lost all he had ever hoped for?

And this day appeared to last forever. He did so long for night! for he was weary, and more exhausted by the loss of blood than he would have cared to own. His hand was very sore. Seating himself upon a little stool, he untied the handkerchief that bound it; the blood, so long repressed, gushed out again; all round the wound the hand was swollen high.

He washed it carefully, cooling it in the water; then he clearly saw the marks of Laurella's teeth.

"She was right," he said; "I was a brute, and deserved no better. I will send her back the handkerchief by Giuseppe to-morrow. Never shall she set eyes on me again." And he washed the handkerchief with the greatest care, and spread it out in the sun to dry.

And having bound up his hand again, as well as he

could manage with his teeth and his left hand, he threw himself upon his bed, and closed his eyes.

He was soon waked up from a sort of slumber by the rays of the bright moonlight, and also by the pain of his hand; he had just risen for more cold water to sooth its throbbing, when he heard the sound of someone at the door. Laurella stood before him.

She came in without a question, took off the handkerchief she had tied over her head, and placed her little basket upon the table; then she drew a deep breath.

"You are come to fetch your handkerchief," he said. "You need not have taken that trouble. In the morning I would have asked Giuseppe to take it to you."

"It is not the handkerchief," she said quickly. "I have been up among the hills to gather herbs to stop the blood; see here." And she lifted the lid of her little basket.

"Too much trouble," he said, not in bitterness— "far too much trouble. I am better, much better; but if I were worse, it would be no more than I deserve. Why did you come at such a time? If any one should see you? You know how they talk, even when they don't know what they are saying."

"I care for no one's talk," she said, passionately. "I came to see your hand, and put the herbs upon it; you cannot do it with your left."

"It is not worth while, I tell you."

"Let me see it then, if I am to believe you."

She took his hand, that was not able to prevent her, and unbound the linen. When she saw the swelling, she shuddered, and gave a cry: "Jesus Maria!"

"It is a little swollen," he said; "it will be over in four-and-twenty hours."

S. S. II-8

She shook her head. "It will certainly be a week be-fore you can go to sea."

"More likely a day or two; and if not, what mat-ters?"

She had fetched a basin, and began carefully wash-ing out the wound, which he suffered passively, like a child. She then laid on the healing leaves, which at once relieved the burning pain, and finally bound it up with the linen she had brought with her.

When it was done: "I thank you," he said. "And now, if you would do me one more kindness, forgive the madness that came over me; forget all I said and did. I cannot tell how it came to pass; certainly it was not your fault—not yours. And never shall you hear from me again one word to vex you."

She interrupted him. "It is I who have to beg your pardon. I should have spoken differently. I might have explained it better, and not enraged you with my sullen ways. And now that bite—"

"It was in self-defense; it was high time to bring me to my senses. As I said before, it is nothing at all to signify. Do not talk of being forgiven; you only did me good, and I thank you for it. And now, here is your handkerchief; take it with you."

He held it to her, but yet she lingered, hesitated, and appeared to have some inward struggle. At length she said: "You have lost your jacket, and by my fault; and I know that all the money for the oranges was in it. I did not think of this till afterward. I cannot replace it now; we have not so much at home— or if we had, it would be mother's. But this I have— this silver cross. That painter left it on the table the day he came for the last time. I have never looked at it all this while, and do not care to keep it in my

box; if you were to sell it? It must be worth a few
piastres, mother says. It might make up the money
you have lost; and if not quite, I could earn the rest
by spinning at night when mother is asleep."

"Nothing will make me take it," he said shortly,
pushing away the bright new cross which she had
taken from her pocket.

"You must," she said; "how can you tell how long
your hand may keep you from your work? There it
lies; and nothing can make me so much as look at it
again."

"Drop it in the sea, then."

"It is no present I want to make you; it is no more
than is your due; it is only fair."

"Nothing from you can be due to me; and hereafter
when we chance to meet, if you would do me a kindness, I beg you not to look my way. It would make
me feel you were thinking of what I have done. And
now good-night; and let this be the last word said."

She laid the handkerchief in the basket, and also the
cross, and closed the lid. But when he looked into her
face, he started. Great heavy drops were rolling down
her cheeks; she let them flow unheeded.

"Maria Santissima!" he cried. "Are you ill? You
are trembling from head to foot!"

"It is nothing," she said; "I must go home"; and
with unsteady steps she was moving to the door, when
suddenly she leaned her brow against the wall, and
gave way to a fit of bitter sobbing. Before he could
go to her she turned upon him suddenly, and fell upon
his neck.

"I cannot bear it!" she cried, clinging to him as a
dying thing to life—"I cannot bear it! I cannot let
you speak so kindly, and bid me go, with all this on

my conscience. Beat me! trample on me! curse me! Or if it can be that you love me still, after all I have done to you, take me and keep me, and do with me as you please; only do not send me away so!" She could say no more for sobbing.

Speechless, he held her a while in his arms. "If I can love you still!" he cried at last. "Holy Mother of God! Do you think that all my best heart's blood has gone from me through that little wound? Don't you hear it hammering now, as tho it would burst my breast and go to you? But if you say this to try me, or because you pity me, I can forget it. You are not to think you owe me this, because you know what I have suffered for you."

"No!" she said very resolutely, looking up from his shoulder into his face, with her tearful eyes; "it is because I love you; and let me tell you, it was because I always feared to love you that I was so cross. I will be so different now. I never could bear again to pass you in the street without one look! And lest you should ever feel a doubt, I will kiss you, that you may say 'She kissed me'; and Laurella kisses no man but her husband."

She kissed him thrice, and, escaping from his arms: "And now good-night, amor mio, cara vita mià!" she said. "Lie down to sleep, and let your hand get well. Do not come with me; I am afraid of no man, save of you alone."

And so she slipped out, and soon disappeared in the shadow of the wall.

He remained standing by the window, gazing far out over the calm sea, while all the stars in heaven appeared to flit before his eyes.

The next time the little curato sat in his confessional, he sat smiling to himself. Laurella had just risen from her knees after a very long confession.

"Who would have thought it?" he said musingly— "that the Lord would so soon have taken pity upon the wayward little heart? And I had been reproaching myself for not having adjured more sternly that ill demon of perversity. Our eyes are but shortsighted to see the ways of Heaven! Well, may God bless her, I say, and let me live to go to sea with Laurella's eldest born rowing me in his father's place! Ah! well, indeed! l'Arrabiata!"

TO LOVE AND TO HONOR

By OCTAVUS ROY COHEN

It was rather amazing to discover a deep vein of sentiment in pudgy little George Potter. I had been his friend and attorney for thirty years and had watched the always stout, and once wideawake, little man settle into a domestic rut. Success had come to him in a modest way: a success which would have enabled him to retire from business and travel about the world a bit had he cared to do so. But instead he and Esther were content to sit night after night in their cozy living-room; she busy with her sewing or reading; he poring over his very excellent collection of postage stamps.

Looking back over the years of my friendship with Potter, I can see that the streak of romance had probably been there all the time. There was, for instance, his youthful and frantic courtship of the stately Althea Deane—an affair which had skirted the borders of scandal. And just when the forked tongue of gossip began flickering at highest speed—George married her.

That marriage appeared to extinguish George Potter's last spark of romanticism. It never had a chance to be successful, and when Althea left him abruptly, George's friends considered it good riddance. Later came the news of Althea's death abroad, and a couple

of years later George started paying stolid court to
Esther. Our set was mildly interested—it is difficult
to be genuinely keen about a prospective marriage in
which the principals are both humdrum.

The marriage was a very nice affair. There followed
the usual round of entertainments. Then it seemed
that George and Esther retired from life. Even his
business affairs ran so smoothly that there was little
need for my services in a legal way—and while my
liking for the man never lagged, we found less and
less in common as the years rolled on. I couldn't
fancy that they were happy: contented, perhaps, but
not really happy. Not enough sentiment. . . .
That's the way I figured George. And nothing happened to alter my opinion until a few weeks before
their twenty-fifth anniversary.

It was then that he waddled into my office, fat little
face alight with enthusiasm, and informed me of his
unique plans for the silver anniversary. His bright
little eyes shone as he outlined the thing and I'll confess that I was pretty well dumfounded: not alone
because his scheme was richly sentimental and profoundly impressive; but chiefly because it was stodgy
old George Pot⁺er who was planning this thing—the
very George Potter who had lived a hermit life since
his second marriage, and who had shunned social
contacts.

According to what George told me, he was doing
this thing for Esther's sake. "It'll sort of tickle her,"
he explained. "Women like that sort of thing, you
know—and this strikes me as a real idea. You've
got to be in on it, because you were best man when
Esther and I were married." He grinned sheepishly.

"It's just a gesture on my part—sort of sacrifice to please the Old Lady."

I'll say this for George: he didn't do things halfway. Instead of the conventional party, he staged a perfect duplication of his marriage to Esther twenty-five years before. There was even the same minister—mighty old now—and the decrepit violinist who had played "Oh, Promise Me" at the other ceremony. A good many of the original guests were there: most of us pretty gray around the temples. But the thing was mighty impressive—Esther in the bridal costume she had worn twenty-five years before . . . let out around the hips perhaps . . . and carrying a shower bouquet of bride roses and valley lilies! the bridesmaids in pink, with bouquets of Killarney roses. Even a ring-bearer. It was worlds of fun and queerly stately where one might have expected it to be absurd.

As for Esther, I never saw a woman more radiant. She took on an aura of genuine beauty. Of course she would have been less than human and far from feminine to have failed of response to this magnificent display of husbandly devotion. George himself was as frightened as he had been on the occasion of their wedding. . . .

But finally the ceremony was finished and the guests adjourned to the dining-room for the lavish supper which had been prepared by a firm of caterers. George and I were left alone and he sank limply into a chair. I dropped a hand on his shoulder and congratulated him on the success of his party.

"You really think it was a success!"

"Wonderful! And," jocularly, "you certainly should feel thoroughly married."

"Yes. I surely do." He fell silent for a moment

or two, and when he spoke again it was in a deadly serious voice. "There's something I've got to explain to you: as my friend and my lawyer." He stopped for a second, then asked abruptly, "You remember my first wife?"

"Althea?" I was amazed by the question. "Certainly."

"Did you know," he went on in a queer, strained voice, "that she died only last year?"

"Good Lord! I thought she died twenty-seven years ago."

"So did I," he said quietly. "And when I married Esther, I thought I was a widower. But I wasn't. . . . And in case anything ever comes up—well, I want you to understand that this affair to-night was a real wedding."

THE MUMMY'S FOOT

By Théophile Gautier

I had entered, in an idle mood, the shop of one of
those curiosity-venders, who are called *marchands de
bric-à-brac* in that Parisian *argot* which is so perfectly
unintelligible elsewhere in France.

You have doubtless glanced occasionally through the
windows of some of these shops, which have become
so numerous now that it is fashionable to buy anti-
quated furniture, and that every petty stockbroker
thinks he must have his *Chambre au moyen âge*.

There is one thing there which clings alike to the
shop of the dealer in old iron, the wareroom of the
tapestry-maker, the laboratory of the chemist, and
the studio of the painter—in all those gloomy dens
where a furtive daylight filters in through the window-
shutters the most manifestly ancient thing is dust;—
the cobwebs are more authentic than the guimp laces;
and the old pear-tree furniture on exhibition is actually younger than the mahogany which arrived but
yesterday from America.

The warehouse of my bric-à-brac dealer was a
veritable Capharnaum; all ages and all nations seemed
to have made their rendezvous there; an Etruscan
lamp of red clay stood upon a Boule cabinet, with
ebony panels, brightly striped by lines of inlaid brass;
a duchess of the court of Louis XV nonchalantly ex-

(Translated by Lafcadio Hearn; copyright, 1890, by Brentano's.)

tended her fawn-like feet under a massive table of the time of Louis XIII, with heavy spiral supports of oak, and carven designs of Chimeras and foliage intermingled.

Upon the denticulated shelves of several sideboards glittered immense Japanese dishes with red and blue designs relieved by gilded hatching; side by side with enameled works by Bernard Palissy, representing serpents, frogs, and lizards in relief.

From disemboweled cabinets escaped cascades of silver-lustrous Chinese silks and waves of tinsel, which an oblique sunbeam shot through with luminous beads; while portraits of every era, in frames more or less tarnished, smiled through their yellow varnish.

The striped breastplate of a damascened suit of Milanese armor glittered in one corner; Loves and Nymphs of porcelain; Chinese grotesques, vases of *céladon* and crackle-ware; Saxon and old Sèvres cups encumbered the shelves and nooks of the department.

The dealer followed me closely through the tortuous way contrived between the piles of furniture; warding off with his hand the hazardous sweep of my coat-skirts; watching my elbows with the uneasy attention of an antiquarian and a usurer.

It was a singular face, that of the merchant—an immense skull, polished like a knee, and surrounded by a thin aureole of white hair, which brought out the clear salmon tint of his complexion all the more strikingly, lent him a false aspect of patriarchal *bonhomie*, counteracted, however, by the scintillation of two little yellow eyes which trembled in their orbits like two louis-d'or upon quicksilver. The curve of his nose presented an aquiline silhouette, which suggested the Oriental or Jewish type. His hands—thin,

slender, full of nerves which projected like strings
upon the finger-board of a violin, and armed with
claws like those on the terminations of bats' wings—
shook with senile trembling; but those convulsively
agitated hands became firmer than steel pincers or
lobsters' claws when they lifted any precious article—
an onyx cup, a Venetian glass, or a dish of Bohemian
crystal. This strange old man had an aspect so thoroughly rabbinical and cabalistic that he would have
been burnt on the mere testimony of his face three
centuries ago.

"Will you not buy something from me to-day, sir?
Here is a Malay kreese with a blade undulating like
flame: look at those grooves contrived for the blood to
run along, those teeth set backward so as to tear out
the entrails in withdrawing the weapon—it is a fine
character of ferocious arm, and will look well in your
collection: this two-handed sword is very beautiful—
it is the work of Josepe de la Hera; and this *coliche-
marde,* with its fenestrated guard—what a superb speci-
men of handicraft!"

"No; I have quite enough weapons and instruments
of carnage;—I want a small figure, something which
will suit me as a paper-weight; for I can not endure
those trumpery bronzes which the stationers sell, and
which may be found on everybody's desk."

The old gnome foraged among his ancient wares,
and finally arranged before me some antique bronzes—
so-called, at least; fragments of malachite, little Hindu
or Chinese idols—a kind of poussah-toys in jade-stone,
representing the incarnations of Brahma or Vishnu,
and wonderfully appropriate to the very undivine office
of holding papers and letters in place.

I was hesitating between a porcelain dragon, all

constellated with warts—its mouth formidable with bristling tusks and ranges of teeth—and an abominable little Mexican fetish, representing the god Vitzili-putzili *au naturel;* when I caught sight of a charming foot, which I at first took for a fragment of some antique Venus.

It had those beautiful ruddy and tawny tints that lend to Florentine bronze that warm, living look so much preferable to the gray-green aspect of common bronzes, which might easily be mistaken for statues in a state of putrefaction: satiny gleams played over its rounded forms, doubtless polished by the amorous kisses of twenty centuries; for it seemed a Corinthian bronze, a work of the best era of art—perhaps molded by Lysippus himself.

"That foot will be my choice," I said to the merchant, who regarded me with an ironical and saturnine air, and held out the object desired that I might examine it more fully.

I was surprised at its lightness; it was not a foot of metal, but in sooth a foot of flesh—an embalmed foot—a mummy's foot: on examining it still more closely the very grain of the skin, and the almost imperceptible lines impressed upon it by the texture of the bandages, became perceptible. The toes were slender and delicate, and terminated by perfectly formed nails, pure and transparent as agates; the great toe, slightly separated from the rest afforded a happy contrast, in the antique style, to the position of the other toes, and lent it an aerial lightness—the grace of a bird's foot;—the sole, scarcely streaked by a few almost imperceptible cross lines, afforded evidence that it had never touched the bare ground, and had only come in contact with the finest matting of Nile rushes, and the softest carpets of panther skin.

"Ha, ha!—you want the foot of the Princess Hermonthis"—exclaimed the merchant, with a strange giggle, fixing his owlish eyes upon me—"ha, ha, ha!—for a paper-weight!—an original idea!—artistic idea! Old Pharaoh would certainly have been surprized had some one told him that the foot of his adored daughter would be used for a paper-weight after he had had a mountain of granite hollowed out as a receptacle for the triple coffin, painted and gilded—covered with hieroglyphics and beautiful paintings of the Judgment of Souls"—continued the queer little merchant, half audibly, as tho talking to himself!

"How much will you charge me for this mummy fragment?"

"Ah, the highest price I can get; for it is a superb piece: if I had the match of it you could not have it for less than five hundred francs;—the daughter of a Pharaoh! nothing is more rare."

"Assuredly that is not a common article; but, still, how much do you want? In the first place, let me warn you that all my wealth consists of just five louis: I can buy anything that costs five louis, but nothing dearer;—you might search my vest pockets and most secret drawers without even finding one poor five-franc piece more."

"Five louis for the foot of the Princess Hermonthis! that is very little, very little indeed; 'tis an authentic foot," muttered the merchant, shaking his head, and imparting a peculiar rotary motion to his eyes. "Well, take it, and I will give you the bandages into the bargain," he added, wrapping the foot in an ancient damask rag—"very fine! real damask!—Indian damask which has never been redyed; it is strong, and yet it is soft," he mumbled, stroking the frayed tissue with his fingers, through the trade-acquired habit which moved him to praise even an object of so little value that he himself deemed it only worth the giving away.

He poured the gold coins into a sort of medieval alms-purse hanging at his belt, repeating:

"The foot of the Princess Hermonthis, to be used for a paper-weight!"

Then turning his phosphorescent eyes upon me, he exclaimed in a voice strident as the crying of a cat which has swallowed a fish-bone:

"Old Pharaoh will not be well pleased: he loved his daughter—the dear man!"

"You speak as if you were a contemporary of his: you are old enough, goodness knows! but you do not date back to the Pyramids of Egypt," I answered, laughingly, from the threshold.

I went home, delighted with my acquisition.

With the idea of putting it to profitable use as soon as possible, I placed the foot of the divine Princess Hermonthis upon a heap of paper scribbled over with verses, in themselves an undecipherable mosaic work of erasures; articles freshly begun; letters forgotten, and posted in the table drawer instead of the letter-box—an error to which absent-minded people are peculiarly liable. The effect was charming, bizarre, and romantic.

Well satisfied with this embellishment, I went out with the gravity and pride becoming one who feels that he has the ineffable advantage over all the passers-by whom he elbows, of possessing a piece of the Princess Hermonthis, daughter of Pharaoh.

I looked upon all who did not possess, like myself,

a paper-weight so authentically Egyptian, as very ridiculous people; and it seemed to me that the proper occupation of every sensible man should consist in the mere fact of having a mummy's foot upon his desk.

Happily I met some friends, whose presence distracted me in my infatuation with this new acquisition: I went to dinner with them; for I could not very well have dined with myself.

When I came back that evening, with my brain slightly confused by a few glasses of wine, a vague whiff of Oriental perfume delicately titillated my olfactory nerves: the heat of the room had warmed the natron, bitumen, and myrrh in which the *paraschistes*, who cut open the bodies of the dead, had bathed the corpse of the princess;—it was a perfume at once sweet and penetrating—a perfume that four thousand years had not been able to dissipate.

The Dream of Egypt was Eternity: her odors have the solidity of granite, and endure as long.

I soon drank deeply from the black cup of sleep: for a few hours all remained opaque to me; Oblivion and Nothingness inundated me with their somber waves.

Yet light gradually dawned upon the darkness of my mind: dreams commenced to touch me softly in their silent flight.

The eyes of my soul were opened; and I beheld my chamber as it actually was: I might have believed myself awake, but for a vague consciousness which assured me that I slept, and that something fantastic was about to take place.

The odor of the myrrh had augmented in intensity: and I felt a slight headache, which I very naturally attributed to several glasses of champagne that we had drunk to the unknown gods and our future fortunes.

I peered through my room with a feeling of expectation which I saw nothing to justify: every article of furniture was in its proper place; the lamp, softly shaded by its globe of ground crystal, burned upon its bracket; the water-color sketches shone under their Bohemian glass; the curtains hung down languidly; everything wore an aspect of tranquil slumber.

After a few moments, however, all this calm interior appeared to become disturbed; the woodwork cracked stealthily; the ash-covered log suddenly emitted a jet of blue flame; and the disks of the pateras seemed like great metallic eyes, watching, like myself, for the things which were about to happen.

My eyes accidentally fell upon the desk where I had placed the foot of the Princess Hermonthis.

Instead of remaining quiet—as behooved a foot which had been embalmed for four thousand years—it commenced to act in a nervous manner; contracted itself, and leaped over the papers like a startled frog;—one would have imagined that it had suddenly been brought into contact with a galvanic battery: I could distinctly hear the dry sound made by its little heel, hard as the hoof of a gazel.

I became rather discontented with my acquisition, inasmuch as I wished my paper-weights to be of a sedentary disposition, and thought it very unnatural that feet should walk about without legs; and I commenced to experience a feeling closely akin to fear.

Suddenly I saw the folds of my bed-curtain stir; and heard a bumping sound, like that caused by some person hopping on one foot across the floor.

I must confess I became alternately hot and cold;

that I felt a strange wind chill my back; and that my
suddenly-rising hair caused my nightcap to execute
a leap of several yards.

The bed-curtain opened, and I beheld the strangest
figure imaginable before me.

It was a young girl of a very deep coffee-brown
complexion, like the bayadere Amani, and possessing
the purest Egyptian type of perfect beauty; her eyes
were almond-shaped and oblique, with eyebrows so
black that they seemed blue; her nose was exquisitely
chiseled, almost Greek in its delicacy of outline; and
she might indeed have been taken for a Corinthian
statue of bronze, but for the prominence of her cheek-
bones and the slightly African fulness of her lips,
which compelled one to recognize her as belonging
beyond all doubt to the hieroglyphic race which dwelt
upon the banks of the Nile.

Her arms, slender and spindle-shaped, like those of
very young girls, were encircled by a peculiar kind
of metal bands, and bracelets of glass beads; her hair
was all twisted into little cords; and she wore upon
her bosom a little idol figure of green paste, bearing
a whip with seven lashes, which proved it to be an
image of Isis: her brow was adorned with a shining
plate of gold; and a few traces of paint relieved the
coppery tint of her cheeks.

As for her costume, it was very odd indeed.

Fancy a *pagne* or skirt all formed of little strips of
material bedizened with red and black hieroglyphics,
stiffened with bitumen, and apparently belonging to
freshly unbandaged mummy.

In one of those sudden flights of thought so common
in dreams I heard the hoarse falsetto of the *bric-à-
brac* dealer, repeating like a monotonous refrain, the

phrase he had uttered in his shop with so enigmatical an intonation:

"Old Pharaoh will not be well pleased: he loved his daughter, the dear man!"

One strange circumstance, which was not at all calculated to restore my equanimity, was that the apparition had but one foot; the other was broken off at the ankle!

She approached the table where the foot was starting and fidgeting about more than ever; and there supported herself upon the edge of the desk. I saw her eyes fill with pearly-gleaming tears.

Altho she had not as yet spoken, I fully comprehended the thoughts which agitated her: she looked at her foot—for it was indeed her own—with an exquisitely graceful expression of coquettish sadness; but the foot leaped and ran hither and thither, as tho impelled on steel springs.

Twice or thrice she extended her hand to seize it, but could not succeed.

Then commenced between the Princess Hermonthis and her foot—which appeared to be endowed with a special life of its own—a very fantastic dialog in a most ancient Coptic tongue, such as might have been spoken thirty centuries ago in the syrinxes of the land of Ser: luckily I understood Coptic perfectly well that night.

The Princess Hermonthis cried, in a voice sweet and vibrant as the tones of a crystal bell:

"Well, my dear little foot, you always flee from me; yet I always took good care of you. I bathed you with perfumed water in a bowl of alabaster; I smoothed your heel with pumice-stone mixed with palm oil; your nails were cut with golden scissors and polished with a hippopotamus tooth; I was careful to select *tatbebs* for you, painted and embroidered and turned up at the toes, which were the envy of all the young girls in Egypt: you wore on your great toe rings bearing the device of the sacred Scarabeus; and you supported one of the lightest bodies that a lazy foot could sustain."

The foot replied in a pouting and chagrined tone:

"You know well that I do not belong to myself any longer. I have been bought and paid for: the old merchant knew what he was about: he bore you a grudge for having refused to espouse him. This is an ill turn which he has done you. The Arab who violated your royal coffin in the subterranean pits of the necropolis of Thebes was sent thither by him: he desired to prevent you from being present at the reunion of the shadowy nations in the cities below. Have you five pieces of gold for my ransom?"

"Alas, no!—my jewels, my rings, my purses of gold and silver, were all stolen from me," answered the Princess Hermonthis, with a sob.

"Princess," I then exclaimed, "I never retained anybody's foot unjustly;—even tho you have not got the five louis which it cost me, I present it to you gladly: I should feel unutterably wretched to think that I were the cause of so amiable a person as the Princess Hermonthis being lame."

I delivered this discourse in a royally gallant, troubadour tone which must have astonished the beautiful Egyptian girl.

She turned a look of deepest gratitude upon me; and her eyes shone with bluish gleams of light.

She took her foot—which surrendered itself willingly

this time—like a woman about to put on her little shoe; and adjusted it to her leg with much skill.

This operation over, she took a few steps about the room, as tho to assure herself that she was really no longer lame.

"Ah, how pleased my father will be!—he who was so unhappy because of my mutilation; and who from the moment of my birth, set a whole nation at work to hollow me out a tomb so deep that he might preserve me intact until that last day, when souls must be weighed in the balance of Amenthi! Come with me to my father!—he will receive you kindly; for you have given me back my foot."

I thought this proposition natural enough. I arrayed myself in a dressing-gown of large-flowered pattern, which lent me a very Pharaonic aspect; hurriedly put on a pair of Turkish slippers, and informed the Princess Hermonthis that I was ready to follow her.

Before starting, Hermonthis took from her neck the little idol of green paste, and laid it on the scattered sheets of paper which covered the table.

"It is only fair," she observed smilingly, "that I should replace your paper-weight."

She gave me her hand, which felt soft and cold, like the skin of a serpent; and we departed.

We passed for some time with the velocity of an arrow through a fluid and grayish expanse, in which half-formed silhouettes flitted swiftly by us, to right and left.

For an instant we saw only sky and sea.

A few moments later obelisks commenced to tower in the distance: pylons and vast flights of steps guarded by sphinxes became clearly outlined against the horizon.

We had reached our destination.

The princess conducted me to a mountain of rose-colored granite, in the face of which appeared an opening so narrow and low that it would have been difficult to distinguish it from the fissures in the rock, had not its location been marked by two stelæ wrought with sculptures.

Hermonthis kindled a torch, and led the way before me.

We traversed corridors hewn through the living rock: their walls, covered with hieroglyphics and paintings of allegorical processions, might well have occupied thousands of arms for thousands of years in their formation;—these corridors, of interminable length, opened into square chambers, in the midst of which pits had been contrived, through which we descended by cramp-irons or spiral stairways;—these pits again conducted us into other chambers, opening into other corridors, likewise decorated with painted sparrowhawks, serpents coiled in circles, the symbols of the *tau* and *pedum*—prodigious works of art which no living eye can ever examine—interminable legends of granite which only the dead have time to read through all eternity.

At last we found ourselves in a hall so vast, so enormous, so immeasurable, that the eye could not reach its limits; files of monstrous columns stretched far out of sight on every side, between which twinkled livid stars of yellowish flame;—points of light which revealed further depths incalculable in the darkness beyond.

The Princess Hermonthis still held my hand, and graciously saluted the mummies of her acquaintance.

been the sort of judgment, anyway, with which he'd
brokered his way through Wall Street to a useful fortune. Marriage was his only wildcat plunge and—

So now when he was nearing forty and his gold was
just a heavy weight, and their apartment at home, full
of museum antiques, was after all a lot of old junk,
and his favorite Fifty-seventh Street club was in reality
a den of dodos, and his tee shots were wilder than ever
—he needed a woman, a wife. And all he had was a
doll's face with a wistful half smile on her lips and a
vague wonder-what-it's-all-about in her gray eyes. That
was Marion to a T—when T stands for tragedy.

"Let's hire a hack and drive through the town," he
said to the slender lavender back, tho—and that
was the devil of it—he knew exactly and in advance
what the reply would be—"Very well, Forrest, if you
wish."

Marion turned around with a white dot of powder
on her short nose. Even her husband couldn't quarrel
with her looks. "All right, Forrest," she said. "If you
want to."

Close enough. Too close. He'd been up against that
devastating obviousness for three years: evenings when
he'd come home determined to tell her a story he'd
heard or to pat himself on the back for some particularly smart deal in rails. But who could talk to a
vagueness? Her clothes? Who wants to talk about a
woman's clothes? Her ailments? When he knew perfectly well that they were imaginary? And as for plays
and books, great heavens! He was too dissatisfied with
his own to worry about the troubles of imaginary lives.

How Marion with her background of cultivation, her
years of travel, her several languages, her reputed voice

—well, what was the use? She never had mentioned a foreign place in any language, and she'd never sung a note, and, by George, that little Miss Evans, his secretary at the office, had more spirit. Forrest Windsor had taken Miss Evans out to lunch a few times, and he knew. But that is neither here nor there. He wasn't married to Miss Evans and he had been married to Marion for three entire years.

He remembered the last time he'd found her sitting in their car in front of the apartment house, all ready to take him for another everlasting drive through the eternal park. He had climbed in reluctantly and killed her faint smile with a perfunctory kiss, waiting to ask her what mail had come until she'd had a chance to inquire about his day at the office.

Halfway through the park he'd said, "I like that emerald ring, Marion." He simply had to say something or he'd become one of those queer, dear souls who pass one on the street babbling happily to themselves. "Yes, I think I'll match it with a bracelet for your birthday."

"That will be nice."

"To-morrow, isn't it?" he asked, encouraged. "We might dine out."

"Very well, Forrest, if you wish."

"Where then? Lido? Ten East Sixty?"

"Either will be very—"

"My God, Marion! Can't you—?" And then he had told her. There had been a sort of helplessness in her eyes, but he had told her that he was going to pull out of it. "I'm going to Europe for six months. You're too sick and, anyway, the other side's an old story to you"—

She had shot him a quick, frightened glance. "I

think a change will be good for me, Forrest." But apparently, thought Windsor as he rose to phone downstairs for the "hack," Europe wasn't enough of a change.

Like the arm of one asleep beside a beloved, Tours reaches a bridge over the slow Loire. Their fiacre returned across it toward the scattered and then merging lights of the city, and down below the brown water was blackening because it was near to night. A boat barely moved.

Soon they jogged into town through the narrow aisle of the Rue Nationale. Blue and gold coaches had brightened that passage once, or a Duc de Guise at the head of forty plumes, or the flying hair of Charles Martel with a bishop's prayer on his head, a blunt battle-ax on his shoulder, and a slim maid on his saddle bow to bid him speed on the road to Poitiers.

"Shall we go back to the hotel, Marion?" he asked. "Why not the L'Univers or the Lyonnais for dinner?"

She was startled out of some distant thought—or some distant lack of thought. "Either will be very nice, Forrest."

He shook his head despondently. Country or continent cannot change a woman. "So kind of you to agree," he said. "We shall proceed to the end in the track of every confounded tourist who has ever been here. I thought at least you knew France—but you've a tourist mind, Marion."

She flushed. Presently she said, "Very well, then. We shall dine elsewhere. Tell the driver to go to the Faison Doré."

"Why didn't you say so before?"

The driver knew, tho Windsor thought he'd for-

gotten until at a point he turned at right angles to take
them, it seemed, head on into a wall until they made
out the time-stained and crumbling archway through
which they could pass. The Gilded Pheasant? No gilt
here. They were in a small, stone-flagged courtyard
and they were out of their century. "What sort of
thieves' dive is this, Marion?"

Dim lights penetrated the barred and curtained windows, and when at the door Windsor jerked a dangling
cord a bell rang as if far away inside. They followed
the tottering, chattering old one who admitted them
through a gloomy hall. "Avec moi, Monsieur-dame.
Oui—à la minuit. The birds have—" He snapped his
fingers for the English word—"they have just been
turn. Et quel vin ce soir, Monsieur—"

The parlor in which Marion awaited him breathed a
faint musk, as if it had just been opened after a few
hundred years under lock. A swashbuckling cavalier
grinned from a gold frame above the marble mantel.
A crimson brocade before the windows looked brittle
enough to break at a touch. Somehow Windsor was
depressed. And Marion sitting there vaguely as tho
she didn't even realize she had brought him to a dead
hole!

"S'il vous plait, Monsieur—"

The dining-room was long and narrow and not large.
There were wall mirrors reflecting from every angle an
unbelievable somberness of red and gold. As they followed silently to their table in the far corner, they
caught glimpses through a haze of curtains—as of ages
—of the Rue Nationale. So an eleventh Louis might
have seen it.

A few older and rather pompous French were at the
front tables, and near their own were two men, an

English personage for one, and the other—? Well, not French. His back was turned.

Windsor felt sorry for Marion. She had doubtless been here before the place began to run down. Perhaps an aperitif would cheer her a bit. "Vermouth Cassis," he said when the waiter's grizzled head bent down. Was this an old men's home? It gave him the creeps.

"Vermouth Cassis," repeated the fellow. "But Madame will prefer vin blanc citron, n'est ce pas?"

Marion nodded absently. "I'm feeling rather faint, Forrest," she said.

So she was going to add to it all with one of her precious spells. He said something about a last trip to Blois, but he knew she wasn't listening. That Englishman was doubtless an ex-undersecretary or a defeated M. P. The younger man had the blackest hair he had ever seen. Indistinctly he caught the word "Americans." Well, what of it? Windsor had no liking for being discussed.

The aperitif brought a little color to Marion's cheek and that maddening half smile to her parted lips. It was the fixity of the expression which got on his nerves. A low but resonant voice came from the other table, apparently careless as to whether or not it was overheard. "But their women, my friend! That is their genius, for no others have so much to offer a man."

He was tall and proud, that man, so much from the set of his shoulders and head. Windsor wondered about his face, and then, chancing to look up, he saw it in the mirror on the opposite wall—a lean face set with hot eyes and a striking texture of skin, under which ebbed and flowed with passing feelings the

patrician fire of some southland. Spanish, he thought,
and then doubted it. He wasn't quite that.

The ex-undersecretary was laughing. "Your enthusiasm suggests a personal experience. Carlos—"

Marion was asking the boat they would take to Blois.
It was like her to be a magpie when he wanted to listen
to someone else, and a sphinx when he didn't. "There
are at least half a dozen boats, my dear. What's the
difference?"

"—you will perhaps take me seriously when I tell
you that I count all other experiences as nothing. Your
democrats are right about one thing: A prince is made
of the same flesh and blood as the rest of you—"

Windsor tried to shake the fellow's voice out of his
ears. Prince? What a lot of bunk! He gave attention to the quality of the wine and the rather special
savor of the dinner course. But it takes two also to
make an appetite, and Marion wasn't eating a thing.

"—My father's entourage was on the way to Biarritz
by motor. There is a little place on the coast, just into
France, called Christobal sur Mer. It is not a village.
It is sort of white toy city with a miniature square and
a hotel and tiny tram cars, and a theater, and the whole
of it set before a bright strip of sand against a background of pine-covered dunes. Oh, yes, too charming
to be undiscovered. The little promenades are bright
with the resplendent uniforms of generals and the
parasols of ladies. Have you time, my friend? My
chauffeur is calling for me here later on. But you?"

Some richness deserted the room when the low voice
was still. Windsor picked up a menu and penciled a
word. It was Christobal sur Mer. "Does he interest
you, Marion?"

She smiled without replying. Probably not then. She

was doubtless debating whether they would go to the
boat landing to-morrow in a fiacre or a taxicab. By
George, if she kept on she might go to Blois, or blazes,
alone. Oh, here was the rest of it now—

"—our party had gone on, but I remained behind.
Christobal fascinated me, full of little corners that were
as intimate as stage sets, or as tho one's favorite
bit of Paris were hidden away in the dunes for his
individual pleasure.

"So while my chauffeur was seeking in a shop for my
particular preference in cigarets, I decided to walk
one time around the square, and when I returned, sitting
in the tonneau of my car as though she owned it and
the whole of Christobal as well, was the lady of whom
I shall tell you. Will it not do if I say that she was
the loveliest woman in the world? At least you will
believe that she was the most surprized—when I
opened the door and stepped in beside her. Or, being
cynical, you will doubtless not believe it. No matter.
But please do not smile like that. What is there to
smile at in a broken heart?"

"My dear Carlos, I am smiling at you in the romantic
rôle. I thought it was one you avoided."

"Very well, my friend, call it romance if you must.
I shall call it fate. I asked this lady where I might
drive her, and she replied in a French that put my own
to shame: 'To the gendarmerie. Monsieur, or to the
museum of art, where such a consummate presumption
may be enshrined on a pedestal.'

"I said to her, 'I have no desire, Mademoiselle,
either to disorganize the local gendarmerie, or to pale
the art museum with your presence?'

" 'In that case,' she said, 'I should advise you to
evacuate Colonel Mills-Brackett's car.'

"As if, mind you, that military gentleman had the only car of the kind in Europe. But I was too concerned with hair that was black and red and golden in a dozen lights, and with eyes which were not like the eyes of my country-women and—but I told you she was the loveliest woman in—"

"Yes," interrupted the undersecretary, "the loveliest woman in sight."

"In the world, I believe I said. But I think you will credit me with too much sophistication to be bewildered by a pretty face. If that had been all—well, that would have been all. But it was her compassion—to my utter consternation, at that moment a group of gay young English people appeared and all of them at once began to clamber into my car, which was in reality Colonel Mills-Brackett's car, as you would have known in the first place if you had not been a cynical old dog. Compassion, I said, but it may have been her rare humor. She introduced me to them with a Spanish name. 'My friend Don Pietro Bomero dos Sanchos,' she said.

"Before I could even think the car started and I was being taken high up into the dunes to the little white villa of Colonel Gerald Mills-Brackett, who, by the way, can take a joke.

"Two days later I found my chauffeur waiting stoically at his wheel with a carton of my particular preference in cigarets. I had quite forgotten the good lad.

"But I shall never forget the two days. They were the beginning for Beatricia and me. May I call her Beatricia? It was not her name, any more than Pietro was mine, though she called me that to the end. I

and gave place to great joy. She was here; he would talk with her. Little English he had, but simple words, those with few gutturals, he had managed to pick up; so he rose, the masterful lover, and, with feline movements, crossed the nightmare chamber to claim his own.

If you wonder how Lucy came to be in this bagnio, the explanation is simple. Battling was in training. He had flogged her that day before starting work; he had then had a few brandies—not many; some eighteen or nineteen—and had locked the door of his room and taken the key. Lucy was, therefore, homeless, and a girl somewhat older than Lucy, so old and so wise, as girls are in that region, saw in her a possible source of revenue. So there they were, and to them appeared Cheng.

From what horrors he saved her that night cannot be told, for her ways were too audaciously childish to hold her long from harm in such a place. What he brought to her was love and death.

For he sat by her. He looked at her—reverently yet passionately. He touched her—wistfully yet eagerly. He locked a finger in her wondrous hair. She did not start away; she did not tremble. She knew well what she had to be afraid of in that place; but she was not afraid of Cheng. She pierced the mephitic gloom and scanned his face. No, she was not afraid. His yellow hands, his yellow face, his smooth black hair . . . well, he was the first thing that had ever spoken soft words to her; the first thing that had ever laid a hand upon her that was not brutal; the first thing that had deferred in manner towards her as tho she, too, had a right to live. She knew his words were sweet, tho she did not understand them. Nor can they be set down. Half that he spoke was in village Chinese; the

surrender — deditio onis f

surrender. dedsere dedidi deditum

eat out — erumpo ere rupi ruptem

sally. eruptio onis f.

embassy = legatio onis f.

attack = oppugnatio onis f.

breakthrough — perrumpo ere rupi ruptem

break. — rumpo ere rupi ruptem

ward. — statio onis f

missile = tellum i n.